# All the Forever Things

Jolene Perry

Albert Whitman and Company
Chicago, Illinois

Library of Congress Cataloging-in-Publication data is on file with the publisher.

Text copyright © 2017 by Jolene Perry
Cover art copyright © 2017 by Albert Whitman & Company
Cover art by Ellen Kokontis
Published in 2017 by Albert Whitman & Company
ISBN 978-0-8075-2532-6 (hardcover)
ISBN 978-0-8075-2534-0 (paperback)

Printed in the United States of America
10 9 8 7 6 5 4 3 2 1 LB 22 21 20 19 18 17

Design by Ellen Kokontis

For more information about Albert Whitman & Company,
visit our website at www.albertwhitman.com.

To Amy—
a first best friend
is always a best friend.

# Chapter 1

Mom and Dad wheel the large oak casket up the narrow hallway. Dad pulls from the head (as always) and Mom pushes from the foot (as always). The bereaved stands in a worn, gray suit. His shoulders hunch forward, and he stares at the floor—typical posture of the brokenhearted.

Everything about this moment is familiar. The silent communication between Mom and Dad as they shift the casket into the best position for viewing. The bereaved's sighs, me sliding the soft soles of my shoes over the carpet, and the overpowering smell of condolences that have arrived from companies with names like FLOWERS R US.

I lean on the doorframe between the viewing room and the lobby, waiting to be needed or to wave Mr. Nichols through the doorway to sit with his wife.

Mr. Nichols arrived early, which wouldn't be a problem except that my brain is still fuzzy from lack of sleep—too much online back-and-forth with Bree last night.

The casket jolts as Dad sets the wheel locks. Mr. Nichols flinches beside me and clutches his old fedora-style hat.

A normal person would think it's sweet that the family cared so much. A normal person might also blink a few times and shed a few tears over the family's loss. If I did that, I'd dry out. I've learned that the only way to stay professional is to stay detached.

My toe traces another circle on the carpet, and I stare down at Dad's old dress shoes from middle school. I stifle a groan. Bree will be here soon for the horrid group project that's been looming over my head for the past week. My best friend being part of my group isn't nearly enough to offset dealing with stupid Bryce Johnson.

"Gabriella?" Mom's voice is a little too shrill for this to be the first time she's said my name.

Her brows are raised nearly to her hairline.

"Gabriella?" she says again. "Would you please see if Mr. Nichols would like some coffee while we finish setting up?"

I step forward. This is Mom's subtle hint that I need to get this man out of the viewing room so Dad can open the casket and make sure Mrs. Nichols hasn't adjusted during her trip up from the basement.

Gesturing toward the front of the home, I put on my best work smile. "Mr. Nichols, if you'd follow me, we have snacks, tea, coffee…"

His gray eyes droop in sadness.

I clasp my hands together in full hostess mode, because without that, I start to feel all the weighted grief of the people who come through here, and I can't experience that every day.

"Maybe coffee."

The defeat in his voice tightens around my heart. I step back and take a few long breaths. Three breaths to be exact. I can always shove the sadness away in three.

The man slowly follows me through the large lobby to the table that my cousin and I set up with refreshments for the family viewing. The one that he's two hours early for.

I pour a coffee for Mr. Nichols and stand with a smile until he's dropped in a sugar. Mom gives me a quick thumbs-up from the doorway to the viewing room. I set a small coffee pot and more sugars on a tray in case he sits in there a while.

Pressing my lips together to make sure the red lipstick is still even, I start back across the lobby toward the viewing room, Mr. Nichols on my heels.

My phone vibrates in my dress pocket. It'll be Bree, making sure I'm ready to leave on time. But seriously, this isn't vintage shopping or doughnuts, so she shouldn't mind being a few minutes late.

"Right this way, Mr. Nichols," Dad says. I pause, letting Mr. Nichols walk ahead.

Mom passes me on her way to our closed-door messy family offices, dabbing at her eyes. "Be quick. He wants time alone with her."

*Crap. He got to Mom.* If this man makes me tear up, I'll have to redo my eyeliner. I take three more slow breaths before I walk back into the viewing room and set the coffee tray on a small table. Dad has the head part of the casket propped open now, and the woman looks asleep instead of dead. I'm feeling pretty proud of the job Bree and I did on her makeup.

"We were married sixty-five years," the man says quietly.

"Wow." Right now, the final month before the end of junior year feels like an eternity.

"There's nothing like finding your soul mate." He peers at me before his eyes go back to his wife.

"I'm sure." But then you end up like the woman in the casket, or the man crying above her. Everything is temporary. My hip vibrates again. Bree must be here, pacing in the parking lot.

"Will you show my son in when he gets here?" the man asks, his voice cracking.

*No, no, no.* Cracking voices sometimes make my throat swell. After that come teary eyes, and cat-eye eyeliner is *not* easy to fix.

"Absolutely." I take a couple steps back. "And I'm so sorry for your loss."

He peers at me again, and a corner of his mouth twitches. I swear he knows those words tends to fly out of my mouth without a second thought.

My hip vibrates *again*—I'm for sure running late.

The moment I'm back in the lobby, I sprint to the door of the back offices and snatch the phone from my pocket.

We're not going to be late, Bree texts. Tell me we're not going to be late, G.

Mom blinks a few times through her tears, and I stop.

"I knew Mrs. Nichols," Mom says as she dabs her eyes a few more times. "Hazard of a small community." Mom should be dried out by now for sure.

"Sorry." But I still need to go, and my body leans toward the door in anticipation.

Mom sniffs again. "What do you have going on?"

"US government, meeting for our project. You know, with it being a teacher workday and all…"

"When is this?"

"Like now."

"Okay." Mom sighs. "We're fine. Angel's at the front desk."

As if summoned, Angel steps through the door with his typical larger-than-life smile.

Angel is a nice enough guy. His accent is hard for me to follow sometimes, but he seems to put people at ease. Angel is great with

4

all the people who come through here—both the live and the dead ones. I'm fine with this, until he begins telling me about the conversations he has with the deceased.

"Hey, Angel," I say. "I'm taking off."

"Miss Osborn."

I snatch a piece of gum from the package on Mom's desk. "I'll only be a couple hours. Promise."

Mom looks me up and down. "Might wanna change first. You got taller again. Maybe we need to find some longer dresses."

I glance at my simple black A-line dress with a white collar. Of all the times I need to wear my Wednesday Addams dress, it's definitely when I'm sitting across the table from Bryce Johnson. My gut twitches with nerves at whatever asinine comment he'll come up with today. I'm pretty sure the last time Bryce said a word to me, it had something to do with asking if I kept skulls in my bedroom or something equally stupid.

"I wear this all the time. And anyway, I'm already late." I pick up my large patent leather purse from the coatrack, wondering how good a weapon it would make if I felt the urge to beat Bryce over the top of the library table.

My phone vibrates *again*.

You're supposed to be waiting under the awning, Bree says. COME OUT NOW. We will not be the slackers in our group.

This is so like Bree. On time. Organized. Prepared. Especially because she knows I'll need reinforcements today. Stupid Bryce Johnson.

I run for the door and hope I have everything in my phone that I need for our meeting.

Bree wears a smirk and a pastel miniskirt, her arms folded across her chest. "Did you forget what time it was?"

"No," I say, giving her a more dramatic sigh than I intended. "The husband showed up early for the viewing, and then Mom and Dad took forever with the casket."

"Nichols?" she asks as she opens her car door. Too bad Mom didn't see Bree's skirt, because it's a solid two inches shorter than mine.

I nod.

"Well, then I'm glad I didn't come in. Crying makes me crazy. How do you think we did on her makeup?"

"She looks fab," I say, bumping Bree with my hip. "Of course." Bree and I are a pretty unstoppable team when it comes to making dead people look alive.

"Okay. Let's go." She points to her small car. "I want you to be aware that I'd be making you drive if we weren't already running late."

I make a face. I hate driving, and she knows it. But I have to admit that if it weren't for Bree, I probably still wouldn't have my license. "You know Mom never gives me her car, so we'd have to take the old hearse if I drove."

She laughs. "Yeah, there's that."

The second we're in the car, Bree hits the gas. Her hair is in shiny, thick curls and teased in the back to add to her whole sixties vibe. "I see that you're dressed appropriately to see Bryce."

Shoving away the bits of uncertainty trying to weave their way into my resolve, I pull back my shoulders. "Of course."

Bryce Johnson is the stereotypical spoiled California jock boy. He's only a junior but walks the halls of our school like he owns it. His smirk is annoying. His hair is always perfect. And I hold him responsible for destroying any chance to date Davis, the only guy I ever put effort into dating.

"Can you even believe how long ago that Wednesday Addams thing was?" She laughs a little as she smooths her lips together. "Like, eighth grade?"

I stop breathing. "Yep." Eighth grade. My little eighth-grade heart had flitted like a hummingbird as I'd tiptoed out of my house and into the dark cemetery. Davis lived in the direction of the beach, so we'd agreed to meet at the lower gate of the graveyard.

Davis and I had been friends since the seventh grade, but over the summer, I'd started to notice little things, like the way the left side of his mouth always turned up before the right, and how whenever Bree and I saw him at the park or the beach, he'd always say hi to me and stand closer than he needed to.

That night, I knew something was going to happen between us, and I was so ready. I stood outside in the dark and tried to remember all the things that Bree and I had read about boyfriends. About how to keep eye contact and ask him questions. Also, that I could always walk away if I changed my mind about him. We pored over online stories about first kisses, and I was determined that mine would be perfect—if it came to that. But really, I knew that kiss was coming. *Knew* it.

When Davis came through the lower gate, we sat against one of my favorite flowering trees. He said something about meeting Bryce for a sleepover that night, and the cemetery feeling so different in the dark, but then we laughed about being back at school for another year of middle school, and I remembered that I liked Davis not just because he was cute, but also because he was my friend. Our shoulders touched. Once in a while, his leg would touch mine. And then he asked to read my palm, but he didn't read palms. I'd read *Seventeen Magazine*—he was looking for an excuse to touch me.

There was no way I was going to let that perfect moment of him tracing the lines on my hands pass me by without my first kiss, so I leaned in and kissed his cheek. Davis jerked in surprise, but his eyes were smiling when he moved toward me and pressed his dry lips against mine.

Perfection.

Until—

"Graveyard Gabby, Davis? You can't be serious! She's a Wednesday Addams, not someone you'd *kiss!*" Bryce yelled.

In less than a second, Davis was up and running for the gate where Bryce sat on his bike, arms folded and a scowl on his face. Davis paused when he picked up his bike, and we locked eyes for a moment. Hope crashed something sparkling, warm, and wonderful through my chest. Until Bryce slapped Davis's back. "Come on! We were going to meet at the corner and you didn't show, man."

They took off, and that was the end of Davis speaking to me. But Bryce seeing my first kiss had much worse repercussions.

Bryce told the whole school that I went around kissing boys in the graveyard, and the slew of names began: Graveyard Gabby, Stone-Cold Gabe, Wednesday Addams…

Bree and I spent that week together watching *The Addams Family* movies since I had *no* clue who Wednesday Addams was. We plotted how to get Bryce to shut up. Clearly the Wednesday Addams and Graveyard Gabby talk wasn't going to go away, so Bree said that maybe Bryce would stop making a huge deal of it if I just jumped into who he thought I was. And the thing is, after watching *The Addams Family*, I decided that Wednesday Addams was a kick-ass girl.

With Bree's help, I fell in love with everything dark and vintage. I showed up at school in a simple black shift dress, Dad's shoes, and dark liner on my eyes. That first day, the name-calling grew worse, but by day three of me sticking to the new version of myself, I'd become a boring and far-too-willing target.

Over the next few weeks, I spent every penny I'd saved on a new wardrobe, Bree and I started our blog, and we embraced being different. Together.

Now Bree and I wear what we want, listen to what we want, and do what we want, which makes high school less of a prison and more of a rite of passage. I can't wait until it's over, but at least we're in it together.

"You're quiet over there," she says.

"Yes," I agree. "How many times have you saved me?"

"Don't you mean, how many times have we saved each other?"

I brush off my already-clean black dress. "Yeah."

Bree blows me a kiss. "So many times."

So many.

"Look both ways," I say automatically when she reaches the four-way stop.

Bree's mouth twitches. It always does. "You're more of a parent than my parents."

I snort but don't say anything else. I'm never quite sure what to say when Bree brings up her disaster of a family.

When she pulls to a stop in front of our small public library, her phone sings "Thriller" and she groans before picking it up. "Hey, Grammy…No, I told you I had a project at the library, remember?" There's a pause. "Grammy, it's Friday…teacher workday…Yes…You had bingo last night, not last week…Grammy…" She glances at me and rolls her eyes. "Yes. Friday. Group project. And then I'm hanging with Gabriella for a bit."

Unless I have to work.

Bree lets out a slow sigh. "Okay, Grammy…Yes, I fed the cats, just check the dishes…No, Friday…*Today*…

Her grammy is a mess, but after her dad's numerous affairs and her parents' divorce, he and Bree's mother both moved away. Living with her grammy is Bree's only option if she wants to stay in Paradise Hill.

"What was that?" I ask as soon as she sets her phone down. "You were talking in circles."

Bree slips her phone in her bag without looking at me. "She's just old, I guess. Forgets what day it is sometimes. But she doesn't have much of a schedule, so she gets confused. Mom's no help, of course."

Of course her mom's not helpful. She's in a craphole apartment in LA, living like a runaway teen.

I think about Matthew living with his grandma, my aunt Liza, and know how much work it can be for him. "Do you need any help?"

"Turn back time and tell my parents to not have their midlife crisis until after I graduate?" She exaggerates her smile and bats her lashes.

"Um…"

"Kidding." Bree's smile turns real. "You can keep being my friend and help me with our website, and make sure your parents keep hiring me to do makeup."

"I can do that." I push the car door open, ignoring my weak legs as I steel myself by staring at the library doors. I hate that one person has so much power over me. Maybe wearing my most Wednesday Addams dress was a bad idea.

"You can face Bryce, Gabe. He's just a guy."

I know I can face Bryce, but I hate that I even need her reassurance right now.

"Besides"—she shrugs as she walks ahead—"he's not that bad anymore."

*What?*

# Chapter 2

I chase Bree toward the old library, with its tiled roof that the palm trees seem to be trying to attack from all sides.

"Bree, wait."

She holds open the door for me.

"How can you say he's not that bad?" I hiss.

Instead of answering, she rolls her eyes a little and waves at me like I'm being silly. Me. I walk sideways a few steps, moving through the big white shoulder-height book-tag detectors.

The dusty, mildewed smell of our library accosts my nose, and I sneeze. I hate sneezing. The whole world blacks out just long enough for—

A sharp pain cracks across my nose, and I blink, reach out as the floor flies toward me, and grab the librarians' counter.

"Ouch, sweetie!" Judy frowns from behind the counter.

I look back at the culprit—the stupid detectors. Seriously, the library books are already *free*. The library shouldn't need detectors.

I start to scrunch my nose to survey the damage but wince.

"Gabe!" Bree gasps as she points, her face paling. I must be bleeding.

"You were putting mascara on a cadaver *yesterday*," I point out. "This is just a few drops of…" But I can feel the heat sliding through my palm, so maybe I have more than just a few drops of blood. Of course this would happen just before being forced to work with Bryce.

"You know blood just startles me at first." Bree blows out through an O-shaped mouth. "I'll be okay."

Judy shoves a box of tissues into my hands, and I grab two off the top and scrunch them under my nose. People pass out if they lose too much blood.

"Given the pain on my face, I'm not really worried about you," I tell Bree, and she lets a gaspy little laugh escape.

"You go sit." Judy shoos us in the direction of the study tables. "I'll bring you ice. The boys and Trinity are already there."

"Thanks," I mumble through the tissue. *Wait. Boys? As in more than one?* It's me, Trinity, Bree, and Bryce. That's our group.

More blood leaks through the wad of tissues and down my wrist. "I need the bathroom."

Bree steps ahead and holds open the bathroom door.

The bathroom fan clacks, and the fluorescent lights zap the color from my skin, making the blood on my cheek, chin, and hands look even more startling.

Bree jerks stiff paper towels from the dispenser and runs them under the water as I stare at myself in the mirror.

"What a mess." I groan.

Bree takes the box of tissues and hands me wet towels. "Clean up, Gabe. I promise you'll survive this."

I point to my eye, which has begun to swell.

"Well, hell. Do you want to skip?" Her words come out so slowly that I know Bree does not want to skip out. She wants this over with. *I* want this over with.

"Just gimme a sec." I rinse off my hands and gently swipe the wet towels over my face. My nose, cheek, and eye all hurt and are all beginning to swell.

Bree holds out a few of the soft tissues. I dab my nose a few times and get just a small drop of blood. Better. Crouching down, she digs through my purse and holds up two Advil, which I take using water from the sink.

Dabbing my nose again and again, I come up with just the tiniest spots of blood.

*What a stupid day.* I let out a sigh and start for the door, holding the tissue under my nose.

"You okay?" Bree whispers. "Like, for real? Or should we leave?"

"We're already here."

*Today sucks.*

Bree tucks an arm over my shoulders. "No stress."

She said this the first time we met—I was bleeding then too—the victim of a volleyball hurling through the air in seventh-grade PE. She ran with me to the bathroom and handed me toilet paper and wet towels until the bleeding stopped. Hopefully I'll never have to admit how many more times she's had to make an emergency trip for me than I've had to help her.

A guy leaps to standing from the small table where Bryce and Trinity sit. "What...*happened*?" he sputters.

I don't know this guy. He's spindly skinny and crazy tall. His pants are plaid, and his jacket with rolled sleeves looks straight out of 1985. Dark curly hair hangs over a pale forehead. Glasses cover a face that I sort of expect to see acne on, but there's none. He's thin, and his face is smooth. He'd be a great Addams Family butler if they ever do another movie.

"I'm fine." I wave him away. But I'm completely not fine.

"Are you bleeding?" Trinity asks as she peers over her phone. I'm amazed her eyes reach my face over the screen she loves so much.

Bree waves her away with a forced laugh. "She said she was fine. Tiny bloody nose. No big."

"So." Bryce adjusts his letterman jacket, as if we all don't see it *every day*. "This is Hartman, from Connecticut. He and his mom are crashing with me right now, so Mr. Sandstrom put him in our group."

The lanky guy folds himself back into the chair next to Bryce.

Bree elbows me until I've scooted over enough to sit across from the new guy, leaving Bree in front of Bryce, and Trinity at the head of the table.

"Why don't you introduce Hartman as a regular person instead of a jock? You know, give me his first name instead of his last?" My nose is really starting to throb, but playing down an injury helps other people notice less, so I'm determined to pretend I'm fine.

"Uh…" Bryce says.

I glance at the skinny guy across from me. "What's your name?"

"Hartman Smith."

I blink. And then blink again. "Hartman is your *first* name?"

Bree smiles too widely. Her brows wiggle just before she gives me a subtle he's-boyfriend-material wink, and I cringe. If this guy knows Bryce and is staying with Bryce, then he's the last kind of person I need. Also, I'm holding tissues against my nose, which is probably swelling.

Trinity hasn't looked up from her phone since her first comment.

"I'm Gabriella, but Gabe is fine," I tell Hartman. I blot my nose a few times and drop the tissue in my bag.

"Gabe, like the boy's name?" he asks.

I feel my eyes narrow. "Are you making fun of my name?"

"Were you making fun of mine?" His face is flat and unreadable. Instead of trying to decipher him, I point. "And that's Bree."

"Bryce said"—Hartman glances at Bryce—"wasn't hard to figure out who was who."

Right. Because Bree is the pretty one with her dark eyes, perfect hair, and bikini-model body. The twinge in my chest is pushed away with a single, deep breath. I'm not the pretty girl, and that's fine. My lips are too thin and my eyes too squinty and my skin too pale, and my blond hair too boring. And I'm sure there's another whole list that could go along with that one. Maybe two.

"Yeah," Bryce cackles. "Because Gabriella is dressed up like Wednesday Addams again."

Just like always happens when she's mad, Bree's brows pinch together. "Grow up, Bryce."

He sits back, holding his hands in a surrender gesture and chomping on his gum like he needs to kill it before we start our meeting. And seriously, he'd make a comment if I *wasn't* dressed this way about where my regular wardrobe had gone. There's no winning with guys like him.

At least Bree is back on the same page with me where Bryce is concerned.

I glance around the table. Trinity is still tapping on her phone. Bryce's eyes are on Bree in a way that says he's noticing her. (He's so gross.) Hartman is still staring at my face and whatever misfortune was handed to me by the stupid detectors. Our eyes lock for a moment before his gaze drops back to the table.

"Here you go, dear." Judy hands me a bag of ice wrapped in a scratchy, brown paper towel.

I try to smile, but it makes my nose feel like it's breaking, so I take the ice and slowly slide it across my right cheek toward my nose. It better not be broken. Not when it was my idea to meet here instead of Starbucks. I can't believe I'm stuck sitting across from the new guy where he'll have full view of my bag of ice and swelling face.

Maybe I should have stayed home and helped with the family viewing or hung with my little sister. "I'm swelling up like Mr. Gibson."

Bree's gaze snaps to me. She widens her eyes, holds in a smile like *Of course you'd say this*, and shakes her head. This is what we do. I make sure she doesn't use grammy-speak now that she's living with her grammy, and she tries to keep me from talking about dead people too much. We both fail at least half the time.

"Do we know a Mr. Gibson?" Bryce asks.

I glance at Bree, and she quietly laughs at me. I swear I can hear her thoughts: *You started it. You can't back down now…*

"My parents run a funeral home," I say slowly. "We had a Gibson in who was…swollen," I finish lamely.

Bryce snorts. "Classic Graveyard Gabe."

I narrow my eyes, which earns me another cackle from him.

"Uh…" Hartman blinks a few times. "Okay."

I'm such an idiot.

"What brought you here?" Bree asks Hartman with her superpolite voice. She gives me a quick smile. Bree is so good at redirecting a conversation after my wreckage.

"My, um…" Hartman swallows. "My dad died. My mom doesn't have much family, but she and Bryce's mom are close. Dad is from here, so we moved here."

Instinct kicks in, and I reach across the table, not quite touching his hand. "I'm so sorry for your loss." It's my smoothest, best, most instinctual work voice.

Bree taps my foot under the table, another suppressed smile tugging at her mouth. Clearly, it's too late for me to not sound like a funeral home director.

Nobody says anything, but even Trinity is peering over her phone again, so my words just hang out there.

I need a redo on this day.

Bree nudges me under the table again, and I jump. She subtly raises one brow and does a half glance toward Hartman. And then again with a little more exaggeration. I shake my head just enough for her to hear me silently screaming, *No way*. And especially not after *this* first impression. Her continued slightly raised brows say that she's not going to let the idea of this cute guy go—at least not soon.

"Can we actually *do* something?" Trinity asks.

Group projects are the *worst*. I have to deal with people who aren't Bree, horrible things like bloody noses happen, we've thrown a stranger into the mix, and now, always-on-her-phone Trinity is the one asking us to start.

Hartman clears his throat as he stares at the table. "Yeah. We should…um…get started."

* * *

One hour at the library, and we all have assignments for our "how a bill becomes a law" presentation. The whole discussion made me wish I'd taken government on independent study over the summer, but it's too late for that now. At least we can leave.

"So…" Bryce starts and leans over the table toward Bree. "You're in that after-school touchy-feely experiment that Ms. Bates is running, aren't you?"

Bree sucks in a breath. "Yeah…"

I scoot closer so she knows I'm on her side with whatever comes next. The group is for students with recently divorced parents—something our counselor started for her PhD program.

"I just noticed you, that's all. Thought maybe we could get together sometime or something," Bryce says. To my friend. Bryce Johnson…and my friend.

*What?*

"What?" Bree says, her posture suddenly stiff.

"No big thing." He smiles a little, and I hate that even though I don't like him, I appreciate the perfection of the tanned dimples on his cheeks. "There just aren't that many of us in the group, so I thought it might be cool to be able to say that we actually got together outside of group. Maybe get a chance to skip one of them or something."

"Yeah…" Bree trails off and glances toward me.

I'm sure my face is blank, because my mind is blank. Guys in Bryce's position in our school don't ask out girls like Bree and me. We're not involved in any school activities…*anything*, while Bryce is practically the school mascot. Well, he's the mascot for the upperclassmen who play sports. He's probably hated by everyone else, but by all accounts, that feeling is mutual.

"I know Hartman really wants to get back to his mom." Bryce flicks another piece of gum in his mouth as he leans back in his chair like he's lounging. "But I'm starving if you're up for a burger or something."

Is he seriously asking out my friend? In front of everyone?

Bree's wide eyes grow even wider, her gaze flitting from me to Bryce to me to Bryce…

She pinches my sleeve and drags me to standing. She missed the perfect opportunity for ultimate humiliation! What is she *doing*?

"Um, just a sec?" I say as she pulls me behind a bookshelf.

"Did that just happen?" Bree asks, out of breath. Her hand

rests over her chest, and her eyes are so huge I'm worried about permanent damage.

"You dragging me away from the table?" I say. "Because my sleeve says that just happened."

"Bryce Johnson asking me out."

"I think…" I lean back and peer at him. He cocks a brow at me. Right. We both know that Bree and I are about to decide together and dissect the conversation. He's *so* going down. "Yeah, I think he did."

Bree stares at the bookshelf for a moment. I'm about to tell her that I'll break the news to him, or say we already have plans, when I see the faintest twinges of a smile.

"Not Bryce. Are you *serious*?"

"He is sort of perfect looking, and I just…" Her brown eyes lock onto mine. "I have a major confession."

Bree and I don't have major confessions because we share things. Like *every*thing.

"Remember how I had that big crush on him before the whole graveyard incident?"

Oh, I remember.

"I was mad at him for you, but…" She peeks through the bookshelves, but I have no idea if she can see him or not because I'm not going to look again.

"But?"

"But he's still…He is just so beautiful. And I wanted to tell you that I've always sort of watched him, but with your history, I was afraid to."

I scoff. No one with that kind of ego and reputation could be considered beautiful.

"It's just one quick meal. How many girls get to say that they dated one of the hottest guys in school?"

"*This* particular guy?" I ask. "A dozen? Two?"

Bree whisper-laughs and shakes her head. She is actually considering going out with Bryce Johnson. "He really is just *gorgeous*, Gabe. Can you let your grudge go for one night? For me? Please?"

She smiles, but it wobbles a little. She actually cares what I think. I guess this shouldn't surprise me, but her überconfidence always shifts how I think she feels. I generally assume Bree is great because she generally acts like she's great.

"Don't you remember how he ruined my first kiss? I mean…" I lean in closer. "Come *on*. And he hasn't grown past the stupid nicknames. Not to mention how many girls hate him after dating him."

Bree sucks her lower lip into her mouth. Her eyes plead with me. Asking me to go along with whatever she wants. Which means I will. "Maybe I could talk to him about the name thing."

This is such a disaster.

Bree lets out a slow breath through O-shaped lips. "One quick burger and a drop-off. That's it. I'm just…" Her shoulders fall a little. "I'm a little curious, you know? What it would be like to go out with someone like him."

*Like him.* That should be her first clue. Not like us. Like him. Like the big asshole he is.

I lean back to see around the bookshelf and glance at the table. Barely holding in a groan, I know I'm not going to stop Bree. I never would. But still…everything that comes out of his mouth is so horrible.

"Gabe?" she asks.

I lean back between the bookshelves.

"Look. I know," she continues. "Sisters before misters, and we're here together, but…When will I get another chance at dating one of the coolest guys in school? It's something I should *not* care about, but maybe I do?"

I blink a few times. She really is serious.

"Help a sistah out?" She laughs quietly, her eyes pleading and her glossed lip tucked into her mouth.

"Yeah." I relent. "Fine. Helpin' a sistah out."

She grabs me arm. "*Best.* You. Are. The. Best."

"Once in a while."

Bree pulls back her shoulders, sucks in another breath, and heads for our table. Her hips swing a little extra as she walks.

"Okay, Bryce. Grabbing a bite sounds fine." She leans against her chair as if saying yes to him isn't a big deal, but I can see the stiffness in her shoulders and how she's trying to keep her face just a little too calm.

Bryce glances at me and chuckles. "I'm glad I passed the group test."

He didn't, but I'm nice and keep my mouth shut.

"Hey, Gabe." Bryce taps his friend on the arm, and Hartman's attention turns back to the table. "Hartman can give you a ride home if that's cool."

Oh. That wasn't part of the plan.

Hartman taps the table with long fingers. "Yeah. That's fine."

How has my fate this afternoon suddenly been decided? What if Hartman is a bad driver?

Trinity is gone with a brief wave. The two guys are talking about schedules and family and I don't know what. How am I suddenly stuck with the stranger?

Bree leans toward me and whispers, "Are you actually sure you're okay with this, or are you just doing that thing where you're annoyed but still the best friend ever?"

"As long as you're not trying to set me up with Hartman, I'm not

21

annoyed." I'm a little annoyed. She should *feel* my annoyance. It's so strong that I've almost forgotten about my nearly broken nose.

Bree's smile turns mischievous. "He's super cute, Gabe. I expect a full report of your ride home."

"Yeah, I'll need a report too."

Bryce tosses Bree his award-winning smile—or at least his girl-getting smile—and Bree waves over her shoulder as Bryce leads her to the door. "I'll call ya, Gabe!"

Bryce looks her up and down like he's going to eat a snack off her body.

*Gross.*

He even has this swagger thing when he walks. He's not fooling anyone. He holds open the library door and gestures outside with a long swing of his arm, and Bree blushes.

Oh, this is not good.

# Chapter 3

Hartman holds open the car door for me, and I glance down at his weird old-man dress shoes. Maybe I can't call his shoes weird since they're almost identical to mine.

"Nice car," I say as I slide into the passenger's side of a little Golf GTI.

He scuffs his old-man shoes a little before glancing at his feet. "It was my dad's."

My hand involuntarily reaches out to give him the generic squeeze and to once again say, "I'm so sorry," but I stop myself by clutching my purse to my chest. Bree will be so proud. "Oh."

Hartman walks around the car and climbs into the driver's seat, frowning the whole time. *Well, crap.*

The thing I wish I could say (but never would because the rest of the world doesn't think the same as me) is that people die. People die all the time. Every day. Expectedly. Unexpectedly. Babies. Kids. Adults. Brothers. Sisters. Fathers. Mothers. Aunts. Uncles.

Grandparents. Great-grandparents. Spouses. Some are loved greatly by a ton of people. Some funerals are attended by only a few. It doesn't change how dead people are, so we shouldn't be so surprised when someone we know dies.

This is all harsh and horrible of me to think, but I've seen death every day, my whole life. If I internalize death as more than just something that happens, the sadness of it spreads like black ink on white silk. I'm smarter than that.

"You stopped talking," Hartman says as we pull out of the parking lot. He looks both ways. "I know it's awkward when I bring up my dad."

I let out one of my even breaths to keep my mind and feelings calm and even. "I see death all the time, so I say the generic thing or I say the wrong thing."

"Hmm."

Like right now, I'm curious if Hartman and his mom are the kind of people who had his dad dressed up in a suit he'd never normally wear, or if they put him in a jersey of his favorite sports team. Or maybe he was cremated, and if so, what kind of urn did they use? Something big and ostentatious, something small and unobtrusive, or something that would have suited Hartman's dad?

I point, careful to keep my hand out of his line of sight. "Take a left here."

"Thanks. This town is just big enough to get lost in, but not so big that Siri does well. And…most of your roads follow the lines of the ocean and are winding anyway."

I blink a few times. "That was quite a commentary on Paradise Hill."

He shrugs.

"We go quite a way on this street. And yes, it's a winding one."

He nods, and now that he's watching the road instead of looking at me, I stare. We don't get new students very often, and I can't remember the last time I was in a car with someone who wasn't Bree or my parents.

His profile is nice, and he doesn't look so awkward and lanky from the side. I send Bree a quick text. On someone less interesting, his clothes would look pretty dorky, but on him…I think it works.

Once I hit Send, I realize I probably just encouraged Bree's wiggling her brows over him, like she wanted to do at the library.

The keys in the ignition jangle when we hit a bump, and I glance down.

"Blake Smith?" I ask when I read the tag on the keys.

He clears his throat. "My dad."

I totally should have known the keys were his dad's. *Not smart, Gabe.* I clutch my bag tighter.

Bree still hasn't written! *Grrr.*

"So, funeral home, huh?" he asks.

And here we go…

"Yep." I let my lips pop on the *p*, ready to be irritated over what he might ask next. It's not fair, really, and I should be used to all the questions by now.

"Crazy."

Why does everyone think it's crazy? "Well, there are funeral homes out there, and someone does run them."

"It seems…" He lets out a sigh. "It seems like a very sad profession, that's all."

"I watch a lot of sadness, I guess." And the benefit is that I'm very good at keeping myself from being depressed. I have about a tenth the amount of drama in my life as most of our junior class. Though I owe some of that to my complete lack of guy drama and the rest to Bree.

"You guess?"

"Everything is temporary. I just got to learn that sooner than most." Most of the time I feel pretty lucky. I don't think I'll be as surprised when super crappy things happen to me because I live my life half expecting them.

He blinks so many times that I wonder if he's trying not to cry. I nearly rest my hand on his shoulder. Again. But I don't. Bree is here in spirit, trying to keep me from embarrassing myself.

He makes a quick swipe of each eye that makes me wonder how recent his dad's death was.

"Take a right here." I point to the light.

He glances around at the roofs of the larger homes that peek above the few homes-turned-businesses. "It's nice up here."

Guess this is our very welcome subject change.

"Yep." I point to the palm trees that line the black, iron fence around the cemetery. "And convenient."

He clears his throat a few times, pointedly staring at the road in front of us. "You're not far from the beach." His voice sounds kind of forced or strangled.

What's up with him?

"Yeah," I say. "I'm down there a lot, but we've had too many drowning victims for me to want to swim. That, and it's freezing."

Hartman gives me another strange glance.

This look shuts me down and is one of the main reasons my circle of friends extends only as far as Bree.

"You live a short walk from the beach, and you don't swim?" he asks.

I've already lost him, and it's not like I'm interested in him, so at this point, there's no reason to mask any of who I am. "Seeing the victims was enough. I know how to swim because I'd prefer not to drown. So I swim sometimes. In a pool." I point to the massive house. "This is me."

He scans the exterior of the mansion-turned-mortuary. "You *live* here?"

"Well"—I point to the sign, the archway that stretches across the driveway, and the obviously new front glass doors—"the main floor and basement are both for the funeral home. We live upstairs."

His eyes scan the massive Spanish-style house and the many upstairs windows. "Oh."

I can't remember a time when I didn't live in at least a part of this gigantic space. For a while we were in the apartment to the right over the detached garage, but even that was pretty large. "I'm used to it, I guess. And we really do need the room. The old attached garage was turned into a chapel. The rest of the first floor is the coffin room and the viewing room, and the carriage house is the new garage..."

I'm gesturing like he'll care how we've rearranged the interior, but he doesn't say anything so I stop talking.

He looks back toward the street. "So, you're also close to the school."

"Yeah," I say. "I walk."

He pulls into a parking space and rests his arms on the steering wheel, still looking at the house. "Are you sixteen?"

"Yes, but I don't like to drive, so I don't do it often. I do have my license, though." *Because Bree made me get it.* "But my mom hogs the Subaru, which means I'm stuck using the old hearse, because everything else is insured by the business, and the insurance company says I'm not old enough to drive those..." I trail off when I realize that there's no way he cares about any of this. "But really, I don't like driving."

The corners of his eyes twitch. "Too many people die in car accidents?"

I tap my fingers on my knee. "People are bad drivers. We get distracted." But people die doing all sorts of everyday stupid things, and apparently can injure themselves just walking into a library.

We sit in silence for a few moments, and then he starts tapping the steering wheel. I'm staring at him again. My heart does an extra little *ka-thump*.

"My dad was a teacher. He died of a heart attack at his desk," Hartman says as he taps the steering wheel a few more times.

Guess we're both finger-tappers. I stop.

"Dad was totally healthy. A runner even."

I know I'm warped and twisted because the first thing I think is that if his dad came through here, I'd have never guessed his death right, and Matthew would have won the bet.

Hartman's fingers still, and he turns to face me. "So, will you stop going to school?"

I want to tell him that being careful is such a tiny part of the equation that keeps one person alive and leaves another dead, but then I'd have to try to explain why I'm so cautious. That would lead to me rambling again about just trying to stack the odds in my favor, and then who knows what ridiculous thing might come out of my mouth. There is no good way to answer.

"Thanks for the ride," I tell him before leaping out of the car. "It was really nice of you."

"Gabriella?" he asks.

"Gotta work." I point to my black dress and then to the front door, all without making eye contact. "Thanks again."

"Yeah..." His voice is quiet and almost lost sounding. "Any-time."

My heart is pounding and my head is spinning, and I'm not totally sure I understand why. I don't wait for him to say anything else, just close the passenger door and try to remember my "work walk" (slow and succinct) as my heart shakes.

When I push open the lobby doors, the smell of sympathy flowers hits my nose, so I take shallow breaths because after my incident at the library, I'm not into sneezing again. I pause next to the massive cherrywood desk that sits near the front and try to see this room the way an outsider would.

Big, open area. Chapel doors. Another set of double doors to the coffin room, which Dad calls the salesroom. Aside from the glass windows into the viewing area, it sort of looks like a hotel lobby. Kind of boring, really. I wonder if I'd have earned the nicknames if people knew the reality of what we do.

"You are *in* it today," Angel says as he moves a few vases on one of the side tables. He's pretty meticulous about their placement.

He's in a gray suit, which camouflages his weirdness nicely.

"A little," I admit.

"Mrs. Nichols is happy. Don't worry about her." Angel gives me his professional smile. "We were chatting this morning."

I swallow before sarcasm leaps out of my throat. "Thanks. I gotta…" I point to the back office doors.

His smile widens, and I'm kicking myself for not just walking around him when I first came in.

The second I'm in the back offices, Dad glances up at me, and his eyes widen. "What *happened* to you?"

"What?"

"To your face?" He points.

I grab Mom's mirror out of her desk and groan. The right side of my nose is swollen just enough that it looks like my nose is crooked, and the distinct purple of a bruise underlines my right eye. *Well, that's just great.*

"Library. Ran into the thingies."

"The thingies?" Dad asks.

"You know." I set down Mom's mirror and swirl my hand in the air. "The alarm thingies."

"The big white ones?" he asks incredulously.

I frown. "I sneezed."

Now he's smiling instead of looking worried. "Only you, Gabby."

"It's Gabe, Dad. Has been for a few years." I start for the back door of the family offices that leads to the house. "I'm gonna go get some food."

He leans back and kicks his swivel chair to face me. He's kind of slouched, and his hair is sort of messy around his face. I get this glimpse of what he might have looked like before he got old. Weird. "I need you to please run down the hill and get your sister from Aunt Liza."

I try to hold my groan in my throat, but it escapes in a weird gagging sound, which makes me cough, which makes my face feel like it's splitting apart. "Can't Mickey just walk home on her own? Aunt Liza's house isn't that far."

Dad's gaze is back on his computer, and his fingers are typing away. "Sorry. Your mom's picking up food from the caterer. Your cousin Matthew's touching up makeup, and I need to make sure everything runs smoothly for services."

I clap my hands together and plaster on a shallow fake smile. "And I'll be trotting down the hill with my busted face to pick up Mickey."

Dad kicks his chair around to face the computer again. "Oh," he says. "I have Bree's paycheck. Where is she?"

"Out with a guy," I say. But not just a guy. With Bryce, and that's one of the weirdest life twists I've seen in a while. Why did Bryce ask her out? What does he want? Does he really think she'll be stupid enough to…do whatever it is he thinks he can talk her into?

Wait a minute…She still hasn't texted me back…

"All okay?" Dad asks, making me jump. "I recognize that worried face."

"Yeah. Good. All okay."

Yeesh. My brain must be shorting out. Bree is out with Bryce. This is totally going to be a one-time thing. I have to stop worrying.

# Chapter 4

I head around the side of our huge house and step over the low rock wall into the cemetery. Bree and I used to try to walk along the uneven top of this wall—just one of the loads of things we've outgrown together since we met.

Bree came to my house for the first time a few months into the school year of seventh grade and didn't freak out that I lived above a funeral home. She didn't ask to see a body or ask about ghosts, just shrugged. I swear, it was like someone had lifted the weight of a bus off my shoulders. There was so much excitement in the idea that I could have a friend come over who wouldn't be weird about where I lived—even though I had a hard time leaving the funeral-home part of me at home.

In Bree's eyes, I've never been defined by what we do. And once I jumped into her love of vintage…that sealed us.

Staring at my phone, I will her to text me back.

Nothing.

Having a day off of school and not spending it with Bree is like…I don't even know what it's like, because it's not something that ever happens.

I weave around the familiar headstones, trying to make sure I don't always take the same trail over the grass between my house and Liza's. With kid number two, Mom and Dad are trying to prevent the kind of scarring that might come from wandering around dead people all day and replace that with the kind of scarring that's going to happen by my little sister's proximity to our great-aunt Liza.

Sucks that even my parents look at my life and want to save my sister from the same fate. There's no convincing them that Bree and I *like* being different because we do it together.

A light breeze kicks up from the ocean, and I sneeze, sending pain across my face. This day is crap.

* * *

When I step inside Aunt Liza's massive house, instead of turning left into Matthew's sleek, modern part of the house, I turn right into crazy-town.

The moment I push open the massive, wooden door, music hits my ears. Big band? Mickey listens to…Bieber-like music. Not this. Music vibrates against the wall, but I see no one. Just the insane living room.

Every piece of furniture stuffed into Aunt Liza's crowded living room is dark or velvet or has wooden scrolling details. Some have all three. Stacks of magazines rest around the mismatched furniture, and the bizarre assortment of trinkets from generations past makes the room feel like a dumping ground for lost items instead of the vintage masterpiece it could be. The wallpaper is cigarette-scented red brocade, and the whole thing just feels…oppressive. Or it would without the music and bizarre bits of pop art Liza has collected over the years.

"Hello?" I call.

"Oh dear!" Aunt Liza parades through her hinged kitchen doors in a red strapless ball gown. A tiara sits on her head, and a long cigarette holder dangles between her thin, glove-clad fingers. "I'm so glad you could join us!" Her voice is the low crackling voice of someone who has spent her life smoking. "Cookies are coming out now!"

She twirls twice and disappears through the clacking door into the kitchen. I tug my shoulders back and walk around the curvy living room furniture, pushing through the door behind her. Flour, measuring cups, and bowls line the black granite countertops. Matthew redid this room about a year ago and modernized the whole thing. It still has enough Liza touches in the lighting and bizarre charcoal art on the walls to match the crazy-cakes feeling of the rest of her house.

My great-aunt Liza reminds me a bit of a cartoon character. Her high cheekbones and the wrinkles that have formed a pattern over her whole face, rather than just near her mouth and eyes, only add to the effect. And maybe the fact that she had her thick eyeliner tattooed on makes her appear like more of a caricature instead a person. Every once in a while, I see bits of my dad in her—the shape of their noses and their foreheads are almost identical—but the older she gets, the nuttier she gets, and the more straight-laced my dad gets. Although, he is just her nephew.

My gaze lands on my little sister, wearing a sparkling flapper dress with a feather in her hair. Who knows which family member that one came from, or how much that dress must be worth. Aunt Liza's closet is a vintage treasure mine.

"Mickey?"

"Cookies are almost done. We have to stay. Please?" She clasps her hands together, her wide blue eyes blinking in the way that nearly always works on Mom and Dad. I'm not so easily persuaded.

"You're dressed in an impeccable vintage dress to bake? Were you careful?" I ask as I try to take in the scene of the formal dresses and trashed kitchen. "Where is the music coming from?"

"Look!" Aunt Liza picks up a very modern set of blue speakers. "My little grandson set this up for me!"

Brilliant. I'll have to pinch Matthew for that one later. I was so happy when the turntable broke because I didn't get hit with scratchy, tinny-sounding swing music or fifties pop or whatever Liza's mood dictated for the day. I should have known that would never last. At least the iPod won't sound garbled like the record player sometimes did.

I turn toward my sister. "Dad asked me to get you because he and Mom are getting ready for services tonight, and he wants to have dinner." I'm not sure how cookies are going to play into dinner, but all I was asked to do was fetch Mickey.

Mickey adjusts the feather in her blond hair and pushes out her lower lip in a pout. "Please? Just a minute more?"

I start to protest that I'd really like some time to myself, but the timer goes off and Aunt Liza claps her hands together before shoving vegetable-printed oven mitts over her long, black gloves.

Instead of arguing, I scan the delicate white fringe of the dress Mickey has on, looking for signs of flour or butter or anything else that could ruin the fabric. "Just tell me when you have a plate of cookies for us to take back home."

Mickey twists away. "I wore an apron when we were baking. Seriously, Gabe."

I raise my hands in defeat and lean against the counter.

Over-the-top exclamations, in accents that don't exist, bounce back and forth between my little sister and Aunt Liza. At least they're having fun. When I was little, I played upstairs alone or in the coffin room. If I went outside, I always had to stay two rows of grave markers close to the house so Mom could keep an eye on me. Aunt Liza was still working at Paradise Hill Funeral Home then and not just collecting money for funeral plots like now. I'm not sure if I'm grateful I didn't grow up with Aunt Liza like Mickey, or jealous.

"Would you like one?" Mickey asks me in a French accent that makes it sound like she's choking on her tongue.

The smell of chocolate and sugar has pretty much permeated my senses, so I pull a cookie from the top of the pile. "Thanks, Mickey." I take a bite with a subtle smile because my face still throbs. "See you soon, Liza."

She slips off her oven mitts and picks up the cigarette she left burning on the counter. "Will Matthew be working tonight?"

"Um...I'm pretty sure, yeah."

She waves good-bye, one gloved finger at a time, and Mickey follows me out of the house. The plate of cookies rests in one hand, and she smiles widely as she takes an enormous bite. "Why don't we do fun things like this at our house?"

I glance down at her sparkling outfit. "Where are your normal clothes?"

"I'll get them later."

"I take it you two were clawing around in the basement's massive closet?" The women in our family knew how to dress, and they kept everything. I can't imagine what the owner of Audrey's Vintage Boutique would do to get a crack at some of those clothes.

Mickey jumps and grins at me—a sure sign of an idea I'm not going to like. "You could get your prom dress from Aunt Liza!"

"I'm not going to prom," I say automatically. The whole idea of spending an entire day getting ready for a high school dance with a guy I probably won't still be talking to in six months feels incredibly pointless. Of course, Bree agrees.

"Why can't you be normal and like normal things?" Mickey whines.

I let out a snort. "Normal is boring, and besides, Bree and I have plans that do not include hanging out with high school follower-zombies."

Mickey's face contorts into something equaling me being stupid, but I'm not going to argue about whether or not I'm going to prom with an eleven-year-old, and she seems to know it, so we move ahead in silence.

"What happened to your face?"

"I wrestled a biker gang at the library," I deadpan.

Mickey scoffs but doesn't say anything else.

The sun is about to dip below the horizon, and the shadows stretch long in front of us. I wish that I could spend the rest of the night out here. In the quiet.

"Gabe! Mickey!" Mom calls. "Hurry up! We need to eat! Services start soon!"

Mickey and I break into a run. We have a typical meal where we watch Mom shovel in as much food as she can while watching the door that leads downstairs. Dad doesn't show. He never leaves the guests. Mom finally leaves with a sigh to help Dad. She's always so hopeful we'll actually make it together for dinner. Mickey beats me to the remote, and I check my phone again. Still nothing.

I'm still waiting...I text.

No response.

I seriously need some distraction.

# Chapter 5

Brushing my silver name badge, I put on my best work smile. Distraction achieved.

Before heading into the lobby, I look up Bryce on every social media outlet I can think of to see if *he's* posted anything since Bree hasn't. Of course he has no privacy settings anywhere, so his stupid grin is easy to find. But nothing new about her—or from her either. Did they both just jump off a cliff after they left the library? Seriously. I need updates.

I shove my phone into my pocket and push through the office door into the lobby. Matthew sets a tray of cookies on the table for the people milling around, grabs one for himself, and then turns in my direction. My cousin looks pretty great in his suit, but he has such a huge ego and such batshit hobbies that I'm not sure if he'll ever settle down. Matthew is a traditional early-twenties California hunk—tanned, blond, and I know that he uses clippers to make sure he has the right amount of stubble.

His brows bob up and down in a hello gesture. I give him a quick wave before checking what snacks we have out and what I might need to bring from the back.

"If it isn't the girl with a sarcastic coat of armor around her fragile little brain and cold, cold heart." He grins.

"There's something to be said for someone smart enough to be sarcastic," I say back.

"And what's being said?" he asks, one of his brows shooting toward his hairline.

"That it's a good thing."

Matthew flips a small shortbread cookie into the air before catching it in his mouth. His eyes zero in on my nose. "What happened to your face?"

"What happened to *yours*?" I quip back, even though it makes zero sense.

"Bad talk-back, cousin." He runs a finger down his jawline. "This face is perfect."

I snort.

"So? Face?"

"I ran into—"

He holds his hand up. "Don't even finish. You'll just embarrass yourself."

I turn to walk away. "Don't eat all the cookies."

"Like you could stop me," he whispers just loud enough for me to hear.

I head in search of Dad and flip off Matthew behind my back. He barks out a short laugh behind me.

Dad's talking with a woman whose pinched face tells me she's probably the family member nominated to deal with the arrangements. He keeps nodding, and I can just make out bits of

*Don't worry…*and *Yes, we've taken care of that…*

She seems like one of those people who need to be busy to cope. People like her are why even Bree prefers to be downstairs where the bodies are stored, instead of up here when we have crowds. The deceased are one thing. The mourners? Quite another.

*Why isn't she answering me?*

"Excuse me?" a girl my age asks. She presses her fingers into her temples and lets out a bored sigh. "Of all the crappy ways to spend a Friday night. We drove all the way up here, and…"

I plaster on a smile. "Can I help you?" I ask softly. I'm still in my work voice, which is stupid. She's my age. She could care less if I sound professional.

"Bathroom?" she asks. "I need ah-*way* from these people."

I point back toward the front door. "Just around that corner to the left."

"Okay." She glances up and down at me, giving me a weird eyebrow raise. "I'm not going to accidentally go into a creepy room or anything, am I?"

I shift my weight to the side, sort of like she's doing, but the movement feels awkward. "It's just the bathrooms there."

"'Kay. Thanks." She spins and walks away.

It hits me that she's given up something fun to come here tonight. I have Bree and our blog and our vintage hunts, but my Friday nights are almost always spent here. I slip out my phone to take a quick peek. *Still* nothing from Bree. Her silence is now officially annoying.

Dad touches my shoulder, and I jump. "Can you find Matthew and have him refill the hot water for tea?"

"Yup."

"Where's your mom?"

"Not sure. She left a sandwich on your desk."

I swear Dad's whole face falls just a bit. "Won't have time but thanks."

He could make time, but Dad rarely leaves the lobby while people are lingering. The same woman as before stops in front of Dad, and I go in search of Matthew. The deceased woman really knew a lot of people—or her family did. The place is packed.

I walk in my practiced slow way to the doors of the small chapel. The large silver urn sits up front surrounded by a sea of white flowers. The room slowly fills with people talking in hushed voices. There's an occasional sniff. Maybe Hartman is right. Maybe this is a sad profession. I've been inside it for so long that it's just…Funerals happen. People die.

Mom taps my shoulder. "I know you have homework. I found Matthew. Your dad obviously isn't going to leave." Her gaze flits to Dad with the look of adoration she always has for him. It's tinged with worry right now, which is normal. "The food is set. You're fine to go back home."

I nod once, but do a quick scan of the table with tea, coffee, snacks…It all looks very hotel-like and professional, which is what they want. Mom's right. It's all in order. Matthew emerges from the offices with another large, silver hot-water container. Guess they have it under control. I'll have to find something else to occupy my brain.

Mom points as she studies my nose. "And don't forget to put some ice on your face."

Right, the bruising and swelling is probably worse after all my running around. Of all the stupid things. I make my way through the long faces and back into the safety of our offices. Once the door closes behind me, I rest my back against it. Time for chocolate milk, some good Jeremy Messersmith-type music or Spoon or Guster, and maybe a few episodes of *Project Runway*. I head through the back door of the offices and into the entryway of our house.

My phone finally vibrates with a text from Bree. Having an unexpectedly good time. Will give you a full report tomorrow.

*Tomorrow?*

I have to wait? I text. Are you serious?

Yep! I'm there for work anyway, and you need me to do your brows! It'll be perfect.

I can't believe she's making me wait that long! I jog up the stairs to see Mickey with a full bag of Oreos.

A thought for the night—Do you ever feel like we're missing out on the high school experience?

It's one thing to realize a girl stuck at a funeral has better places to be, but really, high school is something to be endured before moving on to better things.

Nope. And since you're making me wait, you'd better make it good.

Promise

Ok

This is so…strange. And maybe I shouldn't have told her to make her story good. Bree sometimes charges into new things feet first and eyes closed.

Her ex Jacob is proof of that. So is Grant. So is the catastrophe of the red hair she attempted last year.

But Bree has to be smarter than to jump in with Bryce. I think.

\* \* \*

Instead of trying to catch some sleep, I log onto the website I stared with Bree and click on the History of Us section to maybe tweak it a bit. Bree's section is short.

Back when I was given weird looks in middle school for my bright dresses, old shoes, and vintage everything, Gabe thought I was cool. Gabe puts up with my whining. She knows her shiz when it comes to vintage. She can spot a wannabe vintage dress in a heartbeat. She's smarter about boys than me. When I try to help her with something, she actually takes my help, and wants it. And all of that is great and is why we're friends, but the main thing is this: *Gabe makes me the best version of me, and she always knows when I need a doughnut.*

So much of Bree's life is a disaster that I get why her write-up is so short. What she didn't want to say is that when things get rough with her family, she comes here. And stays. Sometimes for days. I don't question. My parents don't question. It just happens.

My section is a bit longer. I'm sure my parents have read it, but I'm pretty sure the rest of my family couldn't care less about my little website.

Before Bree, friends didn't come over often for a lot of reasons:

1. A certain family member generally embarrassed me by making comments about "growing up" and "becoming a woman" even when I was in fourth grade.
2. Because where I live is a business, which means the 'rents are always working so no one was around to supervise—back when I needed supervision.

3. Once my friends knew we had dead people in the basement...that was pretty much the end of them wanting to come to my house unless they thought they'd find a ghost or something equally stupid. So, they weren't at my house for me, but for a peek at death.

So when Bree followed me home after school one day, even after I warned her about living in a funeral home, I was panicking. I really thought that would be the end of our friendship—the one that was based mostly on her saving me from my elementary school clothes and PE.

Instead, we explored the whole upstairs—even the rooms I never bothered to go in. All the places that Mom said were okay. The next day, we explored the whole rest of the house. Even the basement.

I didn't understand until she showed up for the fifth or sixth day in a row how much I'd missed out by never having friends over. My life had spread about eighteen times bigger than I imagined it ever would.

And we've been friends ever since.

Also, she's a great dresser.

There's really nothing to add to this page, though I'm tempted to say she sometimes *sucks* at updating her social media accounts. But I don't.

I close out of my browser. Still nothing from Bree. The universe has tipped today.

* * *

Midnight and I'm blinking at my ceiling, but each time I blink, the side of my head feels a little like it's splitting apart.

*Sucks.*

After a few more blinks that feel like boxing gloves slamming into my head, I roll slowly out of bed and stumble for the bathroom. The hardwood floors are like ice under my feet, so I end up doing this weird prance, which brings my stinging headache to the edge of a migraine.

*Well, crap.*

Shoving a few Advil into my mouth, I prance back to my room, tug sweats over my shorts, slip on a bra, and tuck my feet into slippers.

It's about midnight, and Matthew usually does the embalming at night, so he might still be downstairs. I walk-slide in my slippers to the far side of the living room and open the door to the old back stairs. Having a turret that's just for stairs seems really, really stupid. But at this moment, and on a lot of other late nights, I'm thankful for them.

The small, round room is black because no one bothered adding electric lights to this part of the house. I feel along the wall until I find the iron railing. Once I make it down the two flights, I give the metal door a shove. Its newness is glaring next to the worn plaster, even in the near pitch-black. I open the door and step into the storage room. Cold storage lockers line one whole wall. Three bodies rest under sheets and sit against the opposite wall on gurneys.

The large double doors to outside are closed, so Matthew's probably not moving in a new corpse. As I step closer to the small embalming room, I hear the distinct sound of the pump that pushes embalming fluid through the bodies and give a quick knock before opening the metal door.

Matthew's in full work garb—clear, plastic face mask, scrubs with a plastic bib, gloves, and even his rubber boots. Fits with the sterile-looking room. White walls. White and stainless steel cabinets. Small objects that look something between medical and dental tools on a tray next to the body.

"What up, Cuz?" Matthew asks as I step inside.

"Can't sleep."

He points at me, a metal hook in his right hand. "You're not really dressed to be in here. I'm pretty sure getting body or embalming fluid on your pajamas isn't something you'd like to have happen. And seriously, we have a good air exchange, but not all these chemicals are things you should be breathing."

I roll my eyes because of course I know this.

"Who you working on?" I ask from the door. Only one of the embalming tables is occupied.

"A Mr. Clancery." He peers at the level of fluid in the clear pump. "Cool last name, huh?"

"Very cool," I agree. It's amazing the little details about people that Matthew clings to.

"Wanna guess?" He grins.

I glance at the man's face, a little grayish right now, but it will pink pretty quickly once the embalming fluid fills his veins.

The man is older, but not super old. About ten years older than my dad and pretty overweight. "Heart attack?"

"Two more," Matthew says, as he massages the corpse's fingers. The toes will be next. He thinks the embalming fluid does a better job of making the person seem lifelike when he rubs the extremities. I can't figure out who would take off a dead man's socks to look at his toes, but my cousin is happy.

"Two more…" I mumble. I have three chances to guess right or I lose. Nothing really happens when I lose, but the next time Matthew gives me crap, or pinches me or scares me from behind, he'll bring this up and say that he "won" the chance to make me mad or freak me out.

Matthew moves to the feet, and I snatch a small towel and drop it over the man's privates—dead or alive, I'd rather not see anyone's bits unless I ask for it.

"Come on," Matthew chides. "Don't think so much."

"Maybe..." I tilt my head to the side. The body doesn't look traumatized at all. Cancer victims are usually much thinner, and sometimes turn a little green with the chemo. "Aneurysm?"

Matthew's smile widens, so I know I don't have it yet. "One more..."

Okay. I'm *not* losing tonight.

I slip on gloves really quickly because I wanna check this old guy out a little before I make another guess.

I squint at the man's gnarly toes. Then I move up his side and turn over his hand. There are scabs on his finger pads. Ha. "Diabetes?"

"Damn!" Matthew laughs. "Got me."

"And I'm going to collect."

He squints at the pump before flicking it off. "So, why aren't you sleeping tonight?"

I point to my nose. "Has to do with the face." And a certain best friend being weird about a guy.

"Ah," he says.

"Anything else interesting down here?"

"The one that came in tonight is an old-age death. It'll be a cremation."

"Nothing good to add to the list then," I say. Mom frowns every time our list is mentioned, so it's now on Matthew's phone instead of taped to the white subway tiles on the wall.

"Nope." Matthew agrees as he starts to rinse off the body again. He's meticulous—always giving the cadavers a shower before and after embalming. "Your dad would kill me if he knew you hung out with me in the middle of the night."

Matthew will cover for me, but knowing he lives with my aunt Liza, I really should make an effort to not complicate his life.

"Night," I tell him as I back out of the room.

He's totally absorbed in his world, lathering soap and gently swiping over Mr. Clancery's face. "Night."

I pull open the metal door that leads to the back stairs and start running up in the blackness. Now I *have* to get some sleep, or at least try to plan what I might say to Bree when she comes to work tomorrow.

# Chapter 6

Music echoes off the walls of the steel-and-white sterile room. "Lucy in the Sky with Diamonds" because Bree is going through another Beatles phase.

The deceased, a Mrs. Farmer, rests between us, a bright light shining on her face so we can match her makeup to a photo we've been given by the family.

Bree's frosted, glossed lips move slightly as she sings along and dumps the first bit of foundation onto a small sponge.

"Um, you owe me details," I tell her. "I haven't forgotten that you left me totally in the dark last night."

"Me either." Bree smirks before continuing.

I readjust myself on the stool. Short skirts and stools don't mix well.

"Too dark," Bree says, pointing to the liner I pick up.

I point to the picture of Mrs. Farmer. "I'm trying to match the picture."

The elderly woman is fully dressed but still on the prep table that rests between Bree and me. Her coffin is waiting off to the side next to a few empty gurneys.

Bree lets out a sigh. "That picture is from a big anniversary celebration. I don't think she needs to be so made up at her own funeral."

She pops her lips together a few times as she studies the woman's face.

Narrowing my eyes at Bree's work and then at the picture, I loosen my hold on the brown pencil. "Funerals are sort of like a party," I mumble.

Bree snorts through her dainty nose and gives me a sideways look. "Funerals aren't parties."

"So you, like, dropped off the planet last night."

Bree snatches the eyeliner with a grin. "It was just really late when I finally got home."

"Did your grammy freak?"

Bree rolls her eyes. "Whatever. She goes to bed at, like, eight."

I know I'm not normal in this moment because all I can think is, *Who is going to keep Bree safe if her grammy doesn't even know when she comes and goes?*

"It was..." Bree pauses for a moment. "He was so super relaxed, and we just talked and it was not at all what I expected."

Nerves and bewilderment ping around inside me, making it hard to consider sitting. "What did you expect?"

Bree's smile has to be hurting her cheeks.

Mrs. Farmer has been forgotten.

"I expected...I guess I expected that he'd be sort of loud and conceited and talk about sports the whole time or something. I don't know." She sucks her lower lip into her mouth, but her smile is still there. He's totally going to weasel his way in as her boyfriend or something—at least until he's done with her. "He's just…so cute and so fun. It was totally his idea to set our cell phones aside and hang out. Like, no one does that anymore, you know?"

I fold my arms. "*Everybody* thinks he's sweet until the guys on whatever team Bryce is on start wagging their brows at whoever he's dating and hinting they've seen pictures, or hinting that Bryce is big on embellishing his kiss-and-tell stories."

"Kiss-and-tell stories?" Bree quirks a brow.

"You *know* what I mean."

"Is it so strange that I had fun?" she asks. "He might not even like me past being friends. He didn't make a move to kiss me or anything. We ate, and we just had so much to say that we kept talking and talking. And then we went down the stairs to the beach and walked up and down until we could barely see, so he had to use his dying phone's flashlight to get back up the stairs."

She's all giggly and starry-eyed and…He was supposed to act like his stereotypical self so she'd run screaming. What is his endgame? And how did any of this keep her from writing me?

"You know it's my job as your friend to, like, keep warning you about his reputation, right?" I take the eyeliner back and begin Mrs. Farmer's eyes again.

Her smile doesn't even waver, and her eyes don't lose an ounce of sparkle. "We spent most of the time saying things to each other that we don't say in the after-school group that the counselor does." Bree shrugs. "His dad just stopped coming home for weekends from LA, and they don't talk. I barely talk to either of my parents, so Bryce gets that about me."

There is a feeling swirling inside me that I can't totally place, maybe a touch of jealousy mixed with worry mixed with…I don't know what else. I was the one who sat next to Bree through her parents' divorce. Just like she was the one who sat next to me after my grandparents died. Doughnuts on the beach, sugar and sand, and now suddenly Ego-Bryce has insights I don't?

"I know that look." Bree's smile falls. "Please let me be happy."

I let out a sigh. She helped me pick up the pieces after Bryce's teasing made me want to stop going to school. I don't understand how she could move forward with him now.

Bree shifts on the bed. "I think you're getting weird."

I start to rub my face, but stop the second my finger touches my sore nose. "I'm not getting weird. I'm just worried."

"I'm not stupid, but the really, really vain side of me is doing cartwheels right now. Bryce. Johnson. He's like…*the* guy, you know? He's the guy who would be the unattainable hottie in every teen movie ever made. And the other part of me knows he's got this reputation, but I can't reconcile the guy I went out with last night with this jerk we've painted him to be." Every word of hers is pleading for me to understand. To share her excitement. I just can't. And Bree isn't the kind of person to let herself be fooled this way.

"*Several* ex-girlfriends have had pretty nasty things to say about him," I point out. "So he has to be pretty good at pretending at first."

"And ex-girlfriends' rants are *so* accurate." I wait for the confident Bree to roll her eyes or tilt her head, but she's still staring at me with doe eyes. "This is someone I've wanted to talk to you about, and I never have. Just…"

I stop with the eyeliner and try to think of some kind of argument, but maybe it's stupid to fight against her wanting to be with him. I don't know.

"But it got me thinking a little…" Bree opens an eye shadow

compact. "Like, you and I do our thing, and it doesn't change. I mean, when was the last time you sneaked out?"

"I sneak down to chat with Matthew," I say. And where would I even go if I left here? It's not like I'm going to drive in the middle of the night. I don't even like driving during the day. "And we've snuck a few bottles of wine from Liza."

"Matthew doesn't count." Bree snorty-laughs. "And sipping on wine we don't even like in one of the million spare rooms in this place only half counts. I don't know. I guess…I guess I feel like this is when we should be really *out* there, you know?"

No, I don't know. I have no idea how to respond or what to think. We have fun together. I work a lot. We hang at my house or her grammy's house or at Audrey's Boutique. It's good. I love our routine. A long time ago, we both decided that high school was just something to endure until we could live our real lives. How could Bryce change that in one night?

"Well, anyway. We texted for like an hour after I dropped him off. He promised that he'd drive next time, and…" Her shoulders come up and her smile widens even further and she takes in this long breath. "And I'm happy there's going to be a next time."

I try to shade the violet shadows together over the woman's lids without thinking about the eye caps underneath the skin.

"So. I'm going to ask you for a monster favor because I really need my friend to not make that face." Bree points.

I look up. "What face?"

"The face that says I'm betraying you for not hating Bryce until his death for minor crimes committed against you years ago." Bree's smile turns sheepish. "Please, please consider giving Bryce a blank slate."

I feel my brows rising before I can form words. "A blank slate for Bryce?"

Bree clasps her hands, her eyes back to the same pleading as in the library. "Pleeease?"

We both know there's no way I'm going to tell her no, but seriously, *Bryce Johnson.*

"Ruined my first kiss," I say.

"That same guy took your best friend out on one of the best dates of her life," Bree counters.

"Fine." I push out an exaggerated sigh. "You win. Blank slate."

"Yay!" Bree throws her arms around me. "Now I can actually talk about him."

And I will have to pretend I can actually forget what an ass Bryce is.

# Chapter 7

Bree stands at the doorway of my big walk-in closet, tapping her chin. "I'm so proud, Gabe." She dabs at fake tears. "You've come so far, but how do I forget how much black you have?"

I step beside her, glad my closet is so massive. "I need it for work." Which isn't really true. Mom and Dad only wear black about half the time.

"But…" She steps inside and starts tapping some of my favorite things—almost all of which I bought while we were shopping together. "What about this?" Her fingers stop on a turquoise dress she bought me for my birthday.

"I love it…" But then I falter. "I feel neon in it."

Bree's gaze flits to her own outfit. Lime green, orange, and yellow flowers dot the 1960s shift dress.

Her fingers tap a few more things. "Next time we hit Audrey's, I'm going to make you branch out a bit."

Branch out?

Bree's phone chirps in "Brown Eyed Girl," and she steps out of my closet with a face-splitting smile.

I cross my arms. Every piece of clothing in my closet is a mix of Bree's funky, vintage style and my need to blend. And it's not *all* black. I have some charcoal plaids and a few bits with ivory or white on them. Almost everything in here was purchased while I was with Bree—how can she be criticizing my closet?

Tweezers snap in front of my face. "I haven't forgotten…" she singsongs.

I groan, but she's totally right. My brows need help every couple weeks.

"You." She points to me and then to the small white chair that sits in front of the antique vanity Mom bought me. "Sit."

I flop down like a petulant kid, pushing out my lower lip. This is going to be extra painful with my sore face. I'm going to have to try super hard not to flinch.

Bree snorts. "You'd die without me doing this for you."

"Truth." There is no way I can tweeze my own brows because every time I pluck a hair, I jump, and pretty soon I'm jumping before I pluck. I stabbed myself in the eye once and had to do medicated drops for a week.

"You try to relax. I bet the pain meds you took for your face will help." Bree taps her toes on the hardwood floor as she studies my face with tweezers in hand. "Your nose doesn't look quite as bad as I thought it would. Little shiner. Little purple. Not horrible." She snaps the tweezers a few more times as she squints and gets closer to me. "How was your drive home with Hartman? You got my text, right?"

"Yes, I got your text. I have no idea how to take *interesting*, but I guess I'd say the same thing about him. It was sort of awkward but fine." I close my eyes because I'd rather not know when she's going to start.

"Hands under your butt," she directs, and I do as she says.

I've been known to jerk at unfortunate times.

"And that's it?" she asks. "*Fine?* He totally seems like your type."

"I have a type?" I ask.

"You prefer Q to James Bond. You're obsessed with *The Sorcerer's Apprentice* because you like that skinny guy. After that movie night with your cousin, you made me watch *Nick and Norah's Infinite Playlist* because you think Michael Cera is hot. So yeah, I think you have a type."

"Hartman is the new guy. Weird or not, girls are going to think he's awesome because he's new. I'm not into competing for the interest of a guy I probably will barely remember when I'm thirty." *Besides, he's friends with Bryce.* But since I just gave Bryce a blank slate, I can't say that.

A sharp pain slices over my eyelid. "Ouch!"

"Relax!"

"Hartman's sort of strange and awkward anyway," I say.

She plucks a few more brows, and I attempt a relaxed breath out, which hiccups when she pulls another brow.

"You know I love you, but *you're* sort of strange and awkward, Gabe. Or crazy aloof at the very least. I mean, I think the guys at our school have pretty much given up trying to get your attention."

*Guys have tried to get my attention?*

"Thanks to Bryce." I clamp my mouth shut.

"No," she says, jerking out two hairs with a little too much force. "Thanks to your reaction to his juvenile comments over *three years ago*. And blank. Slate."

"I liked Davis!" I laugh to try to show I'm over it, but the memory still pinches a little, so I'm not really over it.

She plucks a few more hairs, and I wince again.

"It was middle school," she says. "Davis moved away three months later anyway."

I hate that she's right. But it's still Bryce's pattern of jerk-off behavior.

"Bryce texted," she says, and I can tell by her tone she wants me to ask her about it, but...

I choke before the words come up my throat. "And?"

"We're maybe getting together later."

"But—" But I had to share Bree yesterday.

"Seriously." She bends forward to look me in the eye. "You're not at all happy that I'm happy?"

"I'm..." Still at a complete loss as to what I'm supposed to say right now.

Bree stands. *Stab. Stab. Stab. Stab.*

"I don't care about my brows!" I yell.

"Two more."

"Liar."

"Really, it was Bryce's comment about Wednesday Addams that made you research movies to figure out who he was talking about, and that research led you into heaven on earth."

Audrey's Vintage Boutique.

"And led you to the fabulous sense of fashion you have now—aside from all the *black*."

"Job hazard," I say automatically, and jump off my hands when she plucks out another hair. "Stop! I want to be Oscar the Grouch. Stop!"

"I'm done." She snaps the tweezers a few more times. "I just want to point out that maybe you have Bryce to *thank* for your quirky and fantastic sense of fashion as well as our disdain for everything high school, and maybe even, in a small way, our friendship."

I point up at Bree. "*That* is completely ridiculous."

She rolls her eyes in the way that says I'm not going to be able to convince her of anything. "So, you're not really giving Bryce a do-over, are you?"

"I'm…trying?" I offer.

Two knocks are followed by Mom.

"Hey, Bree."

"Hey, Mrs. O." Bree smiles. "What's up?"

"Make sure you write down your hours before you leave, so we can get you a check, okay?"

Bree gives her a salute, and then Mom's eyes turn toward me. "I have two more things to finish up, but I'm sure your sister is ready to come home. Can you go pick her up?"

"At Liza's?" I ask with a groan. "When will you let her walk home on her own?"

Bree snorts. "It might be fun, Gabe. Maybe Aunt Liza will grab your chest again and remark on your growing bosoms."

"Please, Gabe," Mom says.

I let my head fall back in mock exasperation. "Fine. But I'm digging through the snack closet before I go."

"Thanks, honey." Mom smiles before leaving.

Bree drops the tweezers in her bag. "Your parents are the best."

"They're…something," I offer, but I clamp my mouth shut before I complain too much. Bree's parents are pretty much the worst right now.

The need to apologize is still bugging me.

"Hey, I'm sorry," I tell her. "I'll try to, like, be excited for you."

Bree says nothing, just goes back to looking at my rows of

clothes. She's silent for so long that I'm scrambling for something to fill the space between us.

"You're being quiet. Guys don't come between us," I say, even though evidence is now supporting the opposite.

"No, I know…" But her gaze doesn't find mine.

"Website?" I ask, knowing that working on our vintage-y blog is the one thing we can always agree on.

Her eyes brighten immediately, and she leaves my closet before crawling onto my bed and sliding my laptop off the nightstand. I join her. Now, we're back in our Bree and Gabe zone.

Bree shows me a new photographer she found who takes for-real Polaroids from one of the original cameras instead of all the new knockoffs. Her comments go from the really fantastic pictures to something else Bryce said, to the pictures, to something Bryce said, to a dress, to *Bryce*…

I do lots of smiling that involves my jaw being tighter than it should be for a smile. This isn't what it's like to hang with Bree. When I hang with Bree, I don't have to put on any kind of face or front or politeness. How has that shifted with one Bryce date?

She's in a lot deeper with him than she'll even admit to me. Bree's smarter than to fall for someone like him. I'm going to have to really watch out for her.

# Chapter 8

I stand in front of my closet Monday morning, the weirdness with Bree still clinging to me. I run my fingers over the little turquoise ModCloth dress. Okay, I can wear this bright color. I totally can.

When I slip on the dress, it looks as sickly as my pale skin under the fluorescent lightbulbs Mom got. If I didn't have to be awake before the sun came up, I wouldn't feel so grossly pale in the morning.

I turn on my bedside lamp and then turn off the overhead light.

The dress isn't bad, but wearing only one layer when I'm not in something dark is…exposing. I grab a black cardigan and push my arms through it, tugging the soft fabric over my shoulders. My whole body almost tingles in relaxation, and the dress doesn't feel as far outside my normal.

I tap my foot on the floor and scan my shoes. I could wear Dad's old ones with this, but…

Maybe—I reach down and pull out a pair of black wedges that Bree talked me into—maybe these. She'd be so proud of me. And making Bree proud of me will maybe gain me some leverage with the whole Bryce situation. Sitting on my bed, I buckle the straps and stand. My foot immediately tilts to the side, my stomach leaps into my throat, and I sit down.

"Definitely not those…" I toss them back into the closet. "Clumsy girls should never wear heels."

I slip on my over-the-knee black socks and then shove my feet into the familiar worn leather of Dad's old shoes.

Makeup takes forever because of my sore face and stupid bruise. After five minutes messing around to make my foundation cover the discoloration, all I bother with is mascara, liner, and red lips. I really hope this shiner goes away fast.

I jog down the stairs and see Mom and Dad sitting in the kitchen doing that gross googly-eyed thing at each other.

"You're not sixteen. Knock it off," I tease as I pull open the fridge.

"Well, don't you look cute?" Mom teases back. "Who's the guy?"

My cheeks heat. Did I overdo it? "No guy." I make a face. "I'm trying to take attention away from my bruise."

Dad stands and stretches, his tie still hanging loosely around his neck. "You're looking far too grown-up."

In that case, I'm for sure wearing this today.

His eyes narrow as he studies my face. "The bruise is a little better."

"Half a bottle of foundation later," I say.

"Are you really heading down to work already?" Mom asks, tugging her bathrobe more tightly around her.

Dad rubs his forehead. "Farmers will be by in about an hour. We got a new body in last night, and Matthew wanted to ask me something before he started. We also need to check on our shipment. I think we're out of eye caps and a few other things. And there's the new..." He pauses as he gives Mom a knowing look, a dead giveaway that he doesn't want me to hear something.

That's fine. I've already shuddered thinking about eye caps. Worse would be the eyes of the deceased looking all sunken in, but still... Thinking about setting eye caps and sealing eyelids crawls under my skin like nothing else we do.

"I'll take care of that," Mom says. "You really should have told the family that we're not open until after nine." Mom's voice echoes the same worry it does every time Dad does special favors for people, which is all the time.

"It's fine. They're picking family up from the airport and..." He shrugs.

It's convenient for the family to come at this time, so Dad'll make sure it can happen.

Mom glances at her phone. "I should wake Mickey up for school soon."

Dad kisses Mom's head and squeezes her shoulder. I shouldn't be subjected to this kind of display before seven in the morning.

I grab a yogurt. "I'm gonna head out."

"Eating on the run?" Mom asks.

"Yep."

"You have more meetings after school for your project?" she asks. "Tomorrow? Or do you and Bree have things going on?"

I shake my head.

"Anything else going on?"

I shake my head again. "Wait. Today or tomorrow?"

Mom sighs. "Tomorrow afternoon."

"Do you *need* me to be gone..." but I clamp my mouth shut. Matthew usually warns me when we have a kid in because Mom and Dad both act strange and don't always want me to help. "I'll hole up in the library after school until you give me the okay. And I can get Mickey from school if you need."

Mom gives me a small smile.

"Infant or kid?" I ask.

Her smile disappears. "Does it matter?"

"I always know, Mom. It's not like you're saving me from something by asking me to hide in the house."

She nods once. "I know, but it makes me feel better. He was ten. Died when his bicycle weaved in front of a truck."

I flinch and then tug a corner of my mouth up. "And here you thought I was crazy for having no interest in learning to ride bikes."

Mom's face is unreadable for a moment, and I freeze, wondering if I've gone too far. "Please don't," she says. "Being alive is only worth it if you're actually living."

She says this a lot, and I only half understand what she means. I'm living right now. Breathing up the air in our kitchen. I'm about to go to school. Breathe in the air there. Talk to people. Or, well, talk to Bree. I'm so very *living* right now.

* * *

I cut through the football field, even though some of the more serious jocks are out here running in the morning.

"Gabe!" Bree waves from the bleachers.

This doesn't compute. At all.

When did Bree turn into one of the bleacher bunnies, the girls who sit and ogle the jocks? Meghan and Jessica are here watching their boyfriends—junior class royalty this year. Senior royalty next year.

"You look soooo cute, Gabe! Come 'ere!"

I shift my messenger bag higher on my shoulder and walk toward Bree. The spring rain feels more like mist, but my guess is that she's internally having a panic attack over the frizz that's going to start wreaking havoc with her smooth hair.

"Why are you here?" I ask as I hit the bottom step.

Bree is smiling so widely and so fully, and she's so happy that I'm smiling back before I realize it. "Bryce just asked if I'd come. No biggie."

But it *is* a big deal. This isn't our routine. Our routine is to hang at her locker or at my locker until school starts. That shifts a little when Bree's dating someone, but here? The football field? This is a different world of people than...I guess, us.

Bryce and the guys are doing tag football this morning, and way more than half of them have their shirts off, so they're not doing shirts and skins, they're just showing off. Of course Bryce is without his shirt. So's his friend Jeremy, who Bree used to crush on, and Theo, whose dark skin and big muscles make everyone else look like skinny, little white guys.

"He's just..." She lets out a sigh as we lean against the half wall next to the field. "Look at him. He has *abs*, Gabe. Abs."

"Yep."

Abs really aren't my thing. Everyone has them—some are just buried more deeply than others.

She leans closer to me, her perfume as overwhelming as flowers sometimes are, but I hold in my sneeze.

"Gah!" She grips the top of the half wall. "So much hotness in one person."

I watch the guys laughing and then setting up in lines again. I mean, they're cute for sure, but I can't get past the fact that some of them act subhuman in school. Without his looks, Bryce would just be another egotistical asshole who'd be sent to the counselor to make sure he was stable.

"I'm kind of getting excited about the possibility of him." Bree's attention is on the mess of bodies in front of us. "He's not what I expected. Sometimes we have to pause our conversations so he can help his mom with his baby brother, and…I don't know. He's more than a pretty face."

I turn my attention toward the guys, but there's yelling and grunting, and they're all shiny from sweat or the small bits of rain. It doesn't much matter which, because it's gross either way. I'm totally baffled by the idea that my friend might start dating this guy.

But I recognize the far-off look on her face. It happened with Jamal and again with Peter and sometimes with the lifeguards at the beach who are far too used to starry-eyed looks.

There's really no good way for me to tell her *again* that I don't trust him, but I don't want to see Bree get hurt.

"How's your mom?" I ask instead of saying anything about Bryce. Bree goes very still. "I don't know," she mumbles.

Now I feel like a jerk for asking. Bree would have said if anything had changed. "Sorry."

She stares at the ground for a minute. "And my dad is really busy with his new job, in case you were wondering. My check hasn't come again this month, so he must have had to renew his golf club membership or needed a new car, or who knows what else."

My stomach shrivels. I get annoyed with how involved my parents are, but I can't even wrap my head around how I might feel if they split and then left me behind. "I can see if Mom and Dad need more help," I say quietly. Her grammy lives on social security and Bree said something about property taxes going up again, so money has to be tight.

Bree would never say she needed more hours outright. She'd just laugh it off or shrug and ask if I wanted to work on our website.

Bryce grins at Bree from the field, kisses two of his fingers, and then points at her. She gives him a smooth smile back and shifts her weight a little—almost like she's posing.

He may not have kissed her yet, but kissing his fingers is a pretty big sign of how he wants her to think he feels about her.

"You ready to go in?" I ask, not wanting to see any more Bryce displays of pretend affection.

She shakes her head, still smiling. "I'm gonna stay out here for a bit."

"You sure?" I ask.

Bree's gaze is firmly planted on Bryce. "I'm sure."

I bet she'll be tardy. These guys all have PE first hour. I know this because they all have government second hour, and they come in smelling like either BO or too-thick cologne.

"Okay, see you." I pause, waiting for her to say something, but she's still totally focused on Bryce.

Happy flippin' Monday.

# Chapter 9

My morning pain medicine has kicked in by second period, so my nose just aches instead of throbs.

I stop at the door to US government when I see Hartman standing at the front of the room talking to our teacher. He probably has a lot to sort through since he transferred so close to the end of the year. That must suck for him. He turns a bit to the side. Bow tie today. Skinny black pants. Same curly, messy hair. I forget to breathe for a moment. His style at the library wasn't a fluke.

Bree giggles to my right, and I look just in time to see Bryce grinning at her while sitting sideways in his seat across the aisle.

Could he be any more obnoxious?

I sit in the seat behind Bree, and she turns to face me almost immediately.

She's giving me a look that I can't decipher.

"What?" I ask.

"Two things," she whispers.

I lean forward on my desk and whisper back. "One?"

"Bryce asked me to prom."

What?

Bree blinks. "Come *on*, Gabe. You need to show the proper amount of excitement instead of looking like I just ran over a puppy."

We had a plan. The whole night planned out to hang together. We don't do school dances. Ever.

Bryce leans in to our conversation. "Excitement over what? You flaking on prom already?"

Bree pushes on his shoulder with a wide smile until he slides back in his seat.

"You're still giving me that look." Bree leans in. "This has nothing to do with sisters before misters, Gabe. This is *prom*."

Instead of arguing that backing out of plans with your sister for a mister is *totally* putting misters before sisters, I figure it's best to move on. We can discuss the horrible way she's letting me down later.

"Two?"

Bree sits a little taller. "I got a text from Jill."

"At Audrey's?" I ask.

Bree rolls her eyes. "Is there another one?"

I shrug instead of answering something that doesn't need to be answered.

"Big shipment this week. We can*not* miss seeing the new stuff."

I plop my notebook on my desk. "Of course." I can't remember the last time we missed shipment day at Audrey's.

Hartman folds himself into the chair behind Bryce.

He gives me a quick nod, and Bree's eyes are suddenly on him. And then me. And then him. And then me. And now him.

The air leaves my lungs in a rush. *Oh no.*

"How you settling in?" Bree asks Hartman with a too-big smile.

He shrugs. "Okay, I guess."

"His mom just found them a house, which is cool," Bryce says. "Or my mom did. Or something."

Bree leans over my desk again, and I almost lean away because I'm pretty sure I do not want to hear whatever she's about to say. "You could at least *think* about him," she whispers. "Bryce already knows him, and we could double to prom! It would be perfect!"

My heart pounds in my throat. That's not really my idea of perfect. My idea of perfect was to hang with crazy Aunt Liza and try on everything in her closet with Bree. We figured that since we gave ourselves a while to work up to spending that much time with my crazy aunt, we could handle her for a few hours—especially if we could talk her into a few glasses of wine. We already had a prom-night plan. A perfect Bree-and-Gabe prom-night plan.

"Come *on,* Gabe!" Bree whisper-yells. "He'd be perfect for you!"

"Bree," Mr. Sandstrom says. "We're trying to start class."

"Sor-ry!" she sings.

My poor heart flutters at the thought of actually going on a *date* with Hartman, and my thoughts turn fuzzy. Wonder if this is how people feel just before they have a heart attack?

I've only sort of dated before. There were a couple weird hookups at beach parties, and last summer I was on and off with this guy up here from San Diego, but people go their separate ways after that kind of thing. Starting with *prom*? That's like learning to swim by being dumped in the middle of the ocean. Not really my style. I mean, I've kissed a couple guys before, but nothing that stilled the earth, much less my heart or any other organ worth mentioning. I glance at Hartman, pretty sure that the world would still for whatever girl he kissed.

My neck and cheeks burn.

I have no idea what's discussed in class because all I can do is stare at Mr. Sandstrom and count the minutes in my head. The way I feel makes no sense.

Maybe just for today, I should try to avoid Bree. Just until I can figure out how say no to her prom double-date scheme.

But it turns out I don't have to be careful about avoiding Bree. She's only at her locker for seconds between classes. She doesn't meet me at our corner next to the cafeteria.

I sit off to stage left and search the cafeteria for her orange dress. Bree and I love to sit here. The theater kids rarely bother us, and the cafeteria is spread out below us so we can watch everyone and poke fun at their sheep-like tendencies.

A squeal pierces the gym, and my attention snaps to the right.

*Oh.*

No wonder I didn't see Bree. Her orange dress is covered up by Bryce's letter jacket. Not two weeks ago, she was laughing at how Jeremy's letterman jacket looked on Jessica, and how primitive that kind of "branding my girlfriend" is. And now...

I crumple my sack lunch and dump it before walking off the stage.

# Chapter 10

At the end of the day, I lean against my locker waiting for Bree to show up so I have a ride home. And I wait. And I wait.

Where on earth is she? I flip my phone over in my hand before starting a text to her. Just before I hit Send, I have a text from Bree. Got caught up in something. Sorry! Distracted in a fab way! Sending a replacement driver...

Oh no. It'll be one of the costume kids from the theater department or maybe someone from her photography class. Or worse, one of Bryce's lackeys.

I can just walk home. That would be totally fine. I head for the front of the school and then stop at the front doors.

The rain is coming down so hard that it's bouncing off the cars in the parking lot, creating a sort of watery halo around each of them. I need to step out in that to get home, and the rain will create a watery halo around me as well. I'd really, really rather not have a watery halo today. Or any day, really. Why didn't I wear my trench coat today?

I lean against the glass door of the school, wishing that I could blink myself home. That doesn't seem like a lot to ask. I'm just one person. I wouldn't abuse that gift by robbing banks or anything, just for minor inconveniences and maybe a few trips to Paris.

"Hey."

I jump at the sound of a male voice and slam my hand over my chest. "Geez."

"Sorry," Hartman says. He points outside with a long finger. "Is this normal for here?"

"It's not totally abnormal but pretty unusual."

I glance at his plaid button-down and wonder if *he* has abs—not that it matters.

He shifts his shoulders underneath his old-man cardigan and pushes his glasses up on his nose.

"Can I give you a ride?" he asks.

Bree totally put him up to this. "You just *happen* to show up when I need a ride?"

"Bree said she's your normal ride, and she got caught up."

*Of course she did.* So Hartman's her replacement, and this is probably because she wants me to go to prom so I won't be mad about her ditching me. She's so getting a text later. She probably didn't give me a ride just to force this situation.

"Well, don't worry yourself." I frown. "I've walked home in worse." I think.

"Really?" he asks, peering through the window at the sky.

"Maybe. I mean…probably." I'm squinting again, which makes my nose ache.

"I don't mind." Hartman glances at me.

I have no idea what to make of this guy. We stand and stare at each other for a beat. Another beat. Another…Is it my turn to talk or his? I don't remember.

"Okay then." He shoves out the door, and the second he's not under the awning, he dashes for his car. Rainy halo.

*Dang it.*

I sprint out behind him yelling. "Wait! I changed my mind!"

It's pouring, but he pauses at the passenger's side door and holds it open for me.

"Get in!" I yell. He doesn't. Just stands there and waits until my feet are in before closing the door and running to the other side.

"Whew!" he says as he jumps into the car and tries to swipe water from his curling hair. "I was told it didn't rain in California."

"You were told wrong." I laugh. "We're too far north for perfect weather."

He shakes his head, making me duck away on my side of the car to avoid the water droplets flying off his hair.

"Well, I *was* going to make a remark about you being polite and holding my door, but I take it back," I say as I make a show of swiping my arm and face.

"Did I get you?" His eyes widen. "I mean wet. I didn't get you wet, did I?"

I want to feed him a line like I'd do to Matthew about wet dogs shaking at the worst times or something, but instead just say, "Thanks for the ride."

"So…" He waits, maybe wondering if I'm going to say something else, and then sits back and starts his car. "You and Bryce are friends?"

I snort. "Not me."

"But your friend? She seems into him."

I don't even mean to sigh, but it comes out long and exasperated. "So it would appear."

Hartman backs out of the parking space.

"Your stuff…" He points under his eyes. "Running a little."

My what? *Oh. Crap.* All that eyeliner and makeup I used to try to cover up my black eye…I flip the visor down to see a face fit for Halloween—drooping, running mascara and liner in rivulets down my pale cheeks, and a bruise that's making a more dramatic appearance as my makeup smears. I press under my eyes and try to smoosh the black mess away with my fingertips—so much for "waterproof."

"Crap!" I yell when I hit my sensitive eye too hard.

Hartman pauses at the parking lot exit. "Let's see."

I turn to face him, and he studiously looks at my face for a moment. "That's quite a bruise you have."

I close my eyes. "I'm not the most…graceful person ever."

"Well, only one person is the *most* graceful, so you're one of several billion people."

I'm laughing again. "I guess so."

The rain beats against the roof of his car. I keep softly swiping underneath my eyes, hoping that I'm actually doing something with my light touches.

"So…" I start, only no more words come to mind. "The government project…"

"It's more interesting than I thought it would be."

I lean forward and stare at him. "Really?"

"Yeah. I had no idea there were so many steps and blocks and committees for new laws, and…It really is a mess, isn't it?"

"I guess." I hadn't looked at a single thing in class. I'd counted seconds and tried to ignore Bryce and Bree.

More silence as Hartman fumbles with his phone and the plug into the radio, and when his phone drops between the seat and the center console, he hits the radio. Music blasts into my eardrums. I jump. He jumps, swerves, and hits the radio button, silencing the music.

"Sorry."

I press my hands over my frantic heart. "My odds of making it home alive might have been better if I'd walked."

"In *this* rain?" He does this weird half-laugh choking thing.

I have no idea what this guy's deal is. He's so...strange. He drives straight to my house. Must have a good memory.

We pull to a stop under the awning, and Hartman leans one way a little and then the other, ducking forward like he's trying to see through the glass doors.

Why will it feel weird if I just get out of the car? That part should be easy.

"So, thanks again. I'm impressed you remembered where to go."

He clears his throat. "I've...I've been up this direction a few times since moving here."

I glance outside and then back toward him, unsure of what good protocol is in this situation. "Oh."

"Um...Can I..." He swallows, and I notice it because his Adam's apple really sticks out of his thin neck. "Can I come in for a sec?"

"Are you serious?"

The only people who want to come in want to see bodies out of morbid curiosity, or ask a bunch of stupid questions about ghosts. I don't know what happens to a person after they die, but they don't become ghosts. I don't care what Angel says.

"You're not, like...I don't know...just fishing for information about dead people or something, are you?"

His eyes flash to mine and then dart away. "I don't know anyone in California my age but Bryce, and you can imagine how interesting those conversations are. I sort of know you. That's all.

I'm just…I don't know. Is it weird if I come in? Do you never have people over?"

*No. I only have Bree over.* But that's not something I'm ready to admit. "Sure. Whatever. We always have loads of snacks because sad people eat a lot."

"Okay. Cool." He nods and taps on the steering wheel again. "Why don't you get out under the awning, and I'll park in the lot so I don't crowd up the drop-off place?"

How long does he plan on staying? I don't realize I'm staring until his eyebrows dance up in that universal gesture that says something like *I'm ready for my answer any time now…*

"Okay." I stumble out of the car and tuck my fingers into my hair, trying to fluff up my little bit of curl after the rain.

The second I step in the door, Angel grins like we're in on some secret. I've never been more relieved that he's on the phone. I walk back toward the chapel. I can't remember if today is the child's services or tomorrow. Maybe I shouldn't even be here.

Mom steps out of the chapel, closing the door behind her. "How was school?"

I lean away. She's also smiling too widely. "Um…good?"

"Who dropped you off?" she asks just as Hartman's lanky frame comes through the door. What kind of crazy "mom sense" does she have if she knew a guy dropped me off?

I spin to face Angel. "Did you seriously call my mom from across the room?"

Angel shrugs in innocence and points to the phone he's still holding to his ear, but I'm pretty sure it's a fake call.

Hartman's hands fan over his curly hair, brushing off water. With the way his gangly arms are jerking about, he looks sort of orangutan-like.

"This is…um…Hartman."

How weird is it that I've never introduced my parents to a guy before? Not that he's a *guy* guy, in the sense that we're dating or whatever, but the last thing I need is the twenty questions from my parents over someone who is *maybe* friend material.

His eyes dart around the open room, which looks much more modern than our place from the outside, and I'm so thankful it's empty now. Well…aside from Dad who I can hear in the salesroom, or the *How much do you love your loved one?* room, because the nicer the coffin or urn, the higher the price.

"I'm Jenny Osborn." Mom stretches out her hand and Hartman takes it.

"Great to meet you," he says.

"What are you two up to?" Mom asks.

"That's a good question." I guess I'm a crappy host to people who I'm not being paid to serve.

"Where's Bree?" Mom looks around me as if she somehow missed her.

"Out." I even manage not to frown.

"I'm just…I asked if I could kill some time here." Hartman winces like his words actually slapped him on the back or something. "Or… not *kill*, but…"

Mom laughs. "We've heard every bad pun and watched people flubber over much worse things than the word *kill*, so relax. I'm going to try to finish up the paperwork for Mr. Nichols before he leaves today."

"He's back?" I ask, my heart squeezing a little. *No, no, no, no, no… cannot feel the vice-grip feeling.*

When will they bury her? I know this is selfish and horrible, but that sweet, old broken man is going to break *me*.

"Burial is tomorrow morning, just before the services I asked you to miss," Mom answers. "He asked for another hour in the viewing room with his wife today. You know your dad would never say no to that."

She walks back toward the office, and I forget Hartman is with me. I have to see Mr. Nichols. I walk quietly across the lobby and pause in the doorway of the viewing room.

Mr. Nichols sits on a chair, his eyes closed, but I'm sure he's not sleeping. Just sitting.

The warmth of Hartman hits my back just before the grapy smell hits my nose. *Huh. I wonder what that is?*

Mr. Nichols's eyes open and they're on me.

I suck in a breath and grab my chest. "I'm so sorry," I blurt out.

His mouth twitches. "I know she's not here." He gestures to his wife in the casket. "But...she'll be buried tomorrow, and...and it's hard to imagine days when I won't see her face anymore."

I step into the room. My heart is trying to bang its way through my ribs. Normally I take off when this happens. I should get out of here. I really, really should. Closing my eyes briefly, I try to slow my heart and my breaths—such a generic reaction to everything. "I'm really sorry."

"I bet those words are pretty automatic for you." A corner of his mouth pulls up.

"Um..." I glance back at Hartman, but he's staring at the woman in the casket. "A little, yeah."

"I bet you think I'm crazy."

I shake my head.

"I bet that's automatic too." His smile is a little wider now.

"Yeah, but..." I touch my hand to my heart again. "Some people I notice more than others."

He tips his head in acknowledgment. "One day you'll fall madly in love, and when you do, you'll know why I'm here. Right now you probably see a crazy, old guy in a worn suit."

"I don't think you're crazy," I tell him.

"Me either," Hartman say from behind me, making me startle again.

"This your fella?" Mr. Nichols asks.

"What?" I jump away from Hartman, my frantic heart now fueling my suddenly spinning thoughts. "No. I barely know him. I mean…no."

Hartman is weirdly stoic.

"Tell your father thank you for his indulgences." The man stands up, walks to the coffin, and pats his wife's hand. "Always, love," he whispers.

"Maybe I'll see you again, Gabriella," he says to me before his gaze flits way up to Hartman's face. "And maybe you as well."

"Um, hmm…" Hartman's partial words are mumbled.

The man leaves, his hat still clutched in his hand.

Hartman takes a step forward. And then another one. His eyes are on the woman.

"You okay?" I ask. I barely notice the cadavers anymore, but it's different for everyone.

"I've never seen a dead person before. My mom was against an open casket. I saw my dad before school that morning, and…and now he's buried and I-I wish I'd have been able to say good-bye."

I fold my arms, having no idea what to say aside from the generic phrases I have stored up. And those tend to just pop out. "It'll get easier over time."

He takes another step forward and touches the woman's hand the way her husband just did. "She's cold."

"Yeah." Of course she's cold. She's just a thing now, not a person. I step back so I'm once again in the doorway.

Hartman stands over the woman, his head cocked to the side, and his hands now in his pockets.

"You get used to them after a while," I say. "I've…I mean, I guess I don't remember a time when having cadavers around wasn't normal. Bree and I did her makeup."

He turns to face me. "And what does that do to a person? Growing up like this?"

"It makes them weird." I hold my arms out to the sides and give him a little curtsy. "Like me."

A corner of his mouth kicks up.

"Oh good." Dad sighs. "I was with another wretchedly indecisive customer in the *coffin room*." He emphasizes those words, knowing that's what I call the showroom. "We need to get Mrs. Nichols back downstairs before the next viewing. Today turned extra busy, and you don't need to give me the same lecture as your mother did. I know my days would be less crazy if I started saying no."

"Diabetes guy?" I ask.

Dad presses his fingers to his forehead. "I wish you and Matthew wouldn't do that."

Time to change the subject then. "I can help," I say and then glance toward Hartman, hoping he catches the hint and takes off. "Thanks again for the ride."

"I can help too," he blurts out. "I'm Hartman." He holds his hand out for Dad, and Dad gives him this sideways look like Hartman is an alien or something.

"He's just a friend from school," I say quickly.

Dad's eyes pass back and forth between us a couple times, like he's just now putting together that Hartman is a guy and here with me.

I do not like this look. Dad's eyes catch mine, and I try to give my best *please be normal* look, which is really just me setting my jaw and widening my eyes and hoping he reads me well enough to know what I mean.

"How's the weather up there?" Dad asks Hartman with a half laugh.

I cringe because I'm used to people making stupid comments about my parents' job. Why would Dad make an obvious stupid comment about someone's height?

"Wet today." Hartman ruffs up his dark curls. I wonder if his hair is thick or soft or what.

"I've heard," Dad says as he gently closes the top of the casket and flips the locks down.

Mr. Nichols went all out. These caskets aren't cheap and sometimes take a while to get here. He maybe knew she was going before she died.

I start to think about facing my parents dead in one of these, but shake off the image before it can stick. I'm super good at that. Practice.

"If you two can double-team on the head end, I'll do the feet," Dad says. He jerks off the curtain that covers the wheels, and we start out of the room. "I just need help getting it into the elevator. Matthew can help downstairs."

Hartman has the strangest expression, or maybe this is just what his long, resting face looks like.

"There's a bump here," I tell him just as the casket lurches downward.

Hartman flinches, but I want to tell him that between the weight of one of these premium caskets and the body inside it, we have no hope of keeping it from tipping over if we really mess up.

Though I think the hallway is maybe too narrow for that. Then I think about the awesome irony if someone were to be crushed by a coffin and killed.

I snort, and Dad gives me a strange look, so I shove the thought away. But seriously, the *irony*.

There's another bump as we roll the casket onto the elevator—the metal space can fit two coffins if we need it to.

Dad's phone rings, and he quickly answers. "Yes, this is Mr. Osborn...Yes...No, that's not a problem..." He turns toward the wall, probably hoping to keep his conversation private.

Hartman steps further back in the elevator, and I jerk on the webbed handle, sliding the doors together.

Once the elevator moves, and Dad gives me an odd wide-eyed look while still on his call, I realize that I've maybe crossed a line in bringing Hartman to the basement.

"You should just stay in the elevator when we get downstairs," I say to Hartman. "The room down there is maybe weird." It doesn't feel weird to me, but one thing I've learned from Bree is that my normal isn't normal. I'm pretty sure we're about to see three caskets, and who knows how many bodies underneath sheets. Our town is growing.

Dad continues to talk in his work voice.

Hartman's jaw flexes. "No, it's fine."

But he doesn't look fine. He's pale, and he's staring at the metal wall. He's jiggling change in his pockets. Living people are the tricky ones, so as much as logic says I should understand his reaction, I don't understand his reaction. Being in the basement with the cadavers is simple. Those people are gone, peaceful, and quiet—infinitely easier than navigating this new Hartman situation.

Dad glances back and forth between us a few times, and I very pointedly don't look at him. My dad is a pro at asking questions with his eyes, and I don't want to try to answer with mine—at least not while Hartman is here.

"Yes…" Dad says into the phone. He's seriously staring at me. Yeah…I definitely shouldn't have brought Hartman down. "Yes, we can do that…"

As soon as the slow elevator hits the lower floor, I jerk open the doors and try to take in the room the way Hartman would see it.

Two bodies rest underneath sheets on gurneys. Two closed caskets, one smaller than the other. Too-bright fluorescent lights. White walls.

The double doors into the embalming room are wide open, and my cousin is standing with a light strapped to his head, an apron with a few smudges on it, and gloves that he's got clasped behind his back—probably because he sees that we have a guest down here. It's almost comical in its stereotypicalness. At least the body is covered.

"Hey, Cuz!" Matthew grins, and I cringe. "You should see what we got in today."

His eyes flit to Hartman and then back to me.

This is not good. It's just…While Matthew is the one I hang out with when I want to feel *less* weird because he's *so* weird, I'm really not sure how Hartman is going to react to him.

"What did…What did you get in?" Hartman asks. He gives me a quick look. Licks his lips. Jingles his change. Just when I think he's going to bolt to the back of the elevator, he steps out and toward Matthew.

Dad waves from the side, still on the phone, but I pretend not to see. I'm now curious how far Hartman's curiosity will take him, even though I'm all jumpy inside. Hartman is somebody from the outside world, now inside my life. It's…I feel like he just stepped inside my head, not the embalming room. Bree is the only friend allowed in both places.

I see immediately why Matthew called me over to see. The man's head is caved in on the right side. I can tell by how Matthew is chewing on his lip and waggling his brows at me that he wants me to guess. I step closer, Hartman almost forgotten in my quest to win our little game.

"Motorcycle?" I whisper as Dad maneuvers the casket against the wall, phone still held to his head.

"Try again," Matthew says.

"Cliff diving?" I ask.

He shakes his head again. "They're hoping I can fix him well enough for an open casket, so that's a call I'm going to have to make in a little bit, because he won't look…alive unless they want to spend a lot more money."

With the way the man's head is crumpled, and his tissue is damaged, Matthew is right. It would take major reconstruction. I bite my lip. I only have one more guess.

"Rock climbing?" Hartman asks.

"Dammit!" Matthew laughs. "The newbie gets it right on guess *one*! He was free soloing."

"Oh-kay!" Dad gestures in large circles with his arms toward the elevator. "Out. Now. Everyone but Matthew, who has a job to do. You two were *not* supposed to have come down here."

"This is science, Dad," I say.

"And he was a good one for our list," Matthew adds.

"Please, no morbid jokes." Dad's mouth curves into a frown. "I'll start to feel like a bad dad for raising my little girl in the middle of this."

"Ew, Dad." I grimace as we step back into the elevator. "No little-girl stuff. I'm sixteen."

"And you'll be my little girl until you're thirty. So will your sister." Dad grabs me in a sideways hug that I shrug out of. "Or forever."

I open my mouth to say there's no such thing as forever, but the last time I did that, Mom and Dad sat down and had this long talk with me about how death is part of life. I nodded and tried to pretend I was taking it all in. But in reality, that's the stupidest line ever. Death is not part of life. It's not living. It's *dying*. That's the opposite of death being part of life.

Hartman pauses at the door of the elevator before stepping inside.

"Sorry about that," Dad says. "I'm distracted today. This is probably highly inappropriate. Tell your parents I'm sorry."

Hartman shakes his head. "It's fine. I offered to come down and help, and..." He glances at me. "I was curious, I guess."

"We're so..." Dad shrugs. "I sometimes forget how macabre our job is."

The elevator lurches upward.

Dad doesn't forget. He's desensitized like we all are. When he's in the lobby or the chapel or the viewing room or even the salesroom, he's so cautious. Once he's "backstage," he stops protecting people from the more practical side of what we do.

"I guess it's macabre," Hartman agrees. "But it's a service everyone needs at some point."

"Hopefully not until they're much older than the two of you."

Hartman shoves his hands in his pockets and stares down at the wing tips he's wearing.

Dad recognizes the signs immediately. "I'm so sorry."

"Me too," Hartman says quietly.

I fold my arms across my chest because riding in an elevator with an odd guy and my dad isn't something I thought I'd be facing today. Add in a dash of Matthew's morbid talk and bringing up Hartman's dead father, and awkward becomes the understatement of the year. I tighten my arms as the service elevator makes its usual squeaking, jolting protests.

"So what are you kids up to?" Dad asks.

"I gotta get home," Hartman says quickly.

Huh. So…I'm confused because he was pretty determined to come in, and he played our guessing game, but now he's taking off. I can't figure this guy out—not that I need to.

"He just gave me a ride home," I say. "That's all."

"What happened to Bree?"

"Busy with a guy," I answer.

"Ah." Dad nods. "Good thing you're not allowed to date until I can't call you my little girl anymore."

I rub my hands up the sides of my face. "Geez, Dad. Way to embarrass."

"Wait," Dad says as the elevator stops. He puts his hands on the door, but makes no move to open it. He turns and looks at Hartman and then at me. "You two aren't dating, are you?"

"No!" I yell. "Seriously."

Hartman shakes his head but doesn't really look at either of us. There's probably a lot going on in his brain right now, and I wonder what it is. Or maybe he just gets that our situation in the elevator took a giant leap past awkward.

I can't wait to talk to Bree about all this. If she's not too busy, anyway.

Although, any talk about Hartman will just encourage her scheme. The elevator jolts to a stop, and I now have sympathy for the lumbering piece of equipment because with the realization that

I suddenly have something I'm not sure I'll share with Bree, I for sure feel jolted.

Dad slides the door open, but he's looking at Hartman in a totally different way—with fatherly suspicious eyes, and that puts a fluttery, panicky beast in my body. I need to get Hartman out the door. And then I need to figure how to tell Bree enough so I feel like I'm sharing, but not so much that she'll keep pushing me and Hartman together.

"I'll walk you out." I reach out to grab Hartman's arm or hand or wrist or something to make sure he follows me, but then remember Dad's words about dating and let my arm drop. No need to touch the guy and bring on a round of questions from my parents.

I once again cross my arms and head up the hallway, through the viewing room, and into the lobby.

Mom steps out of the back offices. "Did you help Dad bring up Mr. Clancery?"

I shake my head. "Matthew was down there with the new one, and Hartman helped us take Mrs. Nichols down."

Mom gets this really weird expression. "Ah."

"So, Hartman's headed home."

"Thank you for letting me drop in," he says from behind me.

Mom looks up at him. "Of course."

I hold open the front door. At least the rain's let up a little. Hartman shouldn't get totally soaked running for his car this time.

"So…" I say once the door closes behind us. We're both under the awning, the rain still slapping onto the pavement. "This is my life."

He looks back through the door. "It explains a lot."

I cock a brow as I take him in again. "What?"

Hartman chuckles, his heavy mood seemingly gone. "I'm kidding, Gabe. I'll see you tomorrow."

I take a step back. "See you."

"Thanks," he says.

"For?" I lean my back against the glass door.

He tucks his hands into his pockets. "Letting me in."

He's acting like I invited him over to hang out or something. My cheeks warm. "It's a business."

"Thanks anyway."

"Yep. Polite." I feel my lips purse together. "Polite guys usually have cool moms. I'd like to meet her."

Hartman runs a hand over his curly hair, messing it all up so it sticks out around his head, but under the uncertain gesture is the beginning of a smile that feels like some kind of victory. "Yeah. You know. When we're settled…yeah…"

Oh crap. Did I just, like, invite myself to his house? Way to go, me, for shoving us right back into awkward territory.

"Well, see ya." He gives a quick wave before sprinting into the rain.

I dart back inside before I can say something else stupid. I have to call Bree. Figure out what's going on with Hartman. And maybe she can help me act like less of a noob.

"So," Mom says with a smug smile. "Walk with me and tell me who the cute boy is."

What? "What cute boy?"

She scoffs. "The tall one you just walked outside?"

"He's not cute, Mom. He's tall with weird clothes and weird hair."

"Says the girl who purposefully dresses like…you?" Mom laughs a little at her own joke before pulling open the elevator door. "You're welcome to bring him over anytime."

I stay in the hallway. Mom's probably going down to help Dad with Clancery, and I never got my snack. "Oh."

"He's very polite," she adds.

I'm never saying anything about his politeness again.

"Just so we're clear," Dad says as he leaves the viewing room and joins Mom in the elevator. "You and he are not dating."

I throw my arms in the air. "No!"

Tomorrow I'm back to my black clothes, and I'm *not* getting in Hartman's car again. He's not even a safe driver, so whatever.

"Who did he lose?" Dad asks slowly.

Mom's head snaps toward Dad. She immediately frowns.

"His dad."

Dad rubs his forehead. "That's too bad."

Too bad. Yep. One way of saying he got totally screwed out of a parent.

"Have fun down there." I give Mom and Dad a too-big smile and wave as they close the elevator door.

At least no one asked me to pick up Mickey today.

Now that Hartman's gone, I send Bree a text. Hartman not only gave me a ride home, but he ended up in the basement. I think we need to talk.

I wait for her response as I wander through the house.

And wait.

And wait.

And then I toss my phone on my bed and find my snack.

# Chapter 11

"So." Bree slides her arm through mine the second I step into the school. "I heard that you got a ride home from *Hartman* last night."

"Yes, I did," I say flatly. "And I texted you because my parents were all weird about it, and an *hour* later you texted back to say you'd text me later." Which she never did.

"I got home late," she says. Nothing else.

"Um…" I squeeze her arm with mine. "You know that's not good enough, right?"

I waited up. I mean, I can't even remember the last time that Bree wasn't the final person I talked to before dropping off to sleep. And she *knows* how I am with people who aren't her. Bree, of all people, should know that I'll need her help.

Bree shakes her head. "I'm more interested in you and the new guy."

No real explanation for not texting back? Do I just let that slide or call her on it?

"He drove me home." I start to tell her about how weird he acted and how he helped Dad and me with a cadaver, but there's no reason I should reward her with tidbits when she didn't text me back.

"So, he ended up in the basement, huh?" She waggles her brows.

I shrug. "Yeah, but only for a sec. And then he went home."

"Did he give you a hug or ask you out or…anything?"

"Nah." I try to brush off the whole thing. It's petty and stupid to not want to share just because she didn't write me back, but seriously.

"Are you really not at *all* interested in him?" she asks. "He's quirky and kinda cute, and…I don't know…He might actually be interesting enough for you."

"He—" *doesn't like Bryce, so we probably wouldn't go out together, even if I did like him.* But I can't very well say that to Bree. "He…I think coming here has been a bit of an adjustment for him. You'd know this if you'd had time to text me last night."

We stop at my locker, and she leans against the one next to mine. I take a moment and pause. I'm being stupid toward Bree. I do kind of like him. He *is* interesting. These are things we should be sharing and dissecting. I mean, that's what we've always done. I'm waiting for her to try to dig for more information.

"So, if you don't go to prom, I don't really get it, but whatever. But please, please, please, come to the after-party."

Are we really on a new topic already?

"I'll think about it." I can't imagine hanging out with Bryce all night. I probably really should not have promised a blank slate. And why is she not still asking about Hartman?

Bree's arms fly around me as she crushes me against her. "You're the best! I promise it'll be amazing!"

She can't promise that, but she's excited about the whole thing, so I'll think of a really creative way to let her down later. Or, like I often do, I'll go and it'll probably be better than I'm thinking. Or so very much worse.

"So. I'm hanging out with Bryce after school, and then I'm ditching him so we can go to Audrey's!" Bree beams.

Tuesday. Right. I'm finally catching a break. Maybe Audrey's is what we need to slip back into our normal. I need us to be back to normal.

* * *

I spend a few minutes cleaning out my locker at the end of the day because I'm alone. I have no desire to try to navigate the student lot when everyone's trying to leave at once or watch Bree with Bryce. Once the hallways are mostly clear, I slide the two books I need for homework in my pack and heft it onto my shoulders.

I've done this part of my day without Bree before. I mean, she's dated guys on and off and been busy, but this feels...different. Usually she drags her guys to our lockers or to our table in the caf or to our meeting spot in the hallway. Or just ditches them in favor of us once school is out.

I'm not sure that'll happen with Bryce. He's the one dragging her off with his friends. But I don't really want to see him, and she knows this...Gah. I hate that he asked her out. I hate that she said yes. I hate that because of one guy, I'm worried my days won't be the same. I slam my locker shut and jerk my pack higher on my shoulder. When I get to the top of the stairs, I pause. Slump. Sigh. Lean against the wall. It's not Bree's fault. And I'm probably being paranoid anyway. It'll be fine. We'll be fine.

* * *

My feet slide along the sidewalk as I slowly head for home. One foot in front of the other. All that's waiting for me is maybe work or maybe having to pick up my little sister and take her to Liza's.

I cut through the cemetery just to change up my walk a little. There's a new grave under the oak tree, and I pause for a second. Mrs. Nichols's name is on the front, and the plot next to hers is empty. I know it belongs to her husband without looking at the books.

I look at the marker again. It's nice. Special order. Mr. Nichols must have really planned ahead. Though, my granddad did too. I think we have about fifty family plots in this place—room enough for everyone! At least for a while.

We'll fill them up eventually, and maybe by the time we do, people will be doing something more creative with their dead. Maybe the whole earth will fall apart before then. I don't know.

I walk from the older part of the cemetery to the newer and stop next to another recent grave. I can always tell because the sod is a little greener than everywhere else.

BLAKE SMITH.

"Whoa." I clap my hand over my mouth.

Hartman's dad is buried *here*?

I let out a sigh and stare. I'm thinking they didn't have services here. Or maybe they did, and it just blended into the one before and the one after.

*Beloved Husband and Father.*

Even if he weren't beloved, it would still probably say that. No one would ever write: *Great-Aunt Margie. A wretched hag.*

"You're everywhere," Hartman says, and I let out a weird squeaking noise. Once again clapping my hands over my chest.

"How did you get here?" I ask.

"Um…" He glances behind him. "I walked. From the lower parking lot."

"Right," I say. "Just didn't see you."

"Yeah."

"I'm…You know…I live there." I point to what is obviously the back side of my house.

"Yep," he says. "Saves on gas for the hearse."

I want to laugh. I want to smirk. But I cannot read him. At all. This whole conversation is just…I don't know what it is. "Uh, yeah…"

His gaze slips back toward the headstone. "Dad grew up here and my parents met here, so…yeah…that's why he's buried here."

Hartman steps back, so he's about a grave away from me. It's an awkward distance. One that makes me think he really wants his space and that I should probably leave.

I want to ask him a million questions about things he probably doesn't want to talk about, but I'm going to be smart and exit before I say or do something stupid. "I should get home."

"Yeah." He slips his hands into his gray coat pockets.

I want to tell him that I'm sorry. I want to say that I think it would be so hard to shift schools at the end of junior year, or any year, really. I want to tell him I think it's cool he's so polite and that he drives his dad's car and uses his dad's keys. And ask him where he finds his clothes. I watch Hartman for a minute longer as he continues to half look at me and half look at the grave marker I'm next to. His *dad's* grave marker.

As much as I work in a business that has to provide sympathy, I find it awkward around people I know. The polite distance from a stranger is several person widths, but with a friend? I don't know where the grief barrier is that I shouldn't cross. "Well…sorry to take up your time here."

He's blinking again. Staring at the headstone.

I take a few sideways steps to see if he says something else, but he doesn't. I start back toward the house and hope Bree is ready for Audrey's. I need her to help me figure out why I have no idea what to do when Hartman is around.

# Chapter 12

Bree drives through Paradise Hill while I sit rigid and tall in the passenger's seat. I'm afraid to ask about her confused grammy or her parents. I definitely don't want to talk about Bryce. Today was supposed to be us getting back to normal. Instead, Bree sings the Beatles, and I just take up space in the car.

When Bree finally parks in front of Audrey's, I shove out of the car. The drive has never taken so long.

Cigarette smoke tickles my nose as we walk up the sidewalk, and I sneeze. My hand flies over my nose as if it'll stop the throbbing. "Dang it!"

Bree laughs. "Just smoke, Gabe."

"My nose still hurts from the detectors," I whine.

She points with a grin. "At least your black eye is almost faded."

Yeah. To yellowish.

When I finally release my nose, I see a few girls from our school outside the nail salon, smoking. One of the girls leans toward another, slipping a mini alcohol bottle into her pocket. I can't help but stare. The girl who just got the bottle pulls it out and takes a small sip before passing it back.

I turn away and walk behind Bree into Audrey's. "What are they even doing?"

Now is when Bree will do that little partial snort thing she does and say something about respecting your body, but she's silent.

"You here?" I ask.

She holds the door for me, but my toe finds the threshold, and I lurch forward, barely catching myself before hitting the floor.

"Graceful." Bree reaches a hand down to help me up. "They're just sneaking a few sips, Gabe. It's not like they're out driving around with a fifth of Jägermeister."

My jaw drops. Guess I was right to wonder if our day together would feel normal or not. This is not normal.

"Jill?" Bree calls.

"Back here, girls!" Jill says from near the dressing rooms.

"So, about your Hartman deal," Bree says over her shoulder. "He's just adjusting. I bet he'll seem extra awkward for a while, or maybe he won't, and you two can be adorable together anyway."

"Um…" That's not help. That's an observation.

We wander through the racks—with labels like Twenties to Die For, Forties Made for Rosie Girls, Twisty in the Sixties (which is paired with a black-and-white picture of the Beatles), and Find Your Groove in the Seventies—until we're near the dressing rooms.

Five wardrobe boxes are crammed against the wall, blocking two of the three dressing rooms. The top corners of the boxes are cut away to reveal hangers full of vintage goodness.

Jill wasn't kidding when she said they'd gotten a big shipment in.

"I just…" I start but stop. It's not like Bree needs a reminder that I say stupid things at stupid times.

"If he didn't like you, he wouldn't have offered to drive you." Bree's brows waggle again.

"Hey, girls." Jill grins. "Pretty great shipment, huh?"

"I think we need pics for the blog," I say.

Bree shrugs. "Okay."

"Just okay?" My heart is starting to race at all the possibilities of how we could angle a fun post—"Sorting through the Stacks" or "Finding Treasure amid Chaos" or "How to Keep Your Shopping Time Short When the Selection is Large." So many ideas…I bet we'd get a ton of likes and reblogs if we angled it right. Normally this is where Bree's the best.

Bree pauses in front of the first box and flips a few hangers. "Promise me that if you buy something, it won't be black."

Right. I'm supposed to be stretching myself today.

Jill chuckles a little as she taps on her tablet, probably adding the new stuff to her inventory.

She's sort of forties-fifties today in rolled-up denim and saddle shoes. More casual than normal, but then she probably knew she'd be doing inventory all day.

I'm touching dresses and blouses and jackets that have the very distinct feeling of being something *different*. I stop breathing when I reach a section of sixties shift dresses and hope that at least one of them fits me.

Bree pulls out a lacy, silky piece of lingerie.

"A peignoir?" I ask. "Really?" What on earth would she…*Oh. Oh no. No, no, no…Bryce?*

I have a cream dress tucked under my arm, and Bree is biting her lower lip and flipping through hangers of tiny, silky nothings.

"So…" Bree breathes out. "He kissed me today. One of those nice, long, slow…I mean, everything between us just gets better and better." She hangs up the tiny scrap of silk and lace, a faint smile on her face. I'm pretty sure this is what a "dreamy" smile looks like.

I'm supposed to want to hug her or squeal or fake slap her for not telling me immediately. Instead my mind goes totally blank.

Her phone sings "I Want to Hold Your Hand" (another of her oldie Beatles favs) to signal a text, and she giggles. I glance over her shoulder and catch part of her responding text.

…knew I was thinking about you…

I step closer, and she hits Send before tucking her phone back into her bag.

Bree looks up at me. "What's that look?"

"I don't know." Because I don't. I don't know what I look like. I guess I'm in shock or something that she and Bryce are a for-real thing. Does falling for a guy make you completely oblivious to all the lists of things that could go wrong? To the guy's questionable history?

Her eyes stay on me for a minute longer before she starts fingering the dresses in front of me. "Remember when I asked you if you thought we were missing out on the high school experience?"

I do remember. I didn't know what to do with that comment then, and I don't know what to do with it now. "You sound like a brochure."

Bree slides her fingers over more silk. "I just mean that we…I don't know. Bryce isn't someone I'd have ever even tried for."

"Right," I say. "Because his reputation sucks."

Bree shakes her head. "More than that. You know. I'm not the kind of girl that guys like Bryce notice. I'm not…*mainstream* enough, I guess. But he did, and when he talks about all the adventures he's had up the coast and making banners to attach to the other high schools' bleachers, and how they got Theo's car stuck on this trail because Jeremy's grandparents have this cabin..."

All of this sounds like the stupid stuff that we've tried to stay away from. Now our happy routine of Audrey's, which was shifting us back to *us*, feels...different. Like Bree's moving in a direction I don't want to go.

"Oh!" Bree grabs at a scrap of something on top of one of the boxes. "This is so cool!"

I step closer, still unsure of how to comment back. She's holding the tiniest bikini I've ever seen. A crochet bikini. "Seriously? You might as well be naked."

Bree fingers the fabric with a smile. "I wanna be able to talk to my best friend about things, okay? So don't make that face, and please don't be a prude."

I can hear myself sputtering, even though I didn't give my mouth permission for that kind of behavior. "The word *prude* makes you sound like a granny."

Bree turns to Jill, seemingly totally unbothered. "I can say *prude* without being a granny, right?"

Jill glances at me, her red ponytail swinging over her shoulder. "It is more polite than the alternatives I can think of."

Because there are worse things to call me than a prude?

"Oh." My heart shrinks because Bree is supposed to be safe. "Fine. Whatever."

Bree squeezes my arm. "I don't want to hurt your feelings, Gabe. But we can't just talk about clothes forever. And you're so judgmental about Bryce that I'm afraid to say anything. And I get it, I do. I just..."

She's getting bored with me.

"I…" I just can't imagine putting so much effort into a relationship with a guy that won't last. And there's nothing else I can say about Bryce right now. "Clean slate." I'm a liar.

"Okay," she says before turning back to the box she was peeking in. Her phone sings again, and she bounces as she types Bryce back. Way back at the library, she'd said that she didn't trust him. Has he wiped that fear away? Has she been taken in so quickly? Broken hearts. Naked pictures. Cheating. How big does his trail of destruction need to be before she listens?

"You want the cream dress?" Jill asks me.

I glance down at the garment in my hands. The quilting is pretty awesome, and if I wear my cardi with it, I can still wear my black shoes. "So very much."

She laughs. "It's in inventory, so I can check you out."

"Just this for me," Bree says, showing Jill the tiny crochet bikini. "And no comments from Gabe there." Bree spreads her hand wide and laughs as she holds her hand against my face, pretending to block my view. Normally I'd grab her hand and pull it away, or grab it closer and lick her palm to gross her out, and then we'd both laugh at each other. But her hand blocking me doesn't feel like as much of a joke as it normally would. It feels like I'm being twisted and dried out.

"I'm done," I tell her. "It's fine."

I'm so not done and so very far from fine. And I don't even know what to think about my friend maybe seriously falling for a guy who is going to destroy her.

Jill runs our PayPal info, since we rarely have any cash, and most of her business is online anyway. It is far too easy to spend money. I hope this dress fits, but with all the guy talk and Bree's weirdness, I'll just try it on at home.

Bree tucks her tiny bag into her monster purse. "Thanks, Jill!"

Jill continues with inventory on her iPad. "See you girls next week."

"For sure," I tell her as we head for the door.

Just then Bryce runs in and grabs Bree so fast she screams, and then laughs as he pretends to eat her neck.

He's so disgusting.

"I really need to get home," I say flatly.

"Well, I"—Bryce cradles her against him—"was gassing up my car when I saw yours, and now I wanna hang out with you."

Bree glances my way. "I gotta take Gabe home first."

I fold my arms. "Sisters before misters and all that."

Bryce frowns in a pout, his stupid blond hair all gelled and pushed up, making me wonder how much time he spends trying to look like an asshole. "Hey." Bryce's eyes find mine. "Why don't you just drive Bree's car home, and I can drop her off there later? You can help a sister out." He winks.

How does he even think he can be involved in this?

"What a great idea!" Bree starts digging in her purse. "You don't mind, do you, Gabe?"

"No," I say flatly. "Not at all." She knows I hate to drive. What is with her? Just a few days ago at the library, she was watching out for me with the driving thing, and today she's shoving me off on my own.

"Not so stone-cold after all." Bryce laughs a little.

I grit my teeth. He would just look so much better with a black eye.

Bree elbows him with a giggle. "Stop it!"

I get another twist in my chest, and it's not good. She can ditch me and be weird. Fine. But we always stand up for each other.

Always. Her brows are supposed to be pinched, and her voice should have that snap to it that Bree's voice gets when she's mad. Instead she's wrapped up in the offender's arms.

Bree finally finds her green rabbit's foot key chain and holds it toward me. "You're the best! This'll be so good for you. Just leave the keys on the floor."

I'm waiting for her to look at me long enough to know that this is just not cool. Audrey's is our thing. We come here, we go home, we update on *all* our social media... But this? Her leaving with a *guy*? With *Bryce*?

Suddenly her arms are around me, squishing me to her. "I owe you huge, Gabe. Huge. Thank you, thank you, thank you."

I let out a breath, my frustration already depleted.

"He's important to me," she whispers. "I don't have a lot of people. So thanks."

I open my mouth to answer, but she's under his arm and out the door, leaving me standing in Audrey's with a dress that I really wanted to be giddy about buying. Instead, I'm thinking that I might be losing my only friend, and I have no idea how to stop it.

# Chapter 13

Mom's in her nicest funeral dress, so the customers must be well-paying ones. I sit at the dinner table—another Saturday night at home and working. She shovels in a sandwich before going downstairs to be the pro. I should just hang out, do my homework, and watch TV. It's what I've done with my nights, every night, since Audrey's. Since I drove Bree's car home at like twenty miles an hour with white knuckles. I'm not even sure how late it was when Bree finally got her car. I fell asleep before she made it to my house, and we've barely talked at school.

Bree hangs on Bryce all day, and I'm...I feel like I've let go of something I really wanted to hold on to. Bree's always losing track of time or not realizing that forty-five minutes go by between when I text her and she texts me back. How is that even possible?

Once Mom heads down to help Dad, I go to my room and change into my blacks. Tonight is fallen climber guy, and I'm curious to see what his crowd is like.

When I make it downstairs, the lobby is emptying into the chapel. There are people of all ages, but a lot of twentysomethings in too-trendy outfits. I wonder if they're here to pay their respects or to show off their new heels. Guess I'm judgy and annoyed tonight.

The churchgoers usually have us transport the bodies to their churches, but the nonchurchgoers use our chapel. We've had rock 'n' roll funerals, Elvis funerals, Hello Kitty funerals…So, really, I was right: funerals *can* be parties.

"Gabriella?" Hartman calls from behind me, and I whip around, trip over my feet, and stumble twice before catching myself.

"Crap," I mumble because this is so typical of me—and so not what I need right now.

"Sorry! I'm so sorry!" His hands hover-flutter around me like he wants to fix my clumsiness but doesn't know where to start.

I wave him off and brush off my dress. "It's fine. I'm fine. It's not like I hit the ground."

*Wait a second.*

"Why are you here?" He's been pretty silent in school this week, which is fine. It means that whatever weird plan Bree has to get us together isn't working.

He's in a white shirt, black sports jacket, and dark jeans and looks…*good*. A little mainstream for him, but very, very good. "I don't know."

"I'm…" I tug down my blouse and then point to my name tag. "I'm working, and once I'm done, I'll have to go pick up my little sister."

He sorta twitches forward like he's gonna move but hasn't quite made up his mind.

"Can I help?" he asks.

*Help? Is he serious?*

"Why are you here?" I ask.

He takes a few steps toward me. Close enough that I have to really tilt my head.

"I looked at the schedule on your website. There's a funeral." He blinks and then stares at his shoes. "I just want to sit in the back, but if you need help, I could help."

I scan the room because the last thing I need is Mom or Dad questioning Hartman's presence. "*Why?*" This is just so very weird.

"How sad are you when someone dies?" he asks.

"What?" I take a step back. Too many dead people come through here for me to even know how sad I am.

"I'm not…" He presses his fingers to the bridge of his nose. "I thought…"

I stand. And wait. And wait. "Hartman?"

His eyes are pleading. "I thought maybe if I saw a bunch of people go through what I went through, that it would hurt less. Or that I'd find a way to turn off how hollowed out I am."

My jaw goes slack, and I get a swirling in my gut. I take the standard three even breaths to sort myself out.

"Is that weird?" he asks slowly.

I don't know if that's weird or not. The pain in his eyes taps against my heart the way that Mr. Nichols did, which is maybe not good for my sanity. It does mean that I can't turn him away. "Come sit with me in the back if you want. This is the guy you guessed right on anyway. You know…downstairs." On the other very odd day that Hartman came inside.

His face relaxes in relief. "Thank you."

"It's open to the public." I turn and Hartman follows me into the chapel. I'd totally text Bree to see what comes next, but I think the stress of her maybe not texting back, paired with Hartman's proximity, would be too much.

Hartman and I sit in the back. The rows of pews on either side are nearly filled with people. Guess our climber was a pretty popular guy. Closed casket. The dollar figure to fix his head was steep.

Churchy music I've heard a million times plays, and one of the ministers Mom and Dad hire most often says just enough words to be present.

A young guy gets up and talks about his dead brother being so full of life.

I've heard this so many times. It's stupid, really. Everyone is full of life until they're dead. I tap my toes together and stare at my feet.

"What?" Hartman whispers.

I lean close enough that I hope my whisper doesn't carry. "People say the same things over and over. People die all the time. Every minute people die." I tap my feet a few more times. "They're still surprised."

"Of course they are."

I look at him long enough that I start to feel his brown-eyed stare tingle in my stomach. I grasp my waist and jerk my head to face forward.

"This…" The guy at the podium sniffs a few times and wipes his eyes. "This was his favorite climbing song."

He closes his eyes.

Some rap song I've never heard comes on, and the guy up front wipes his cheeks again. All I know is that no radio would ever be able to play it over all the bleeping they'd need to do.

Hartman's mouth pinches, and I get that he's trying not to smile. His body convulses once like he's trying not to laugh. I use the back of my hand to lightly slap his shoulder, but I can feel my shoulders start to shake as I try to hold in the fit of giggles pushing its way to the surface.

I cannot let the giggles out right now. Cannot.

He stares at his lap and laughs a few more silent laughs. Then he blinks. Oh, crap. Is he *crying*?

In seconds, he's on his feet and walking from the chapel. I leap up and follow, trying hard to do my slow and succinct don't-see-me walk out the open chapel doors. The thumping bass of the song follows us out, but at least we're free of the words.

Hartman's on the other side of the lobby.

"Whew." He blows out air while resting his hands on top of his head. I still can't tell if he's trying not to laugh or trying not to cry.

"You…Are…" I'm never sure how to help people I know. "You okay?"

"I laugh, and then my body wants to cry and everything I feel is all mixed up." He has tears on his cheeks, but he's still sort of shaking in laughter. "I feel like shit when I'm happy because I shouldn't be happy when my dad is dead, and I'm sorry I'm dumping this on you."

"Shhh!" I push on him as I look over my shoulder at the double open doors to the chapel.

"I'm sorry," he whispers, swiping at his eyes.

I grab his arm and drag him behind me, then pull open the coffin room door and hold it, gesturing for him to step inside.

He walks into the dark without pausing, and I flick on the light as the door closes behind us.

"Whoa." He stands in the center of the room, surrounded by caskets, urns, and epitaphs for the dead. There are eight caskets in here; the room is not quite big enough for ten to look anything but a bit squished together. Add in all the fancy pots and vase-looking things, and it makes kind of a mess.

"This feels…strange," Hartman says quietly.

I make a slow circle, looking over the room and trying to figure out what it would look like to someone who has never been in here before, but…I can't. This room has always been one of my favorites.

"Are you using me? Because coming here for a glimpse at a dead body, which you already got, and to see what we do here… That really gets old. There are no ghosts. I'm not taking you back downstairs."

He touches the side of one of the caskets. "What do you think happens to people when they die?"

So, I guess we're ignoring my question for the moment.

I want to tell him what I hear people say all the time: *People go to a better place.* But I don't want to feed Hartman a line. "They go to a better place," I still say automatically.

I cringe, and he turns around, his face distorted in skepticism. "Do you believe that?"

"I don't know what I believe." I'd rather not think too deeply about it because then what I do everyday might feel different. Bigger. More. And I already sometimes need to excuse myself for my three breaths and refocusing.

He runs his hand over the smooth interior of a coffin. His brows pinch together almost like Bree's do when she's upset, but the rest of his face is so relaxed I guess he's just thinking. "When I think about my dad being buried, sometimes I can't breathe. And then I get so frustrated and want to ruin everything in the room I'm in, but I can't let go and do that. I know better." His voice is more strained with every word. "There's this practical, pragmatic side of me that I sometimes wish I could push away so I could act stupid and crazy or whatever people are allowed to do when they lose a parent."

His eyes are wide and almost desperate, and his knuckles are white from clutching the edge of the coffin in front of him. We just stare at each other for a few moments. And a few more moments. I half expect him to grab an urn off the wall and throw it. Instead his face starts to relax around his brow, and then the tight line of his mouth droops and the white on his knuckles starts to fade.

"I used to take naps in here when I was little," I say quietly. I don't know how to address anything else he hit me with.

His brows shoot up. "*What?*"

I lean over the white lacquer casket and peer inside.

"They're cozy little cave holes. Dad always has the head half open for people to see the inside, but I'd crawl into the foot part and go to sleep. Mom and Dad couldn't find me for hours once." This is one of the stories my parents always tell that always makes me want to disappear, but here I am telling this story to someone else.

He wipes his hand over his face and shakes his head. "I'm kind of envious. I didn't…I mean…I didn't know what to expect when Dad died. And now that it's all done, I wish I would have spoken up. Had some say."

"I did with my grandparents." I tap my nails on the casket surface. "I picked out their caskets for them when I was six or seven."

"*With* them?" he asks with a weird kind of laugh.

"Yep. They were both totally healthy, and my granddad used to joke that he didn't care what we did with his body. I was thirteen when he died, and I wanted to bury him with a clown nose just to prove a point, but my parents got all worried about my sense of humor after I mentioned that. I had to see a counselor for a whole summer."

"So you were thirteen when you fooled this counselor into thinking you were okay?" he teases.

"Ha, ha."

Hartman smiles back, and his whole face seems lighter.

I lean against my favorite white casket. "This'll be mine one day. I think. Although cremation sometimes sounds better, so maybe I should be picking urns instead. Though, I don't really like the idea of any part of me being trapped that way."

Hartman smooths down the lapels of his jacket. I wonder where he got one with arms long enough for him without it sagging over his narrow shoulders.

"You're looking at me funny," he says.

*Crap.*

I turn away from him and tap my fingers over the top of the casket.

Hartman's hands are clasped behind his back. He peers at the satin interior. "I sort of want to crawl into one of these."

I feel a smile tugging at the corners of my mouth. "And that comment just got added onto the reasons you might be a little bit unbalanced."

"Of course I'm unbalanced." His eyes flash to me for a second before going back to the casket in front of him. "I love my dad. He died. We moved. My mom is recovering slowly, but she's a mess. My life is upside down. There are days when I want to snap."

I'm not sure how to react to his snap comment, so I don't. Instead I open the door between my home life and my outside life a little further.

"Crawl on in." I gesture around me. "Any one you want. They're made for people, you know."

He reaches out and touches the black lacquer surface. "You sure?"

"Yep. I used to do it all the time." *I still do...*

"And you call me unbalanced?" he asks.

I shrug in return.

"Hmmm…" He taps his finger on his chin as he scans the room. "Which one…"

"This one's mine." I hoist myself onto the edge of the white lacquer coffin and then let my bum slide down until it hits the bottom of the inside. I kick off my shoes before sliding my feet into the bottom. "The fact that these things have cushion on the bottom cracks me up."

"Wouldn't want the deceased getting stiff." He snorts a little at his own joke.

I've already heard them all.

Hartman, slips off his shoes, lifts a long leg up, and sets himself inside a cherrywood casket without needing to jump.

"Nice choice," I tell him.

"You too."

I scoot down until my head rests on the little pillow, then let out a breath. It's silly but this is childhood and hide-and-seek and finding ways to spend long days within sight or sound of Mom and Dad while they worked. The too-sweet smell of flowers is in the background and the weird white noise that hushed voices bring (now that the song is finished)…It's all part of me, and now Hartman is in the middle of it.

Hartman glances at me and then slides down until he too is lying down. "I keep imagining Dad waking up and being buried alive."

"Not possible," I say.

"People have been buried alive."

"But I spend a lot of time in the basement here, and we'd for sure know if someone was alive before we started the embalming process."

I hear him sigh but nothing else. "I never know how to take what you say."

"Right back at ya." I clasp my hands together over my stomach. "I see death every day. And I'll generally say one of the worst things a person could say at any given time. People at school don't even bother making fun of me anymore...for the most part."

"I wonder if it would hurt less if I saw death every day."

I think about my dad lying lifeless in one of these caskets. Or my mom's jaw being clamped shut by someone like Matthew. The thoughts feel like someone standing on my chest. I close my eyes and pull in my three breaths. "I'm good at finding ways to get rid of sadness."

"I guess I'll get good at it too," he says quietly.

The door clicks open, and I sit up so fast my head spins.

"Gabriella!" Mom snaps. "What on *earth* are you doing?"

Hartman sits up.

"Hartman?" Mom asks as she holds the door closed behind her back. At least she used more surprise than annoyance when she said his name.

"Sorry, we were..." I start, but how do I even answer? Hartman was being weird so I offered him a casket to rest in for a minute?

"I'm..." Hartman's mouth pops open and then closed and then open.

"Just..." Mom sighs. "Please get out of the caskets. I sometimes really wonder what we're doing to you here," she mutters.

We both sit still for a moment before Mom leaves, closing the door carefully behind her.

"I hope I didn't get you in trouble," Hartman says.

I rub my hands up and down my thighs a few times. Living thighs. Not dead ones. He stops next to my casket. That was fast, but with legs as long as his, it was just a step down instead of a jump.

"Need a hand out?"

I stand up in the casket and lean down, resting our hands together, palm to palm. His hands are surprisingly strong and warm. I slip down without tripping or anything. It's a lot easier to step out of one of these with help.

"Thanks." I take back my hands and tuck my feet back in my shoes, sliding my warmed palms over the fabric of my dress.

He glances around the room again. "I guess I should go."

"It's been…strange," I tell him.

He does this breath out his nose like he's almost laughing, but he's staring at the floor and his hand makes a swipe across the back of his neck. "Yeah…I guess it has."

I have no idea what to make of this guy. "You're super weird, Hartman."

His brown eyes finally meet mine. "You're super weird, Gabriella."

I gesture to the door and follow him out of the room.

Once we're outside, I figure I should pick up Mickey. Then I can come back in and refill snacks if I need to. "I'm headed this way." I point behind the house.

"Can I…" He gestures the same way I pointed.

"Seeing my aunt Liza is a pretty sure way to make you afraid to ever come here again, so how would you like to proceed?"

"So I guess my question got bigger, huh?" he asks.

"What do you mean?"

"Well now, if you *want* me to come, then maybe you're trying to scare me off…"

Something deep in my stomach is getting all tingly with how he's watching me. "I warned you. I'll leave it up to you."

As surprised as I was to see him tonight, now I'm not sure if I want our night to be over. This is when I need Bree.

"I'm going to chance your aunt Liza because I'm curious." His voice is hysterically formal. "And she doesn't live *in* your house, so

I'm thinking that she won't actually prevent me from wanting to come back, no matter how crazy she is."

I respond in my best formal voice, but my lips are betraying me and attempting to smile. "Very well then." I gesture toward the cemetery. "Out this way."

Hartman asks me a few questions about the house and my grandparents and how my family got into running a funeral home. The questions are all ones I've answered before.

We move through another gate on the far side of the cemetery, and I pause at the steps that lead to the door of Aunt Liza's place. The music isn't loud enough for me to hear words, only for me to know it's loud.

"Here?" He points to the large wooden door.

Instead of answering, I steel myself and start up the steps. I knock a few times and then push open the door, veering right into Aunt Liza's living room.

She's in a silk robe and is holding another one of those long, black cigarette holders that I used to think were just for old movies. Her hair is tucked underneath a fur cap, and she gestures wildly as she shares a story.

"…and his hands were all over me! On the dance floor! But you know what?" She leans closer to Mickey, and I'm so stunned that I'm frozen. "…I didn't care because he was just that good at it."

Mickey giggles, and my face burns. "Aunt Liza!" I yell. "What are you…I don't…" I don't have words for this situation. "It's time for Mickey to come home."

"Oh!" Aunt Liza jumps up, her pale-blue silk robe billowing around her ankles. "And what a lovely young man you've brought with you." She slips the cigarette holder between her teeth and looks him up and down—not unlike the way Bryce looks at Bree.

*Gross.*

"Mickey." I shove my face into a smile. "Let's go home, please."

Mickey checks the grandfather clock in the corner. "The funeral is still happening, right?"

"But it's close to done, and you sit upstairs during funerals all the time."

Mickey frowns. "But she was just telling me how many beaus she had, and how unusual it was for someone to share a bed with their beau before they were married!"

*Oh perfect.* I rub my forehead.

Hartman's smooth cheeks suddenly have dimples.

"Fine, fine!" Aunt Liza waves us toward the door. "You go. Have your lives. But you…" She points at Hartman. "It's not often I get a handsome young man through here that isn't my grandson. Give a sweet old lady a kiss?"

She tilts her head, aiming her cheek toward Hartman, whose face is about eight shades of scarlet.

He leans over quickly and pecks her cheek.

"A timid one." She waggles her brows at me. "Hold on to him, dear."

"Go, go, go!" I shove Mickey out the door, Hartman following close behind.

The second the door is closed, I try to take my three calming breaths, which slow down my heart and cool off my cheeks.

We walk down the steps in silence.

"You're super tall," Mickey says. "That might be a problem for kissing."

"Mickey!" I yell, having no idea what else I could possibly say to make this more or less awkward. My face is heating up too fast for me to make sense of my thoughts. At least it's dark outside.

"Do you go to the same school?" Mickey asks, totally unbothered by my outburst. "I don't recognize you. Are you from here? You seem sorta pale for living in California."

I grit my teeth. "Mickey. Please stop."

"What?" she asks innocently.

I try to glare at her, but it's so dark I'm sure she doesn't see. "Never mind."

"Well…" Hartman starts. "I just moved here, and yes, I go to your sister's school."

I pause to look at him in the dim light, his mouth twitching in a partial smile. I also notice he didn't answer her kissing question. The weakness that comes from relief that he's not embarrassed or angry makes me stumble. He laughs and grasps my hand, holding it just longer than he needs to. Our eyes lock as I find my steps again.

"I'm not afraid to come back to your house"—he leans so close that the delicious grape smell tickles my nose again—"but I might let you pick up your sister on your own from now on."

Laughter bursts out of my mouth, because with all the tension bouncing around in my body, it's all I can do. "Yeah. No problem."

# Chapter 14

I'm not having my best morning. I nearly crawled back into the white casket after Hartman left and slept there. I'd have probably gotten more sleep than I did tangling myself in my sheets as I flopped over last night. No one but Bree has ever shared the funeral home part of my life—at least not without an ulterior motive. Though Hartman has a slight one, I'm just not sure his plan of being around death will help him feel any better about his dad.

I slump on the kitchen chair, which is freezing and makes me wish even more that I were still in bed.

A loud rapping comes from our front door, and I blink at the kitchen table a few times. Mom peers out the window, still in her robe. "Bree's here! That's nice. I feel like we haven't seen her in ages!"

Yeah. Me too.

I snatch a yogurt from the fridge and head for the door. *Finally* back to normal.

Mom and Dad each say a different version of *love you* and *see you after school*, and I give them a quick wave before shutting the door behind me.

"Hey!" I jerk the lid off my yogurt.

"Oh good!" Bree grins too widely—a sure sign she's up to something.

I frown. "You're way too chipper for morning."

She shifts her weight to the side, slipping her already very short skirt up a few inches, but it's some boring, short denim skirt I've never seen before. "I've decided you need to learn how to drive better."

"Yeah. Sure." I blink a few times, still a bit in shock that she's here. The good kind of shock, but still...shock. "Once summer vacay has started, and I have more time, or—"

"Nope. Now."

I stop.

Bree steps behind me and begins shoving me forward.

"What are you even doing?" I sputter.

"You're driving my car to school."

I shake my head frantically. "It wasn't super fun to drive here from Audrey's. You know that, right?"

"But it was for a good cause. Anyway, you're like the safest driver in the universe, which is maybe the *only* reason you passed your driver's test. I'm willing to set aside the fact that your driving is super annoying because it would be really nice if you could drive." Her smile is so damn hopeful, but there's something in her eyes...I'm entirely suspicious.

We might not be operating on the same wavelength lately, but I do still know my friend. "You have a purpose. You're doing this for a reason."

"Yes." She places her hands on her hips, gives me a smile, and does this great wide-eyed exasperated stare. "I'd really like my best friend to be able to drive."

Nope. There's something else. I start for her car. "You know when I drive, I drive the hearse. Almost always."

"But…" Bree shrinks back a little, and I know…I just know whatever's going to come out of her mouth is not going to be cool. "Bryce thought it might be fun to ride in the hearse to prom?" Her voice gets all squeaky at the end.

Bree has never, ever, ever opted to take the hearse anywhere. I think I've driven us in the Subaru twice. But…but if I were to be her driver, I could maybe watch out for her better.

"I'd just be the chauffeur, is that right? I don't have to go to the dance?"

Bree sighs. "I'm still going to try to talk you into it. You're maybe into Hartman, yeah?"

"I'm *maybe* into him."

She claps her hands together and grins.

I make a big show of slowing my trudging steps when I get near the driver's side of her car.

"Just get in." Bree laughs.

Once we're inside, I buckle in and rest my hands on the steering wheel. There are so many ways this could go disastrously wrong. At least I'm hanging with Bree. She seems to think we're all okay. She's acting like we are, so maybe it's just me who's moody and strange right now.

"Earth to Gabe." Her fingers snap in front of my face, and I jump.

"I'm here." *I think.*

Her phone sings, and she starts typing.

"What's up?" I ask, pointing at her phone.

"Um…" She bites her lip.

I check the time and slowly put the car into Drive, my foot still firmly on the brake. Now that I've checked all directions, I ease my foot off the brake and head for the parking lot exit onto the street.

"Bryce is just being sweet."

*Gag.*

I check the street both ways, once, and then again before pulling out. I can tell Bree wants to tell me to just *move already* with how she's leaning forward but she won't. She won't because she wants me to drive her to prom, in a hearse.

"Gabe. This last year has been so crappy. I'm finally having fun. *Please* let me have fun without that frowny disapproval." She sticks her finger against the corner of my mouth and wiggles it. "Don't think I can't tell when you're thinking things you don't want to say out loud."

The problem is that I can already feel the heartbreak from him coming. Will I feel more responsible if I don't keep warning her? Or do I need to find ways to let my frustration go so I can be happy with her now?

A little blue car speeds around us to the left, and I jump in my seat. Why are there so many other people on the road? It's way early to be out and about. What could they all possibly be doing?

Bree blows me a kiss, and I try to relax as I grip the steering wheel. My heart pounds and my mouth dries out at every light. I watch for drivers on their phones, or drinking coffee, or generally not paying attention.

"This is good for you. You hate that I force you out of your comfort zone, but you also secretly love it." She pinches my cheek, and I pull away to keep my eyes on the road.

"I don't love it right now," I tell her as I hold the steering wheel tighter.

"So…" She trails off, biting her lip. "Since you'd be driving Bryce and me to the prom anyway, we sort of hoped you'd be cool with taking the group."

My foot slams on the brake so hard that the seat belt crushes my left boob.

"Gabe!" Bree yells. "Drive!"

Two horns honk before cars zip around on our left.

My hands shake at my stupid driving move, or maybe at Bree. Having me drive was a dumb idea. Grasping the steering wheel, I try my three breaths as I let off the brake. She's just talking about a couple more people. That I don't know. That I don't talk to in school...

She sits back in her seat and taps her phone on her chin. Her face is flat. I can't believe my stupidity in hitting the brakes in the middle of the road.

"Yeah. Okay. Sorry," I say. "I was just surprised."

"Well..." Bree says with a smirk. "No guessing where you fall on this issue. But you'll come around. You always do. It'll be good for you. They're all super nice."

I'm sure they are. I'd just rather not find out on prom night, in a hearse, while I'm *driving*. Normally, I'd ask Bree for reinforcements for a group situation, but she's the one dragging me into it. I'm used to having a *partner* for horribly uncomfortable high-school situations, not a small crowd.

I flip on the turn signal when we get to the student lot, but it's sort of a nightmare for me with cars buzzing in so many directions.

Bree's lips are both sucked into her mouth as she tries to not yell something like *Just park already!* To her credit, she holds it in. Maybe I need to try to do the same.

"Driving the group could be...fun," I choke out.

"Liar." But she laughs a little when she says it, so I think we're okay.

I park way near the back of the lot so I don't have to navigate through student traffic. "This good?"

"Perfect." She's lying, but at least we made it to school.

Once the car has stopped, I put it in Park and turn the thing off. *Finally.* My shoulders ache from the tension. Bree holds her hand out, and I drop the keys in.

"What else has been going on?" I ask. "I feel like I've barely seen you."

"Oh, I don't know. I guess mostly—"

Her car door is jerked open by Bryce, who growls and jerks her from the car.

*Seriously?*

I stand up, and Bryce is now growling into her neck.

"Can we have a minute?" I snap over the roof of the car.

Bryce stops and his eyes meet mine, his mouth dipping into a frown.

"A minute?" I ask again.

Bree looks back and forth between us a couple times.

Bryce takes back his hands and backs away. "Whatever."

Bree scowls.

"I…" *Crap.* "I'm sorry. I just thought we might talk or something."

Bree glances over her shoulder. "Can we catch up later?"

Bryce high-fives one of his friends and then fake humps the front of his car. I gesture toward Bryce. "Really?"

Bree smiles a little and rolls her eyes, but it feels more endearing than annoyed. "They're just screwing around."

"I thought you were smarter than that."

Her smile falls. "I'm sorry, what?"

*Crap again.* I tuck my hair behind my ears. "That didn't come out right."

"But it's how you feel. Isn't it?" The look she throws me forces me back a step.

"I'm sorry." But I don't know how to fix what I said.

Bree backs up and then sprints away from me and slams into him. He picks her off the ground, she wraps her legs around his middle, and even from two car lengths away, I can see their tongues as they kiss. *Gross.*

I have no idea what the balance is between supporting my friend and warning her, but I'm obviously screwing it up.

\* \* \*

When I go to classes, I don't see Bree. And when I text her at lunch, she doesn't text back. Did she seriously skip school and isn't answering me?

After school, I stand on a bench to try to see the whole school parking lot. Bree's car isn't here. And no texts…It's just not like her.

And then, predictably (because he seems to be popping up everywhere), Hartman's car stops next to the curb.

"Gabe!" he calls through the window. "Let me give you a ride?"

I pause like I need to think about it.

"Come on!" He gestures with his head.

I jump off the bench, and he leaps out of the car to get my door. "Seriously?" I ask with a laugh.

"Seriously." He shuts my door and crawls into the driver's seat—his long limbs and all. "A ride home? Something else?"

His smile still doesn't quite reach his eyes, and even though I'm never exactly sure what to say aside from the generic lines that slip out, I don't want to tell him no.

"A ride home would be great."

# Chapter 15

The breeze is really coming off the ocean today, and there's nothing that makes the air feel cleaner. The sun has heated the hood of Hartman's car almost to the point where I'm ready to slide off, but not quite yet. My back and head rest against the windshield, and my nearly bare legs are soaking up the heat from the black paint of his car. The view of the ocean from this part of the parking lot at my house is too good to move.

"So, Bree and Bryce are quite a thing," Hartman says.

I make a face. "I don't trust him."

"Does Bree know that?"

I let out a long sigh. "Well, yeah, she definitely knows I don't trust him, but I'm not sure how much she cares. Now I'm just trying to figure out how to be her friend, but also to keep warning her that he's not the best idea." And I'd like to be able to talk to her about what's happening in my life. Like, it would be nice to talk over this afternoon with Hartman.

Hartman shifts his weight—I know this only because I hear the movement, not because I actually open my eyes. "You can't force her to not like him."

"I know," I say. "But our rhythm is totally off, and our rhythm has *never* been off. It's me and Bree and all the things we love versus everyone and everything else. Has been since seventh grade."

"Until now."

We sit in silence for a few moments, and I let the sun keep soaking into my tired body.

"She wants me to drive the hearse to prom. With them." Just the thought of it makes my palms sweat.

"You're going to prom?" he asks, his voice a shade higher with surprise.

"No. Just driving."

"Oh."

Silence.

A breeze rustles through the tree leaves. I had no idea that I'd ever be able to relax around Hartman. Something else I'd like to share with Bree, but I'm not sure how anymore. It's not like I can open with that, can I?

Wait a minute…If I want a partner in this stupid high school situation, maybe *Hartman* could be my fix instead of Bree.

I sit up. "Could you come with me? Help me drive, I mean? Like…be my buffer?"

He blinks. "Are you asking me to prom?"

My insides topple. That's totally what I just did. "It's that…" My neck and cheeks burn. "Bree's usually my partner for stuff like this, but we're not really in the same groove right now and…you and I…" *are.*

Hartman doesn't speak. He turns to face me fully, but the car isn't nearly long enough for his tall body, so he looks like he could topple off with one small move. He readjusts his elbow a few times before sitting up and crossing his legs on the hood. Still silent.

I'm such a moron. "I'm sorry. Forget it. It was a stupid ide—"

"I'll go. With you. Yeah." He swallows, his face sort of flat and maybe in shock.

I just wasn't thinking that by asking him to drive with me to prom, I'd also sort of be *asking him to prom.*

"I'd vote for no photos," he says. "Aside from whatever our parents need. And I also vote we only stay as long as we want, and…"

Oh, photos…prom stuff…no. "I wasn't even sure if I was going to go inside, you know?"

His head falls to one side. "Your plan was to sit in the car and actually be a chauffeur?"

I stare at my lap. "When you say it like that, it sounds kind of…"

"No, I get it, I think. But…" He taps on his knee. "But if we're already there…"

My chest is doing that tumultuous rolling, flipping thing where I'm not positive how to breathe, so I press my hands to my chest and start my three-breath thing.

"You okay?" He laughs a little. "You did ask me, and now you look like you're panicking."

I wave him away. "I'm weird."

"Better than being normal."

My mouth tugs into a smile, and my hands drop into my lap. "So, you're saying I'm not normal?"

He snorts. "I'd think you'd be used to that by now. You used to take naps in coffins, Gabe. That's not normal."

"Uh…"

His long hands sort of flop around in front of him as he gestures and sputters for a moment. "That came out wrong. Weird is what makes our world worth living in."

"While we're here," I add.

He gives me another one of his odd stares. "While we're here."

My gaze floats over the rest of the parking lot and the open garage door, which reminds me there's one more catch. "We're... We'll be driving a hearse."

"A hearse?" He sits back a bit. "Why not a limousine? You have one or two, right? I thought I saw them the other day."

I nod. "But I can't drive them because of the insurance company. There's an older hearse that Dad switched to our personal insurance."

"Uh..." He suppresses a smile. "Okay, then. Prom in a hearse."

"And I might beg you to drive." I bite my lip waiting for his response, but instead of rolling his eyes, he just smiles.

"So you don't really want to go to prom, but you've asked me anyway, and I'm coming." He slides off the hood and stands. "But I have this feeling you'd take back the invite if I said I didn't want to drive."

He's pretty much spot-on, but I'm not ready to admit that to him. "Thanks?"

Hartman nods once, his outrageous hair moving with him. "Walk?" he asks.

There's a beat of silence, but it's not like I have something else going on today. "Sure."

"Can we walk through the cemetery?" he asks.

"Do people go to other places to take walks?"

His mouth twitches. "I'm sure they don't."

After scooting off his hood, I breathe in the warm, spring air. "My sister will be home before too long, so ya know..."

"I've been warned."

But now we're walking, and neither of us is really saying anything. The last thing he wants is to hear me talk about how I'm worried about my friend with Bryce. And even though he seems okay with all the funeral home talk, I'm still waiting for a time when he's not okay with it. Or if I say something weird, or something that makes him sad again over his dad…There are just a lot of ways I could screw up. I can't believe I just asked him out. I want to tell Bree so badly that my fingers itch to pull out my phone.

When we reach the fence around the cemetery, he holds open the small gate for me to step through.

"This was my park when I was growing up," I say. "Because it was close enough that Mom and I could get back if my dad or my grandparents needed help."

Hartman smiles a little, and I feel myself warm up at the way his face changes with the subtle movement. "But your sister spends a lot of time with your aunt?"

"I think a lot of it has to do with my summer of counseling, and maybe my general callousness toward death." We're in the oldest part of the cemetery now. Late-1800s dates on the headstones. "My parents are just trying to limit exposure or something. Make sure daughter number two isn't as strange as daughter number one."

Hartman scratches his head. "And your aunt Liza's is a better place to be?"

"That's what *I* said!" I laugh a little.

Then he sighs. And then he looks up for a few steps. And we're still just walking.

He takes his hands out of his pockets and accidentally brushes mine, spinning heat up my arm. I fold my arms. We walk. I start to ask him about Connecticut or his mom or his old friends, but stop myself. Maybe he doesn't want to talk about those things.

Hartman stops. I stop next to him.

We're now in front of his dad's grave. I'm not sure if he meant to come here or not.

I press my lips together because I've seen worse tragedies. Kids on bicycles for one.

"Let's head back." His eyes rest on the stone for a few moments longer. "Before I have another one of those moments when I want to break everything around me."

He spins and starts walking back up the hill.

"Wait!" I call as I jog to catch up to him. I reach for his arm, but last time touching him made me all flushed, and I need to think.

Hartman pauses, and we watch each other for a moment. And watch is a much better way to say it than stare, because it's more than staring. I'm trying to get a better read on him. On who he is. What he wants. Maybe he's doing the same. Our eyes aren't locked—I'm scanning his face, and his gaze floats over mine. I don't notice the tension around his eyes until he relaxes and then his lips turn up in the slightest of smiles.

"Sorry," he says. "I'm kind of a mess. I feel…Everything inside me feels raw and mixed up. I'm just decent at putting on a normal face."

"S'okay."

We start walking in silence, but it doesn't feel awkward anymore, just kinda nice. New. Different. We slowly weave through the headstones, and once in a while I point at a name I like, or at someone who died really young, and he does the same.

There are a few people buried here whose families I remember, and we pause at those for a minute so I can tell Hartman a detail about their life or their family. His dark eyes lock with mine often enough that I know he's taking it all in. Actually listening instead of cringing away.

"Isn't it awful to watch people grieve over and over?" he asks quietly.

I lick my lips once before answering. "I turn it off." I've turned a lot off. "Matthew thinks this is where my sarcasm comes from." *And my cold, cold heart*, but I leave that out.

Hartman gives me a curt nod, which gives me exactly zero insight into what he's thinking.

After a few moments he pauses. "You're a puzzle."

"Puzzle?" I ask.

"You and Bree spend a lot of time putting yourselves together." He gestures to my little black dress and red lips. "But you really do give off the air that you don't give a crap about anything."

I'm not sure how to answer.

"Part of me wonders if it's a mask." He shoves his hands further in his pockets. "If all of it is. I'm being honest when I say that I'm totally putting on a mask everyday."

"I care about things," I say. "People, I mean."

He scratches the back of his head before shoving his hand back in his pocket. He's still watching his shoes. "I know. I didn't mean to sound like a jerk and say you didn't care. That was bad phrasing or something. But you are... You're a puzzle, you know."

"I don't mean to be." Or maybe I do. My life is much simpler when I have just Bree and me and my family. Fewer people in my life means fewer chances for me to lose someone I'm close to.

When we reach the small gate near my house, he once again holds it open for me.

"I'm gonna head for home, I guess."

"Thanks for the walk."

"Don't worry too much about Bree." Hartman shrugs. "Just be her friend."

"Yeah, but…"

"But people do stupid things when they like someone." He stops next to his car and grabs the door handle.

"Like what?"

"Like…" He opens the driver's side door and smiles. "Agree to drive an old hearse just to get a date."

And then he's in his car and driving away, and I'm left in the nearly empty parking lot feeling like firecrackers are pinging around inside me.

I jerk out my phone and text Bree.

I have news.

Flipping my phone over in my hands, I walk toward the back of the house and text her again.

This is one of those "call now" kind of news bits.

My cheeks hurt from grinning. I really need her to answer. She'll be so proud of me for going to prom.

Bree?

Leaning against the rock wall that marks the edge of the cemetery, I stare at my phone. Silently will Bree to text back. Flip the phone over.

Nothing.

# Chapter 16

Random mumbling conversations pass me in the halls as the school slowly fills up. My brain stumbles over thoughts from another night of too-little sleep. I stare at the inside of my locker, like that'll somehow help me focus.

The more I think about Bree and Bryce, the more scared I am for her. Some things you can't take back. She never answered my texts last night *or* this morning, and that's just weird—especially since I told her I had news. Involving Hartman. Answering late is one thing. Not answering? I'm not even sure how to react.

I flick my locker shut and start for Bree's.

"Gotcha!" Bree leaps onto my back from behind, and I shriek.

"Holy crap!" I spin, clutching my chest. "What was that about?"

"You're it." She snorts and I cough.

"What is that *smell*?"

Bree rolls her eyes and sets her hands on her hips. She's in dark-wash designer jeans and a boring white tank top. This is not Bree.

"What smell do you think you smell?" she asks.

"Toothpaste and...*whiskey*?"

Her eyes get wide, but they're not really super focused either. "Wow. You're good."

"Are you *drunk*?" I hiss. "At *school*?"

She pinches her fingers in front of her and squints. "Maybe a little."

I grit my teeth and step closer. Everything Hartman told me about relaxing and being a good friend evaporates, unlike the smell around my friend. "What the hell is *wrong* with you? I had big news last night, and you never wrote me back." Friends share. Friends text back. She's wanted me to be involved with someone, and now that I'm sort of stepping that way, she's not even around for it because she's drunk? Am I hurt? Mad? Confused?

Bree snorts and pushes my chest lightly. "Lighten *up*, Gabe. I was busy."

I jerk back.

She waves her hand loosely in the air. "Not all of us have perfect parents and great lives and..."

"What are you talking about?"

Bree wobbles a little before leaning in again. "I was out too late, and the best cure for a hangover..." she sings.

Now is when I need to say it sucks that my feelings are being hurt by my best friend because she isn't paying attention to me. Instead I say, "I'm just worried about you, because this Bryce thing is—"

"Oh!" Bree throws her hands in the air. "I'm so done with the same stupid conversation!"

I step back. "What?"

"Leave Bryce *alone*, Gabe. Why can't you just be *normal*? This would be so much easier *if you were more normal*."

Bree has never asked this of me. Ever. And I'm not that strange. We do the same things. We're a team. Or we used to be. My throat swells, and I'm blinking over and over as liquid fills my eyes. "We're...friends."

She grabs my shoulders. "And you talk about dead people and past lives and families I don't know, and you can't lighten up enough to even allow *me* some fun." If she makes another move, my blinks won't be enough to keep tears from falling. "You don't even get how good you have it. You just...you just don't."

"I'm just watching out for you," I whisper. This conversation doesn't feel like it could actually be happening. Bree and I are solid. We share things...I thought we did.

"Yeah. Well." She stands up a little taller, dropping her hands. Her body wavers a bit from side to side. "I don't need you to watch out for me. I stayed with Bryce last night. Do you know who noticed I never came home? *No one.*"

That's it. Bree isn't the problem. It's Bryce. And he's almost always in the same place before school. There are no words for Bree in my head, but I have a lot of things I'd like to unleash on Bryce.

I leave Bree and run through the halls, across the gym, and out the doors next to the field. I'm not losing my best friend to stupid *Bryce Johnson.*

Bryce laughs, tossing the ball into the air, and the bell rings. I don't know if I'm tardy or if that was our warning bell. I don't care.

"Leave my friend alone!" I yell. "Getting her drunk before school? Are you stupid on top of being an asshole? She can't afford to be in trouble! Her parents will come take her back! Her grammy will send her away!"

Bryce's smile falls. "Hey." He takes a step closer to me. "I was trying to help. Her dad's being an ass over her grammy and the kid he's having with his girlfriend, and I wanted her to be able to forget about all that for a while. And don't for a minute think either of her parents will come running back here to take her away. Her grammy isn't with it enough to call them anyway."

I'm stunned still for a second because I don't know about Bree's dad or her grammy. How is this possible? Confusion twists in my chest and then turns to anger the second I realize Bree's told *him* things she hasn't told *me*. What on earth has happened to her common sense since she started dating this guy? When did she so fully let go of me? "Do you seriously think that getting her drunk before school is going to help *anything*?"

"No!" he shouts back. "I don't! But, unlike you, *I* don't try dictate what she does or doesn't do!"

"You just gave her a place to do it!" I yell back.

And the thought hits me in a rush—*she didn't ask me to be her safe place. She didn't tell me about her grammy, not really. I didn't know about her dad having another kid.*

Bryce's voice lowers. "Damn right I did."

"This isn't like her!" I shout, gesturing wildly back toward the school.

He leans back, folds his arms, and smirks. "She seemed to be *all her* last night at my house."

I don't think, just swing. Pain shoots through my palm and up my arm. I jerk my hand back into my chest, but if it hurt me, it *had* to have hurt him. I lunge forward and swing again. A large hand grabs me from behind, and I yell, flailing my arms until I hear Coach shout the *f*-word.

Stumbling a few more steps, I stop and lean against the gym doors, gasping for air as the world comes back into focus. I've wanted to hit Bryce for so long. So many years, months, weeks of humiliation were stored up for that punch.

"You." Coach points at me. "I saw that. You're coming with me."

"She attacked me!" Bryce points out.

He's totally unscarred. Like, doesn't even look like...*anything* happened to him.

Damn.

"Look at me!" I yell as I hold up my swelling wrist. "I'm half your size!"

"Enough!" Coach yells. "Both of you with me. Principal's office! Now!"

It hits me about halfway there that someone from the office will be calling one of my parents. I further know that there are services around lunchtime today, so when Mom or Dad comes to the school to collect me, they'll be dressed exactly like the school assumes they dress every day.

Also. My wrist really freaking hurts.

I'm ushered into Mr. Conner's office, and he frowns as I step inside.

"Ms. Osborn."

Coach steps forward. "She came running outside from the gym, yelled at Bryce Johnson, and then slapped him on the face. Two or three times."

I sit across from the principal and try every trick I know to keep myself calm. Pressing my hands on my thighs, I take three deep breaths—that should work even though my heart's speeding on the verge of panic. I'm fairly certain that if I let myself really take in my surroundings, I might lose my composure, and that doesn't feel like an option with Bryce here. "I was trying to punch him, but...but I've never hit anyone before, so I guess it could have been a slap."

Mr. Conner blinks a few times. "Thanks, Coach. Take Bryce to the bench outside. I'll take it from here."

The door closes behind Coach and Bryce, and I feel like I'm in a movie where suddenly the door feels like a bank vault and all the furniture in the room has grown, leaving me shrunken and tiny.

"So, Gabriella," he says. "Can I get your version of the story?"

I want to tell him that this guy brought my best friend to school drunk, but then she'll be in trouble too. "I think Coach was pretty close. I don't like Bryce. He's dating my best friend, and he's terrible for her. I confronted him. He was a jerk. I hit him."

He deserves so much worse.

Mr. Conner lets out a long breath before tugging his tie from his neck. "I'm going to have to suspend you."

Heat begins to creep up the back of my neck. "I figured," I mumble.

"We'll have your parents come collect you. Two days suspension."

"Fair enough."

"Did Bryce provoke you in any other way?" he asks.

"I'd check his blood-alcohol level," I say, and leave it at that. Now I just hope he was drinking with Bree earlier.

The principal nods once. "And will you please refrain from hitting or attempting to punch students at this school when you return?"

I fold my hands in my lap and rub my lips together. The answer I'd like to give him is that if Bryce is removed from the school, my promise would be easy. Instead I just say, "Yep."

He runs a hand down his blue-and-red tie. "I'm letting you off easy because your record here is clean."

"Thank you."

His eyes go from his tie to me.

"Nothing else going on?" he asks.

I shake my head.

"Very well." He starts typing into his computer, marking my

clean record. "You can wait in the hallway outside my office for your parents."

*Crap.*

"Thanks," I mumble.

Bryce throws me a dirty look when I step into the hallway, and I grin when I see that his right cheek is a little pink. My swelling wrist was totally worth it.

* * *

I clutch my backpack in my lap as Dad drives us home. His brown hair is swinging weirdly over his forehead, making me wonder how many times his hand ran through it on his way to get me.

"I don't get it," Dad says as he rakes a hand through his hair again. At least we're in the family car instead of the hearse, but he is very predictably in a black suit and tie. He's so old school.

Dad is someone I might actually be able to tell about Bree's drinking and how much I think Bryce is influencing her. Or even about her grammy being so much more forgetful. But if Bree gets in trouble and is sent out of her grammy's house, she'll never forgive me. She'd end up with her mother in LA or her father in Nebraska.

"And this guy is Bree's boyfriend, right?" Dad asks.

I nod again as I watch the houses and light posts and palm trees pass by. Home is so close. It's stupid they made my dad come pick me up.

"That has to be causing some friction with you and Bree." His voice is low, slow, and even—his very best sympathy voice.

I keep my eyes focused out the window. "A little."

"I'm sorry, hon. If I can do anything to help, let me know."

"Make her parents not act like selfish assholes?" I suggest.

"Language, Gabby."

"Gabe," I correct automatically. I want to ask if Dad somehow knows about Bree's dad getting his girlfriend knocked up. No wonder he isn't sending checks—he has another kid to save up for.

Dad eyes me as we pull into the parking lot in front of the funeral home. "You're so grown-up."

I'm never sure what to say when my parents get sentimental, but I'd really like out of the car if Dad wants to talk.

"And does this guy…Hartman…Does he get along with Bree?" Dad asks.

I shrug. "I don't think they've talked much." *She's been busy with Bryce.*

"He seems like…a character," Dad says with a partial smile. Dad's a big fan of characters.

"I asked him to prom. Sort of." And I should maybe make sure I can go. Like, ask my parents.

"And so you are…" Dad stammers. "I mean, are you…Do you…"

I shake my head at Dad. "We're just going to prom. It's no big deal. I'll be home whenever you say. I mean, if you're okay with me going after…today."

"I don't approve of your actions, but I can partially understand. You will do all the boring, stupid jobs you hate while you're home for the next two days, including watching your sister after school, but if the school says you can go to prom, I think it's fine."

There's actual relief that I can go, which is weird, because I didn't even want to go to prom. Though, after today, I obviously need to stick close to Bree. We climb out of the car together, and Dad stares at me over the hood of the car. His mouth opens, and I wait for another partial lecture or question about my day, but then his face changes from sadness to something harsher.

"You can start your suspension by inventorying the snack closet, organizing the snack closet, and making a Costco list. You and your mom can head to Costco when she's ready."

I feel the groan fighting its way up my throat. But my day could have been a million times worse with a parent a million times more pissed off.

"Okay," I manage. "Sounds great."

# Chapter 17

Mom and I pull into the driveway from the special hell that is Costco to find Hartman sitting on the hood of his car near the front door of the funeral home. He's in a blue corduroy sport coat, skinny jeans, and another pair of old-man shoes. I look down at my *Pride and Prejudice* T-shirt, a pair of worn Vans, and my faded gray jeans. Costco isn't worth a nice outfit, but Hartman might be.

"You're *sure* you two aren't dating?" Mom asks as we pull to a stop.

"I think you're dating," Mickey says from the backseat. "I mean, he's here all the time."

I spin to face her. "Why don't you keep that to yourself since we were nice enough to get you from school early. And anyway, what would you know about dating?"

"I watch TV, and Great-Aunt Liza said that—" She snaps her mouth shut as soon as Mom's head whips around.

"I'm sure we're not dating," I say, already feeling exhausted from my time out of school. "We've ridden in the car a few times. That's all. Riding together isn't a date."

"Gabe," Mom says. "You're going to prom with him. He's been here a lot. He's...cute in an interesting way. I don't know. Your get-togethers seem like dates."

"Told you," Mickey says, and I shoot her a narrow-eyed look to keep her quiet.

"Dad said he was a character," I say as I watch Hartman chew on his nails.

He isn't looking at our Subaru. Maybe because we're in the driveway to the house instead of in the parking lot.

"He is that," Mom says.

We get out of the car and Hartman waves. My heart stumbles. That's kind of a weird reaction seeing as we're friends.

"I'm..." Mom frowns. "I think you should be in trouble. I don't think your boyfriend should be able to come over on a day when you were suspended from school."

"Mom!" I whisper-hiss-yell. "He is *not* my boyfriend."

Mickey giggles, which really doesn't help my case.

I grit my teeth as I push a smile on my face. "I'll let you sleep in my room if you stop it already."

Instead of answering, Mickey runs into the house. She probably thinks that by me offering for her to crash with me, she gets to go hang out in there now. I try to quickly catalog anything I might have left out, but it's not like I really have anything to hide, so I should be good.

Hartman slides off the hood and walks toward us. "I wasn't sure if it was okay that I'm here, or if..." His long fingers gesture back and forth between Mom and me.

"I've never been suspended. My parents have no idea what to do with me," I tell him. "They can't decide if I'm actually in trouble or not. Or…" I glance at Mom who is giving me this weird half smile. "Or really how to act when I'm in trouble, or whatever."

Mom laughs a little, but she really can't argue. I've never been called to the principal's office, much less suspended.

"Why don't you two unload the Costco run?" Mom asks.

Hartman jumps forward a little and walks for the open trunk. "No problem."

"And go straight into the office," Mom says. "The family is setting up early for services."

We seem extra busy lately, but Dad's done a lot of work to earn a good reputation and Paradise Hill is growing.

Hartman swallows, and I wonder how much different it is for him to watch people be sad than it is for me. One: I grew up with this. Two: The only people close to me whose funerals I've gone to were my grandparents. Three: His dad died not all that long ago, so being here probably makes him feel sad all over again.

Which makes me wonder why he's here.

He stacks a few items on top of one of the large Costco boxes and walks for the front door. "I can get the rest of it," he says. "I'll be right back."

Whatever. I reach in, stack a few things on top of the other box, and follow him.

"Wait!" I call, and he holds open the door for me.

"I said I'd get it," he whispers.

Angel wags his brows at me the second I step inside. *Not him too.*

Dad shoos us into the offices and presses a finger to his lips. There are more people in here than I'd guess by the few cars outside. Hartman and I running in and out of the lobby is maybe a bit disrespectful, so we'll hole up in the office. Or the house.

"Why are you here?" I ask once the office door closes behind us.

"I wanted to see you."

When I drop my box in front of the snack closet, he sets his next to mine.

I'm not sure how to respond to his simple honesty. "I'm not that interesting."

"I actually find you very interesting." He cocks his head to the side. "So, did you really hit Bryce in the face?"

I bend my wrist a few times and make a face. "It was sort of a blur. I don't remember much. Now I need to try to convince my parents to let me out so I can go see Bree." Hartman's face is scrunched in something that looks like confusion, so I keep rambling. "Bree always tells me everything." Only now she doesn't. "But there's new stuff that Bryce knows." Which is like knives in me. "And that I don't, so—"

Tears well up in my eyes so fast that I start blinking at light speed.

"Have you..." Hartman winces a little. "Have you talked to Bree since this morning?"

"Not yet." I tuck my hair behind my ears and take a quick swipe at my eyes. "She hasn't answered my texts, but with her recent absenteeism from my life, I figure we'll talk when she's not busy anymore. We always do."

"You hit her boyfriend. She's not..." He stops, his gaze darting around the room.

"Is she *mad* at me?" I ask. How could she be mad? It's not like he was actually hurt! And she was drunk anyway.

"She made it sound like maybe she was a bit...upset..." His lips are pursed together in an awkward way. "Or maybe a lot upset."

A strange wailing sound comes from the lobby, and Hartman stands up a little taller.

Bree's mad at me? I mean, being preoccupied with a new boyfriend is one thing. Anger is quite another. And seriously, *she's* the one who has totally ditched me for a guy.

"What is that?" Hartman whispers.

"I guess the family's having a hard time. Some are worse than others." The sound carries through the door again. I've heard this a million times, but I still close my eyes for a moment to push away the cracking feeling of someone else's grief.

When my eyes open, Hartman has the office door slightly open and he's peeking out down the hall toward the lobby.

"What are you doing?" I hiss.

"I'm curious." But he isn't leaning against the wall like he's curious. He's leaning against the wall like…like he *needs* to watch. He clutches the door so tightly that his knuckles are white.

"How…" He glances back at me, his brown eyes seeming a little more chocolaty brown than before. "How do you watch this? How do you listen to people who are heartbroken?"

"I cope." I lean back, watching him. "Didn't we just have this conversation yesterday?"

"*How?*" There's a desperation in his voice that I don't understand.

I stand next to him and lean against the wall. "I do horrible things like keep track of the ages that people died and play guessing games on how they ended up downstairs. It's disrespectful and horrible but…"

He softly closes the door. "It gets you through."

"I'm afraid sometimes that—" But I stop. This isn't something I've ever admitted to anyone.

He cocks his head to the side. "What?" His voice is soft like pillows or my favorite blanket or fuzzy socks.

The words are sticky in my throat before I push them out in a voice somewhere between talking and whispering. "I just don't *feel* like normal people do."

"You don't."

My gut feels as if someone kicked me.

"I don't either," he says. "No one does. We all see the world through a different lens."

"You sound like a shrink."

Hartman shrugs. "Your view of the world is a little more warped than most," he teases. "But that's okay."

"It makes *me* warped. And I've come to terms with that. I just…I don't know how to not be me."

"That." He leans in so close I smell…He smells like the inside of his car, which makes me smile. "I think that's good."

He's so warm and his eyes are so…deep and his voice…I think I'm melting.

"Oh," I squeak.

He slips his hand into mine. "Show me your house?"

I've only held a guy's hand a few times. Does he *like* me? I look at our hands together—his thin fingers, our pale skin—and hold on.

As soon as we open the door between the offices and my house, his phone beeps and Mickey stops at the top of the wooden steps.

Hartman reaches for his phone, but our hands are still clasped together.

"Go! Away!" I mouth to Mickey while gesturing for her to move out of sight before Hartman sees her.

She glances down at our hands, grins far too widely, and waggles her brows.

In this moment, I really wish I were an only child. At least she leaves.

"My mom." Hartman drops my hand and frowns a little, which

tugs at his smooth lips. His face doesn't look as long as it used to. Paired with his perfect eyes and flopsy hair, he's actually...Maybe Mom was right in that he's kinda cute, and cute in more ways than him knowing how to dress.

"Okay?" I ask as he types and then waits.

"My mom is still having a really hard time." His stare is intense. "There are times when she misses me during the day."

"Maybe 'cause you're so cute," I tease and mock punch him in the arm with my free hand.

But the way his eyes are suddenly on me makes me flush from my toes to the top of my head. My throat is swollen. He's a step closer, and he's dropped my hand to put his hands on my shoulders. All I can do is stare at this strange, cute boy in my entryway who is kind enough to carry in boxes and lie in coffins and write back his sad mother.

He bends forward and his lips touch mine.

But I'm not good at this. "Are you kissing me?"

He freezes, inches from my lips. "I'm sorry. Should I not have? I just thought...I mean...I thought..."

Even his nostrils are kind of flared as he shakes his head, his cheeks pinking at a rapid rate.

"I..." I have no idea what to say. Did I just seriously screw up?

I want to feel Hartman again. I'm not sure how all this works. Do I ask, or do I just kiss him back? And now that we've just kissed, how do I know when to expect it again?

"You look like I seriously screwed up." He takes a step back. "I should go. That was stupid. I'm sorry."

Is he sorry he kissed me? Not sorry? Do I tell him I want a kiss? Do I just hold his shoulders and do what he did to me? Why am I feeling like a total amateur?

He pats his pocket and his keys jangle together. And then he slips his phone into his other pocket. He's still staring at the floor. "Should I go?"

"I'm, um…" I touch my lips, but it's not the same as his lips on mine. Not even close to the same. "I'm glad you came."

His head snaps toward me so fast that I jump a little. My heart pounds again at the intense way he's looking at me. "Are you sure?"

He's asking about the kiss, not about staying.

I nod, but that's all I can do.

"Okay."

I take a step closer. I like being close to him because it reminds me how tall he is. So tall that the second I can feel his warmth, I'm craning my neck.

"You're smiling." He smiles.

"Yeah."

"I like you, Gabe."

*I like you too*, but those words don't find their way out. "Can I touch your hair?"

He chuckles and leans forward, his hair flopping in front of me. My fingers slip through his curls. His hair is incredibly soft. Like baby-hair soft. When he stands upright, we smile at each other—me touching his hair felt almost as personal as the kiss.

Hartman begins to bend down, and every cell and every fiber of my body is tensed in the most perfect kind of anticipation. This time I'll be ready for a kiss. It'll be better. This time I'll try not to say something stupid after it's over.

His nose touches mine just before my lips brush his again.

"Gabby!" Dad calls.

I jump away but quickly touch a finger to Hartman's mouth. It's not a kiss, but it's something. His eyes turn about a dozen shades warmer. My finger is still on his lips.

"Matthew can't—" Dad stops in the entryway. His eyes are on Hartman and then on me and then on Hartman again, only a bit narrower.

I drop my hand.

"Matthew can't come out," Dad says evenly. Still staring at Hartman. But also still obviously talking to me. *Weird.*

Hartman holds up his phone, and all the parts of my body that were primed and ready for another kiss are now deflating.

"I really need to go help my mom," Hartman says.

My cheeks ache, and when I touch them, I realize it's because I'm smiling so widely.

Dad taps my shoulder. "Go get dressed, please. Your mom needs help, and you're in trouble anyway."

I want to walk Hartman out. Tell him about how much I loved the kiss. How we should maybe do it again.

Instead, I stand next to Dad like an idiot while Hartman fumbles with the lock on the front door, jerks when the door squeaks, and gives us an awkward wave before leaving.

"I'm pretty sure he's your boyfriend, and I'm pretty sure I'm not at all ready for this." Dad rubs his forehead and stares at the door for a moment.

"I don't *think* he's my boyfriend." But I'm not as sure about that as I was earlier. We did have a quick kiss, sort of two. And I for sure would like to have another one.

I really need Bree.

# Chapter 18

Mickey snores on the small pullout bed. I should have never let her stay in my room.

I've texted Bree like five times about the hearse and prom and that I have news...It seems stupid to tell her I kissed Hartman with a text, but...but she's not answering me. And after Hartman said she was maybe angry, it's like I have to hear from her. Bree doesn't stay angry. I don't stay angry. We work. But it's midnight, and still nothing.

Finally, I write: Are you mad?

You hit my boyfriend! His parents are furious that he ended up at the principal's office. He's grounded this weekend. He might miss prom.

My jaw drops as I stare at her words and type back a quick Seriously?

Silence. More silence. I want to ask why she didn't tell me about what's going on with her dad and the new baby, but she's already angry. I'm blinking back tears again. I'm not sure how we got to a place where we're not talking. This can't possibly last, can it?

There's no staying in bed. I slide up the hallway in my fuzzy socks and pause in the living room. Mom and Dad are droopy-eyed on the couch, watching some show.

I need to tell Bree about the way Hartman's hair felt, and his smile, and his soft lips, and then ask her what we do next. What does the kiss mean? What am I supposed to do when I see him at school tomorrow? I don't remember liking someone the way I like Hartman.

I head down the stairs into the entryway and then into the offices. Grabbing a few cookies, I walk through the dark lobby.

The chapel still has a sickly floral smell to it. The coffin room is closed. The viewing room is closed.

The cool air in the large house brushes against my cheeks, and I jog faster down the long hallway to the large elevator. But when the elevator hits the bottom floor, everything's dark.

I lean against the wall. I still remember when Bree came over to my house in middle school, and the first time she stepped into this room. It was different then. Not as many cold storage lockers. Bree stood next to me and clasped her hand in mine. "It's weird," she said. "But not as creepy as I thought it would be."

Last year, we begged to do the makeup on a girl our age who'd died of leukemia. It took some convincing before my parents relented. Even after embalming, her skin had an odd tinge to it from all the meds in her body. We both cried a little, but we also both knew it was worth it. For us, for her, for her parents. And ever since then, Bree's come down here to help me with makeup.

I'm still standing in the dark room, and I can't imagine never sharing this space with Bree again.

\* \* \*

I don't hear from Hartman all weekend, and that's okay. I mean, he totally knows the family business is busy and that I might be in trouble. He answered my texts, but only with necessary single lines. We haven't had any kind of actual conversation.

And that's kind of weird. I mean, we did *kiss*. I sort of wanted to kiss him again, but maybe…

Maybe now he doesn't want to kiss me.

I send Bree another text. **Need to talk. Come on, Bree.**

Nothing. And still nothing new from Hartman.

My insides crumple at the thought of Hartman's possible rejection. I don't want this desperate, clutching feeling. Is this what made Bree make the terrible decision to date Bryce? To buy that awful nonexistent swimsuit? To come to school drunk? Was she just trying to keep Bryce interested in her? I let out a few slow breaths like I do when pushing away pinches of sadness, but nothing changes. I feel stuck in a really crappy place, and I'm not at all sure how to climb out.

* * *

Monday morning, I lean against Bree's locker. I'm back at school, and I'm really not into being avoided by her anymore. She would never just push me away at school, in the middle of the hallway.

I clutch my books for first period tighter against my chest. Where *is* she? I scan the hall both ways really quickly but don't see her. This bites. I let my head fall forward and rest my chin on my math text. Talking to Bree should be easy.

"Do you need something?"

I jerk my head up to see Bree's bitch face, the one I helped her practice in front of the mirror.

"Just…I'm sorry," I say. "I wanted to say I'm sorry."

"Did you know he was grounded all weekend?" she snaps. "And he didn't even do anything wrong."

He's done plenty of terrible things he's never been caught for. In my mind, this was just karma coming back around—with a little help from me.

"Are you *smiling*?" Bree asks.

Oh crap. "No!" I clutch my books more tightly.

"Just…" Bree shakes her head. "I don't think I can deal with this right now. Not on top of everything else."

Doesn't want to *deal* with me?

We stare at each other for a moment. Bree is my love of vintage, and late-night texts, and online bestie…and who I want to tell about my first kiss with Hartman and ask if his silence might mean something.

How did this happen so fast? We were tight. Not talking or arguing or not dealing together doesn't make sense. "Why didn't you tell me about your dad?"

She swallows. "Because I didn't need any more reminders of how much worse my life is than yours. Because even if I had told you, you wouldn't have understood."

But she didn't even give me a *chance* to understand. "But I—"

Bree turns and walks away.

My throat closes up, my eyes swell about three sizes, and I fall against our lockers.

It was just last summer that Bree's parents both left Paradise Hill. We grabbed doughnuts at the all-night doughnut place and watched the sunrise from the park because that's what we always do for each other when crappy things happen. And now she'll only talk to me long enough to say that she doesn't want to talk to me.

I want to find Hartman. Maybe he'll be smarter at this than me, or have some ideas on how to talk to Bree, or…*something.*

What did she mean by having one more thing in her life not as perfect as mine? I don't get it. I have an annoying little sister, an aunt who occasionally grabs my chest, and parents who work more than anyone else I know.

I don't find Hartman in the hallway. He's not in our shared second period. He's not at his locker after school.

At the end of the day, I stand in the foyer and once again lean forward until my forehead is pressed against the glass. The too-bright sun is not working with my mood.

Pushing my bag against the doors of the school, I walk out into the sun. Bree is probably smashed against Bryce in the parking lot somewhere. And he probably has his gross hands all over her. Hartman is…who knows where. Maybe he's avoiding me too.

One foot in front of the other, and my brain shuts down enough that I blink a few times and I'm home. This is why I don't drive.

The parking lot at home is full, but I still push through the front doors and then stop when several pairs of eyes in gray, wrinkly faces are on me. Frowning. I glance down at my worn shoes, bare legs, and short, faded plaid skirt. *Oops.*

I walk quickly to the back office door and slip inside before I disrupt anything further.

Grabbing cookies, I wander into the house, which feels positively like an oven with the sun today.

Is Hartman sick?

Did something happen with him?

Why can't Bree just give *me* a clean slate?

Instead of totally spiraling into something pathetic, I send Hartman a text. US gov't isn't the same without you. And you were right. Bree isn't happy with me.

After a cool shower and a very quiet dinner with my parents, I finally get a text from Hartman. Sorry about Bree. Chat?

YES! Once I hit Send, I realize how pathetic I might have sounded.

When my phone rings, my hand shakes a little before I answer. All these raging nerves over *one person*. Is it even worth it?

"Hello?"

"Hey…" His voice sounds off.

I clutch the phone tighter. "I…"

*I missed you.*

*You weren't at school today.*

*Are you okay? Are we?*

*How did my friend start hating me so fast?*

"It's been weird at home," he says slowly. "We're packing to go back to Connecticut for a couple days. Long story, but the short version is that Mom wants to sort through a few things in storage there before we pay to ship the rest of our stuff. She also wants to say the good-byes she was too sad to say when we left the first time. And—"

But he just stops. Silences himself.

"How…um…how long will you be gone?"

"A few days. Maybe a week," he says quietly.

Prom shouldn't even matter or be on my radar, but that's the first thing I think. We'll probably miss prom. Tears pool at the corners of my eyes. All of this over one stupid night? One person? How does one person have the ability to make me *feel* so much? Bree makes sense. I've known her for years. Hartman I've known for a couple weeks. I have to snap out of this.

I can't talk to Hartman about Bree, not when he sounds so strange, and Bree isn't available for me to talk about Hartman…Aunt Liza would tell me a crazy story, Matthew would talk about some dead person, Mickey would get starry-eyed and tell me to do something over-the-top romantic. Parents are out because…just…no.

"Okay," I say brightly. I even force myself to smile, which is stupid because he can't see me. "Have a good time with your friends and stuff, and I guess I'll see you when I see you."

"Gabe," he says softly. If he's about to apologize, I don't want to hear it. I don't *want* to feel so attached.

"Thanks for calling to say you'd be out of town. We'll talk later!" My voice is a strangled sort of cheery. All I really hope for is that he can't read through the fakeness over the phone.

"I just…Yeah…It's going to be busy there with stuff, but I'll text you."

"Oh, you know…" I swallow the lump in my throat so I can keep trying to sound normal. "Whatever. It's cool. I guess I'll see you when you get back."

A few moments of silence pass between us before Hartman answers. "Okay."

"Okay. Later." And I hang up before I'm attacked by any more feelings or before he gives me more bad news, or tries to apologize, or tries to distance himself from me. Everything between us, if there's still something between us, feels so completely breakable.

# Chapter 19

Wednesday night I go to the bakery, order myself two doughnuts, and eat one on my way to the beach. It's not the same without Bree. Actually, eating a doughnut by myself is just a smashing reminder of how alone I am.

I pause and consider asking Mickey to join me, but instead I head down the steps to the sand and ocean, my second doughnut at the ready. Maybe I'll figure out what to do or what to say to make everything better after some sugar and sand.

I hope.

\* \* \*

It's Thursday. *Thursday.* Still total lockout from Bree, and nothing more than single-sentence texts from Hartman. I know he's out of town and probably busy, but he hasn't initiated talking once. It's been *four days*. I'm so worried about him and about us that I can't eat, or maybe I can't eat because Bree still won't talk to me. Won't answer my texts. Won't even look at me in our classes or the rare times when we pass in the hallway.

Trying to take three breaths to get rid of this aching sickness that's spreading from my gut is a joke.

After school, I walk to Bree's house instead of home. It's a good mile and a half, but it's not like I have anything to do. I need to talk to her. I need some answers, ideas…anything that's not silence. My doughnut habit is going to force a change in my wardrobe soon.

Why is Bree still so mad about this *one* thing? It's not like Bryce got suspended. So what if he was in trouble for a weekend? We're supposed to be closer than arguments like this.

I turn onto Bree's road just in time to see her run from her house toward Bryce's car. Supershort cutoff jean shorts and those lame white tennis shoes half the senior class is wearing this spring. This is *not* her.

"Bree!" I call as I jog her way.

She pauses and then frowns.

"Just a sec?" I ask.

Glancing back at Bryce, she takes a few steps my way. "What do you want, Gabe?"

"Why are you so mad? I get that I screwed up, but…"

"I can't handle anyone else disapproving of my life. Dad won't…" She bites her lip and looks away for a moment. "I don't have the energy to deal with your constant disapproval of Bryce." Her gaze flashes back toward her grammy's house. "Not right now."

"I don't…" I glance toward Bryce's car and try not to think about him sitting there and maybe listening in. "I'll try to…" Try to what?

Bree sighs. "We really need to get going. The group is waiting for us. I'll see you later, Gabe."

My shoulders fall. "Do you still need a ride to prom?"

"So you can hit my boyfriend again?" She jerks open the door.

"I won't. I…" I didn't even hurt him, so it's annoying that this is even a thing.

Bree looks me up and down like she's seeing who I am outside of us being friends. Her eyes travel from my dad's worn shoes to my unstyled hair. I'm still staring at her generic T-shirt, which is completely not Bree-like. "We'll talk at school tomorrow."

They drive away. Leaving me on the sidewalk. Alone.

Tapping on my phone, I text Hartman even though I don't expect a response.

You around?

I don't wait for his answer because all week it's taken him hours to write me back. At some point, I'll need to give up. Slipping my phone in my pocket, I slowly walk back home.

I'm not in the mood to be the perfect worker-bee daughter or to tell my parents what's going on with Hartman (they'd probably be relieved) or Bree (they'd be far too worried and might contact her parents).

Hartman still hasn't written me when I make the last turn before home. The parking lot is nearly empty when the house is in view, and the relief almost makes my knees buckle.

Even the lobby is quiet when I get there. Dad steps out of the office and gives me a smile and a welcome home before slipping back inside. I walk to the coffin room and stand in the doorway.

"The place is unusually empty of deceased guests today," Angel says as he stands next to me. "Normally they're all talking so loud it's hard to answer the phone. Today it's just Ms. Foster who won't go away. She had cats. Did you know that?"

Since he's not looking at me, I let my eyes roll.

Angel pats my shoulder. "Gotta finish up invoices."

"See ya," I mumble because I feel like I should say something.

I feel just like all these empty coffins and urns. Waiting to be filled. Nothing inside worth...anything. I take back what I said about Hartman being polite. Barely talking to a girl after kissing her is not polite.

Stepping into the dark room, I crawl into my white coffin and cross my legs. My fingers start tapping on my phone as I unleash the millions of things going through my head in a text to Hartman.

I don't get why we aren't talking much. Maybe it has nothing to do with me. Maybe you really are super busy. Bree is barely speaking to me and only to say I don't understand and that she doesn't want to deal with me. I'm just sad. This is stupid. I shouldn't be sending you this. I really shouldn't...I just thought we were friends, but friends talk, right?

I hit Send and my stomach lurches. What did I just do?

I read over my ramblings again, thinking that I've just ruined any chance of anything between us ever because I sound really needy and whiny, and that's not what I wanted. I mean, I'm not sure what I wanted. There has to be a way to take that message back, right? I open my web browser and start typing to try to figure out how to delete a sent message.

My phone vibrates in my hand. I jerk so hard that the phone leaps into the closed side of the coffin. *Crap.*

I lean forward and feel around the satin interior, but nothing. The vibration rattles against my legs, and the light from my phone has slightly illuminated the foot part of the coffin. I slide around until I'm on my stomach before reaching into the bottom of the casket and feeling around. I laugh as I think about what I'd look like from inside the room, legs flailing from the head of the casket and nothing else.

I finally find the phone.

I'm so sorry, he says. I'll call soon, but I'd rather talk face-to-face when I get home.

And that's it. How can that be it? This is so completely unfair!

I take back what I said about you being polite. My finger hovers, but I don't push Send.

"Gabe?" Dad asks.

I wriggle backward until I can sit up. "I dropped my phone."

Dad quirks a brow. "I have customers coming in ten minutes."

"Got it." I jump out of the casket and fluff the small pillow. "All good."

Dad's eyes are on me with an odd look as I walk past him, but it's not like I'm going to talk to him about this. Whatever *this* even is.

"Your mom got tied up. Could you walk to the elementary to get your sister and take her to Liza's?" he asks.

I pause. "Yeah. For sure." Because it'll give me something to do.

Dad's head rests to the side as he looks at me. "All okay?"

My teeth clench together when I try to smile. "Fine."

I stare at my phone. *I'd rather talk face-to-face.* What does that mean? Why can't Hartman call now? Why aren't we texting back and forth? Did I screw up our kiss that badly? Is there a way to tell him I'm just inept, but still wanna try again?

I so need Bree.

\* \* \*

Mickey's bouncing by the time we're in front of Aunt Liza's house.

"I really, really don't want to do this," I say.

"But prom is this weekend!" Mickey's exasperation is strangely satisfying.

I even lean back a little just to see how much bigger her eyes might get.

The problem is that since I haven't really talked to Hartman, I don't know if he'll be home on time, so I can only assume we're not going. "Whatever. I have stuff."

Mickey growls, which makes me snort.

"Go!" she demands as she starts pushing on my back with her small hands. "I want to see you try on dresses."

I want to flop back in my coffin with some music. Trying on dresses is something I should be doing with Bree.

But we're through the door, and Liza throws her hands in the air in excitement and ushers us both downstairs with chatter that doesn't stick in my brain long enough for me to know what's being said.

Liza lights a cigarette as she tugs open the door to the massive room that doubles as a walk-in closet for our family's belongings. Dresses. Shoes. Mirrors...Stacks of hats are on a high shelf that surrounds the room. Two racks of hanging clothes rest in the middle. One wall is nothing but clothing, and the other side is shelves of old military uniforms, books, cameras, photo boxes...

This is the best part of Aunt Liza's house.

"You really shouldn't smoke in here," I say as my gaze floats over the floor-length dresses.

"I know, I know..." She waves me away. "Just this once." Like she always says.

Mickey is already hanging up possibilities in the corner, next to the three-way mirror.

I find it very amusing that Liza has a corner to try things on. But then again, she doesn't work much anymore, so maybe this is how she passes her days. The windowless basement room filled with beautiful things suddenly feels very sad.

"...because you really shouldn't wear black, like *always*," Mickey continues.

As stupid as it is to be looking for a dress that I'm not sure I'll wear, I start toward the wall of floor-length gowns. Bree nearly had an aneurysm when I first brought her here. Liza's cigarette smoke filled up the room almost as thickly as her crazy stories. Bree and I stood between the long, silk dresses, letting the soft fabric slip on our bare arms. It felt like we could have buttoned those dresses up and become princesses.

This was supposed to be our prom. What's Bree going to wear? Who will she shop with? My stomach rolls.

Aunt Liza's cigarette is out, and she's chattering away with Mickey.

"...kitten heels...Here's a bag..."

A deep-purple dress is held up to me, and I stare down at the shiny taffeta.

Boat neck, tie shoulders, full knee-length skirt. This is... "Too poufy."

"Just try it." Aunt Liza pushes the dress against me. "Trust me."

Bree would love it for me.

I stand in the corner, half behind one of the center racks of clothes, and quickly trade out my school dress for the purple one.

"That was my sister's dress," Liza says. "Your grandma. You both have the same blond hair and body shape. I thought it would work."

I tug on the side zipper until the fitted dress squeezes my ribs. Not too tight, but tight enough to know there will be no hiding in this thing.

"Whoa!" Mickey screeches.

I stand in front of the three-way mirror, staring at someone who doesn't look like me. Tiny waist. Curves. Lean arms. The purple actually gives my skin a nice tone—though that could be the soft basement lighting.

Four pairs of short heels are tossed toward my feet. I pick the lowest ones, but they're too tight. On the third pair, I find some T-straps that fit and that I can maybe walk in. If I practice.

Mickey and Liza are still being all loud and weird. My heart is thundering. I feel *pretty*.

I press my fingertips into my palms and stare at myself. It's just a dress. But now I really, really want to wear it. I need Hartman to see me in this. I need Bree to see me in this.

Mickey tucks a thick, black headband onto my head, pushing the hair off my face.

Swinging side to side in the mirror tugs my mouth into a smile. I might be able to pull this off. Might. *If* I still have a date to prom.

# Chapter 20

My eyes are dry and scratchy from lack of sleep. This bites. I'm zombie tired. It feels like I've walked the hallways alone for days, and I'm not sure why that's making it impossible to get good sleep.

With a huff, I toss my blankets off and grab my hoodie from the old desk chair. I'm sure Matthew will be here tonight, so that's something.

I slide across the hardwood floors to the odd back door in the living room that'll take me to the basement. I walk down the familiar curved steps, shivering a bit in the unheated stairway.

The metal door in the basement is cool to the touch. Voices echo on the other side of the door. Matthew better not have a girl here. Dad really hates that.

Pushing open the door, I stop. A rush of cold washes from my head through my toes. The door to the embalming room is open. Matthew is working over another old guy, and standing next to him is *Hartman*.

"What?" I ask. "What?" I ask again. My mouth is about to make the same stupid word again, but my jaw drops instead. I've been carved out from the inside, and it does *not* feel good.

Hartman's eyes widen, and Matthew gives me a smile like everything's normal.

Everything is definitely not normal.

"Hi," Hartman says, giving me a quick wave. "I just got back."

"You've barely talked to me, you didn't say when you were coming home, but you can come to my house in the middle of the night and hang out in my basement?" I ask. "*With my cousin?*"

My body trembles. I've been afraid. And worried. And feeling stupid. And terrified he likes me. Scared he doesn't like me. And now he's just here? Only not with me? This kind of rejection is one that burns and stings all over the surface of my body and begins to sink in.

Hartman cringes. "It's not like that. It's—"

"Whatever!" I yell. He didn't tell me he was back, but he can come over to talk to my cousin. What else do I learn from that except that he doesn't want to talk to *me*?

What is wrong with *me*?

"Gabe?" Matthew's brows shoot up.

"You!" I point to Matthew. "This is not your conversation."

"Listen, Gabriella," Hartman starts. "It's complicated."

I snort, praying tears don't slip down my cheeks. Pathetic answer. "It's late." I turn back to the door. This isn't how tonight was supposed to go. I was supposed to come down here and chat with Matthew and take my mind off everyone and everything else.

"Gabe…" But that's all Hartman offers. No explanations or apologies. My name.

I wasn't supposed to be confronted by one of the two big reasons

I came down in the first place. "You can't just invite yourself to my house!"

"I said he could come in," Matthew says quietly.

I narrow my eyes. Hartman had to have waited for Matthew in the parking lot. So, he can come over and wait for Matthew, but can't send me more than a simple, cryptic text? Can texts be simple and cryptic? *I don't care.*

I jerk open the door to the stairs and start up in the blackness. My tears are cool on my hot cheeks. The door slams behind me, which is perfect. My legs are like rubber and suck at climbing stairs. I lean against the old wall in the dark, close my eyes, and try my three breaths to calm down.

A flash of light and the squeak of the hinges sends my thoughts into a mess.

"I'm not in the mood, Matt."

"It's Hartman."

My feet still won't move. The door closes behind him, enveloping us both in the dark. I swipe at my eyes as if he could somehow see my tears.

"Wow, it's dark in here."

I don't speak.

"I meant it when I said it was complicated," he says softly. "A combination of friends I left back in Connecticut, my mom having a rough week, and…I'm sorry, Gabe."

I imagine the way his lips would come together on the *b* in my name. *No.* "Don't use my name."

A frustrated sigh bounces through the small space. "I just needed—"

"Stop!" I can't let him finish. Can't. My insides are dancing around each other making knots.

"Gabe. Just…"

"Look! I'm acting crazy and feeling crazy, and *I don't want that!*" I yell. "I like my normal. I like my simplicity. I can't handle the continuous feeling of inadequacy or second-guessing or panic or whatever it is that clutches at me when I'm thinking about you!" Especially when I'm doing it all without Bree's help. My heart aches for her and me and Hartman—and because of all the crappiness that's suddenly been shoved at me from too many sides.

Our breathing echoes in the blackness. I know his weight shifts, so I squint in the dark, but I wouldn't be able to see my hand in front of my face, so I'm not sure what I hope to accomplish by squinting.

"Okay." His voice is low and sad, but now I'm thinking about what *that* might mean. This is stupid. How does anyone put up with this twisty-turny feeling long enough to be with someone and get *married*?

He hasn't moved.

I haven't moved.

My heart pounds now, and I feel my body start to lean his direction.

No. No. No. No. *No.*

I'm not doing this.

I spin, rest my hand on the wall to guide me, and rush up the stairs.

As soon as I shove open the door to our house, I nearly run into Mom who is standing in her bathrobe, her arms crossed. "What are you doing?"

"Fighting with…Matthew," I finish in a lie.

"You really…" She stops, and I swear she's regrouping. "You should probably go to bed."

Is that it? We stare at each other for a moment longer before I turn toward my room and die a little with needing to talk to my friend.

If I hadn't had to pay for my own phone, I'd throw it across the room. Four snoozes later, and I still feel like I was run over by a truck.

I get dressed in the turquoise dress from Bree—like maybe my cute clothes will counteract my mood. And like maybe wearing the dress she got me will make her talk to me. Prom is tomorrow, so I really should use today to find a way to apologize to Bree in a better way. On top of which, how am I supposed to navigate the Hartman situation without Bree? Or the Bree situation without Hartman?

A coffin sits in the viewing room but I don't see anyone, so I stand in the doorway. Another older lady. Sort of roundish. Matthew made her lips too pink, but maybe she always had really pink lips. Bree would know, if she'd taken the hours my parents have offered her.

"So," I ask her. "What would you do, huh? Suck up to the a-hole boyfriend to get your friend back?"

Even though I never knew this woman alive, I picture her bright lips frowning.

"Yeah, well. It's not like I have a million other options here."

I imagine her giving me some kind of knowing nod, her mouth pursed.

"I'm gonna do that. Friendship should come first, I think." And I desperately need to share my crazy with someone.

"Gabby?" Dad calls.

I open my mouth to correct him, but step back out of the room instead.

Dad's brows rise in question when I walk into the lobby with my bag over my shoulder.

"Just curious. I didn't see her when Matthew was getting her ready," I explain. And getting cadavers ready without Bree just isn't the same, so I haven't been helping.

Dad starts tying his tie. Black tie. White shirt. "Thought I heard voices."

"You turning into Angel?" I tease.

"No." Dad shakes his head with a weird smile. "Everything okay? Mom said you were arguing with Matthew last night. That you woke her up."

"Matthew's fine. I'm peachy."

He does his staring thing like he can somehow see into my brain just by looking long enough or weirdly enough.

"Don't want to be late," I say as I start for the door. I'm not sure I like sunny California in this moment. I'm in the mood for a rainstorm.

"Okay," Dad says behind me.

There's no replacing Bree, so even if I have to apologize *and* sound like I mean it, I should say something to Bryce. I'm going to have to talk to him.

This might end me.

# Chapter 21

I walk through the hallways looking for one of the biggest assholes in school. The one I tried to give a black eye last week.

*Worth it for Bree. Worth it for Bree…*

"Bryce!" A guy's voice crashes into my ears, and I flinch.

I turn to see Bryce giving his friend Jeremy a high five. Jessica is draped against Jeremy like nearly always, and I stare like a moron because now I'm here and I'm doing this and I really, really don't want to do this.

Because I'm still standing in the middle of the hallway like an idiot, Bryce sees me right away.

He has this amused expression on his face. The odd smirk also makes him look like an asshole. I'm not sure how he accomplishes this, and I'm about to make some snide remark to ask him until I remember I'm here to say I'm sorry.

"I'm sorry," I blurt out. "It was stupid. Trying to hit you. I had…a bad day…?" Will that work? And I maybe shouldn't have let it sound like a question. "Bree said you thought it would be cool if I was your chauffeur for prom in the hearse? I can still totally do that. Like…as an apology. I didn't mean to…" I swallow a huge lump that I'm quite sure is filled with every ounce of dignity and pride I used to possess. "…to get you in trouble."

I hope I'm an adequate enough liar to make this total humiliation worth it.

"I'm half tempted to ask you to say this same thing to my parents so they'll leave me alone about it, but…" He strokes his chin in mock thoughtful consideration.

My heart stops.

His head cocks further to the side, and he smacks his gum in his mouth. Bryce tugs at the front of his letterman jacket. "How many people do you think can fit into the back of the hearse?"

I gasp in relief when I realize he's not actually going to ask me to talk to his parents.

"Um…" I resist the urge to close my eyes and do my three deep breaths to reset myself. "Three people could sit on each side facing each other. The floor isn't totally smooth because caskets need to be locked in place, but I still think three would work. Four on each side would be tight." Maybe he won't get that each side means the numbers are doubled. "So, that's six or eight."

He snorts. "I figured that." He steps closer, still chomping his gum. He's also doing that weird pulling-his-shoulders-back thing like I'm a guy and we're in some sort of pissing contest. "You really think I'm an idiot, don't you?"

*Yep. Totally.* "No. I sometimes don't say things very clearly."

This really better save my relationship with Bree because I'm *dying* here.

"Sounds good, Graveyard Gabe." He cackles.

I try to make my smile look real. So hard. I know I fail, but I hold it anyway. We both know why he gave me that nickname, and we both know I hate it. "So. Clever."

His laughter dies, but his smile widens. He knows exactly how painful this is for me, and he's enjoying it way too much. The second he breaks up with Bree, I'm going to find some really creative way to pay him back.

Bryce slaps my shoulder as he walks past me like I'm one of his stupid followers. "Sounds great, Addams. I'll have Bree make sure we all have your number. See you tomorrow."

*Yeah.*

*Asshole.*

* * *

After school, I'm tapping on my phone to send Bree a text when Bryce's car screeches to a stop next to me.

"You want a ride?" Bryce yells over Bree in the passenger's seat.

"Um…" *Hell, no.* "I like to walk, but thanks."

Bree finally looks up at me but there's no familiar smile, just a weird staring look. "Thanks for offering us a ride to prom. Sorry I was kind of bitchy yesterday. We haven't caught up on all the drama with my parents."

"Call me later?" I ask. I hate how much desperation and hope there is in my voice. Maybe I need more friends. Though, if finding friends were easier for me, I might have more than one. I don't know.

"Sure, yeah." Her eyes dart around, and her hands are clutched in her lap.

There are things she hasn't told me about her life, and I don't know if they're new things or if she's always told me less than I assumed she did.

Bryce pulls away, and I let my feet drag on the sidewalk. I'm not sure when I stopped knowing what to do for my friend.

\* \* \*

Just as I reach the empty parking lot in front of my house, I get a text from Hartman.

I'd like to see you.

I can't answer. He might want to move forward and be a couple or something. He might want nothing else from me. Talking to him is unavoidable, but that doesn't mean I can't put off our conversation a little bit.

When I push open the front doors, Matthew stands behind the front desk in a suit.

I pause and glance around at the empty space. "What are you doing here?"

"Hello to you too." Matthew smiles. "Your dad just needed someone here while he and your mom ran errands."

"Angel?"

"Afternoon off."

"So, you're the showpiece, huh?" I ask.

"What does that mean?" He smooths down his tie, giving himself a double chin as he looks down. "I have this feeling you just put me down without me totally being aware of it."

I rub my forehead. "I don't know what I mean."

"About last night with Hartman." Matthew puts his hands in his pants pockets.

I rub my forehead with my fingers. "I really wish we could all just erase that. Can we erase that?"

"Doesn't work that way."

"I know." *I know.* But I so wish it would.

"He's dealing with a lot, Gabe. Cut the guy some slack. His plane landed, he drove his mom home, he came straight here but the house was dark. I pulled in just after he stopped, and he asked to come inside."

Hartman being here doesn't feel quite as strange as it did last night.

"Do you even think he wants slack from me?" I ask. It's my weird way of asking my own cousin if he thinks Hartman cares enough about me to care what I think about him. My life sucks.

Matthew nods. "You are terrifying, Cuz. Don't forget that."

I snort.

"I'm serious. He probably came over here in some kind of wild romantic gesture, but the house was already dark. Then you yelled at him in the stairway before giving him a chance to get his thoughts together."

He even looks serious. Maybe he *is* serious. Did I just totally overreact?

I need Bree. Not Matthew.

"I need a nap," I tell him. Especially if I'm going to have to play nice and be a chauffeur tomorrow night.

"His life is upside down, Gabe," Matthew says quietly. "But he's a nice guy. Talk to him."

"Yeah." But then I'll be back to the feeling that whatever might be starting between us is so fragile. Walking around fragile things makes feeling normal close to impossible. "See ya."

I step into the family offices and stop. I haven't exactly told my parents that I'm going to chauffeur, *or* that I'm not going with Hartman. I didn't text him back. I sort of yelled at him last night. I'm pretty sure our date is off.

It was so very stupid to let Mickey talk me into trying on dresses.

Staring at the TV with my parents and my little sister is an incredibly sucky reminder of the current state of my life. But here I am, staring at some show with guns and serious faces and countdowns.

I don't care about these characters, but it's better than the pukey feeling I get when I think about Bryce or Bree or Hartman.

"Are you excited about prom?" Mom asks as Dad fast-forwards past the commercial.

"Um…" Now is when I should tell her that there's this weird misunderstanding between Hartman and me, but she just looks so… *hopeful.* "I'm all set."

"You're sure?"

"The dress looks *sooooo* pretty on her!" Mickey says, her eyes too wide.

"I have my dress, and"—I glance back and forth between Mom and Dad a few times—"I'm excited to drive for the night."

Dad hits Pause. "What?"

"I thought it would be fun to take the hearse?" I really should have kept the question out of my voice here too…

"You can have the Subaru, or even Hartman's car is nice," Mom says.

Dad's brow furrows. "There are only two seat belts, and the back is big enough to…to…."

"To what?" I cannot even fathom where he's going with this.

"Only two people can ride in it because of the number of seat belts." His mouth opens and closes.

Mickey leans forward. "You could have a picnic in the back of the car!"

I'd like to tell Dad I plan on taking a lot of people, but he'd never allow it.

"What will you do with all that…space…in the back…" He's choking on his words, makes a few quick glances toward Mickey, and then it hits me what he's trying to get at.

"Ew! Dad!" I grab my knees to my chest. "*Geez!* I barely know him!"

His face slowly relaxes as he watches my reaction.

"You know him well enough for a picnic!" Mickey says. "You could make sandwiches and have strawberries!"

I stare at my sister's hopeful little face. Aunt Liza has filled her brain with far too many romantic ideas. "I'll think about it."

Besides, Hartman's probably not coming. I just don't want to have a conversation where Mom and Dad ask me questions I don't know how to answer. And the worst thing I can imagine in this moment is my parents' sympathy over guy problems. I don't *want* to have guy problems. I much preferred life when I did *not* have guy problems. Though, maybe with how I've hardly spoken with Hartman, I don't have guy problems. That should make me feel relieved instead of like I'm shriveling up.

"Well, you should have some sort of curfew or something," Dad says.

All I can think is that Bree and her group probably won't have one. "How about we just stay in contact?" I suggest. "I'm…" How to play this? "I'm a little worried about Bree's boyfriend, so I'd like to stick close to her."

Mom frowns a little. "The same one you got suspended over?"

"He's…I don't know…" I glance toward Mickey, not that I'd give Mom and Dad the full info even if my little sister weren't here. "Newer to her, I guess."

Dad unpauses the TV. "We'll talk more tomorrow."

And between now and tomorrow, I'll need to find a good way to explain Hartman's absence when I leave for prom.

My phone vibrates in my pocket, and I slip it out.

I'll be at your house at six, Hartman says. In my tux. My question is, do you still want to go with me?

My heart leaps into my throat, and I stare at his words. I'm hurt and sort of angry, but...

Maybe give me a chance to explain everything? he asks.

He *is* going through a hard time right now...

**Are you still driving?** I text.

If that's what you want. Yes.

*Yes. Yes.* I bite my thumbnail and stare at his text.

Mickey snickers and waggles her brows. "Are you talking to your *boyfriend*?"

I just smile back at her because I'm not sure, but maybe yes?

# Chapter 22

Nerves have taken my stomach hostage and dried out my throat and mouth. Who knew that getting dressed could make someone feel a little like they could throw up?

A soft knock on my door is followed by Mom, carrying her flat iron. "I figured Bree would be here."

And just that fast, the nerves switch into a sinking kind of dread. "I'm…" *Picking her up*, which I can't say because I only have enough seat belts for me and Hartman. "Meeting her there. No biggie."

"Is everyone doing dinner first, or…?"

"We're doing drive-in burgers for fun," I tell her.

Mom plugs in the iron. "It's already hot. Sit real quick, and we'll give your hair a smooth fifties feel, okay?"

I sit and Mom starts smoothing over my hair when my phone sings "Uptown Funk," and I grin because it's Hartman. And then I force my smile to disappear because we haven't really talked since I yelled at him in the turret. Texts count, but don't count.

"Hi," I say through my suppressed smile.

He lets out a sigh, and I'm afraid to breathe or move or do anything—not that it'll change whatever he's about to say.

"I'm going to be late," Hartman whispers. "I'm so, so, so sorry, Gabe. So sorry. I know I've already screwed up, and I know I'm making it worse. My mom saw me in my tux and lost it. I just…I can't leave her yet, but I'll meet up with you as soon as I can."

My throat is no longer a throat—it's a massive lump I'm not sure I can talk around.

Mom leans over to see me, so I give her a reassuring smile through shaky lips. "Yeah. Sure," I say too loudly, brightly, and enthusiastically. "For sure. Send me a text, okay?"

"You sound way too normal. I'm depressed over this." He laughs a little, but it's in a whisper like his voice. "This sucks. Mom misses Dad. I miss Dad. I need to get her settled before I can leave."

I should think it's super sweet that he's taking care of his mom, but instead of being that sweet girl, I'm feeling a little heartbroken over our night.

"Okay. Well…" My voice is still too high to be genuine. "Just text me."

"You're the best, Gabe."

I'm something like that.

"All okay?" Mom asks as she smooths over my hair with her fingers.

"Hartman's running behind."

Mom sighs. "Is this some scheme to get out of pictures?"

I shake my head, my throat still feeling a little swollen. "No. We'll get pictures."

"Promise?" Mom asks.

I'm not sure how I could promise when I have no idea how my night will go. "Promise."

After adjusting all the pedals, steering wheel, and mirrors, I glance at myself in the rearview mirror. Dramatic cat eye makeup (thank you, patience and practice) and red lips (thank you, Cover Girl). Smooth, shiny hair tucked up with a headband (thank you, Mom).

Jessica lives just up the hill, and that's where the group is meeting, so I head up the winding neighborhood streets, letting my phone guide me. The hearse feels like a lumbering beast riding slow waves. I hate this thing.

When I pause in front of Jessica's, Bree and Bryce are leaning against his car. Or, rather, he's leaning back against his car, and she looks like she's trying to crawl up his body to kiss him harder. Her knee-length, bubble gum–pink dress tugs tightly around her hips, but not as tightly as Bryce is grabbing her ass.

And the dress is so…not Bree. Though, at this point, I shouldn't be surprised.

The headlights hit Bree, and she breaks away from him, giving me a huge grin and a wave. I wonder who was with her when she picked out her dress, or how she paid for it. I shove away the thought and concentrate on her being happy to see me. Are we okay again? Just like that?

"Hey!" I wave.

Bree prances my way in the biggest steps her dress will allow. I throw my arms around her and hold on. Eyes welling. Heart happy.

"Okay, Gabe. You're ruining my hair." She laughs a little.

I slam my arms back to my sides and stare at her. Bree's eyes are unfocused. Has she already been drinking? Now I wonder if we're actually friends, or if she's just saying that we are so the night goes the way she imagined. My heart is split into two parts.

Instead of thinking too hard about Bree, I walk around the back and open the hearse's loading doors. "Your car awaits."

I gesture into the back, which is immaculate because I worked on it all afternoon. Matthew helped me put a carpet over the attachments for coffins, and I added a few pillows and blankets I stole from one of the spare rooms at my house. My parents were too busy to realize what I was up to, so the inside looks pretty great. Since Dad thinks tonight is just me and Hartman, I'm sure he'd have had a small stroke if he knew I was about to fill it with Bree's friends from school.

"This is so cool!" Bryce runs around Bree and leaps into the back. He seems totally unbothered by the idea that he's rumpling his tux. "No seats, just room…" He rubs the carpet in large circles while wagging his brows.

"Maybe we *shouldn't* have invited anyone else." Bree winks at him while holding her waist.

*Really?* "I'd still be here," I remind her.

Her eyes flash to mine, filled with annoyance and then worry. Definitely been drinking. "Where's Hartman?"

"Meeting up later."

Bree frowns, her eyes pleading, but the worry in the wrinkles feels forced instead of genuine. When did we start pretending around each other?

"I wanted tonight to be great for *everyone*, Gabe," she pouts. Like I had some say in this crappy situation.

I shrug, the purple taffeta making swishing noises with every movement.

"Hi, Gabe. I knew you'd look cool," Jessica tells me with a smile. Her floor-length pale-blue dress flows around her like someone crafted it for her body.

I glance down at my old family dress and then to Jessica's sleek gown that looks more appropriate for the Oscars than for prom.

"Um…" I say. "Thanks. You too."

"This is very cool of you." Meghan pauses at the rear doors, her tight dress hugging her knees too closely for her to climb in.

"Oh." I look at these two girls who I've probably never spoken to, completely convinced I'll say something stupid.

Bree compliments Jessica's bag, and then Meghan pipes in as Theo's bulging arms flex while he hoists her into the back of the car.

"You cool driving?" Theo asks me in his deep, rumbling voice. "This car is a trip. I love it."

I nod without speaking.

He pauses for a minute longer with a smile, and then he and Jeremy climb in the back. If I were to crash this car, I'd kill our junior class royalty. That's a crazy thought.

My phone sings as I sit back in the driver's seat.

A text from Hartman: I'm sorry. I'm working on it. Give me a few more minutes.

My heart cracks.

I can't think about him. I need to concentrate on helping Bree have a good night without doing or saying anything too stupid. I'm afraid to believe Hartman will show up.

As I climb in the driver's seat, I recheck all my mirrors and try to drown out the chatter from the back. Should be an interesting night.

* * *

I kick my feet up on the dashboard and flip another page in my book. The light in here isn't really bright enough to be a good reading light, but it's enough. I walked through our prom for a whole three seconds before I knew I didn't want to be there. Hartman hasn't shown up yet, so lying to say that I was going to go pick him up was pretty simple.

My phone buzzes, making me wonder when I turned off the sound.

Mom says, Don't forget to text when you leave prom to go somewhere new!

And then another from Hartman. Finally leaving! Meet you at prom.

I'm the girl in the hearse.

With our weird half conversations and our argument on the stairs, I really want my face-to-face with him.

Maybe I should write something else. Or not. He's driving now. I know he doesn't live far, but how far? Was he on the road when he sent the text or not?

I can't just sit in the car anymore, so I step into the empty parking lot and peer over the tops of the cars. And then walk a few steps in my low heels, but I don't want to be too far away from the hearse, so I start walking back. And then I stop. The parking lot is still silent. This is stupid. I open the driver's side door again and sit down, tugging my full skirt in behind me.

Just as I grab my door to close it, Hartman darts up and rests his hand on the top.

He's gasping for air like he just sprinted. "Gimme a sec…" He grins as he stands taller and sucks in a lungful of air.

This is the boy who kissed me and then barely spoke to me, and then left the state, and then came back without telling me, and then came late to prom. I'm not sure what to do with him.

He reaches toward me, and I take his hand without thinking. Suddenly I'm standing next to him in the parking lot, and I don't really care about anything except for him being here with me.

"Hi," he says.

"Hi," I say back.

Hartman smiles again, bringing my hand to his lips and kissing my knuckles. "I love doing that."

"I see."

"You're gorgeous. Look at you." His brows go up as he holds my hand to the side. "Totally gorgeous."

My cheeks heat up before I think to look at Hartman. The tux is black and fitted, and every inch of it is sixties chic.

"You look great."

Hartman's face falls a little. "I can't believe you're not yelling at me, or slapping me, or doing one of a million other things you have every right to do."

"I'm…" I let my gaze rest on him for a few moments. "I'm confused."

"I'm not." He shakes his head. "I like you."

Heat rushes up my neck again, and I stare at the ground. "I like you too. But I'm still confused."

"It's so late…" He glances around. "I'm sorry. Our short trip was harder on Mom than I thought it would be. I couldn't leave her home alone crying like that."

"How, um…" I steal a quick glance toward the restaurant and let the sound of the pulsing music take over my thoughts for a moment. "How are you?"

"Recovering." He slips both his hands in mine. "I want to dance with you."

"I'm…" Here? In there?

"Oh! *Driii-verrr!*" Bryce yells across the parking lot before laughing. "I believe our party is ready to depart!"

Hartman's eyes narrow. "Has he been this obnoxious all night?"

"It was just a burger dinner and then here. But yes. Yes, he has. At least everyone else in the group seems pretty cool." This should maybe not surprise me so much, but we've never really talked.

"Really?"

"I'm judgy, I guess. I expected them to all be Bryce clones, and they're not." Just Bree, it seems...

Hartman gives the group a single wave, gesturing for them to come to the car, instead of us picking our way through the crowded lot to get to them. Part of me wonders if there's enough light over here for them to see him, but they start moving this way.

"Bryce isn't a bad guy," Hartman says. "He just doesn't think. His parents spoil the hell out of him, and since his dad moved out, it's gotten even worse."

I always forget that Hartman has known Bryce since forever.

"Then why is Bree with him?" I ask, not expecting an answer.

"You'd know better than me."

Hardly.

"How was your trip?" I ask as the group laughs their way toward us.

"Right." Hartman squeezes my hand. "There are things to say. Lots of things."

I have no idea if that's good or bad.

"And I..." Hartman bites his lower lip like there's something else he wants to say. "This is history. This should be easy."

"What should be easy?"

"I broke up with my girlfriend. Well...*we* broke up before I moved here. I'd been—"

"We ready or what?" Jeremy asks as he jerks open the back door.

Hartman had a girlfriend? It's not like it would be weird or unusual. I just hadn't really thought about that before. That he had this whole other life before coming here. I mean, now that I know, of *course* he had a life before here, and why wouldn't a very cool guy like him have had a girlfriend? I just suddenly feel like the kid here, and the world and the sounds that go with this night start to blur a little.

I need to think.

"You're the best, Gabe!" Bree squeals.

I don't feel like the best. I feel like Hartman just sucked the air out of my chest and like I miss my best friend even though she's two steps away.

Jeremy carefully holds Jessica's long skirt up for her so she can climb in. Not too high. Just enough. Meghan's yellow dress comes next. It once again takes both Theo and Jeremy a minute to lift her into the car.

Meghan smiles at me. "Thanks again, Gabe. This was really cool of you."

I just nod, unsure what my voice would sound like if I were to speak.

"You know, Meghan..." Bryce leans forward with this gross, sneering look on his face. "If you slipped out of your dress, getting in and out of this car wouldn't be so hard."

"Don't be a dick." Theo wraps his arms around Meghan and pulls her onto his lap.

Bryce just cackles. "I'd like to see at least *one* naked girl tonight."

Bree slaps him, pretending to be mad, but when I look at her face, she seems more scared than jokingly mad. My body tenses. I imagine smashing my fist into Bryce's face again, only this time actually doing some damage.

"All ready?" Hartman asks with a hand on each door, holding them just far enough apart in the back to stand between them.

"Thanks!" Jeremy waves and Hartman shuts the doors.

"My guess is there's been some drinking?" Hartman asks.

"Yes."

He walks to the passenger door and holds it open. "I believe this was the arrangement? You ride and I drive."

It was the arrangement, but I might need the distraction of driving. I'm desperate to know more about his trip, and…Okay. I'm desperate to learn more about the girlfriend, but I definitely don't want Hartman's past and his confusing "now" to be explained in a car full of people.

I pause and stare at him for a moment, letting my stomach flutter before sitting. Hartman walks around the front of the car, while noise from laughter and jokes I don't get rattle into the front.

Hartman pulls the driver's seat back before sitting. "You're shorter than me."

I laugh a little, but it's a choking, nervous kind of thing. "Yeah."

"So about Connecticut—"

Bryce's face appears between us. "We want to head up to Tanner's Warehouse."

"What?" I ask. "Why?" It's a run-down old warehouse that used to manufacture…something. The place is a wreck, and the view of the ocean is only good when it's light enough outside to see, which it clearly is not.

Bryce gives me a *You're crazy* look. "Because it's fun."

Hartman starts driving out of the lot. "You'll have to tell me where to go."

I nod and then stare out the window. Hartman threads his fingers through mine, but I'm still confused.

"This thing is a *boat*." Hartman chuckles. "No wonder you don't like driving."

That's not the whole reason, but this car definitely doesn't help something I already find awkward.

Another burst of laughter from the back makes me turn around.

Bree waves at me with a bottle in her hand. "Come on back, Gabe!"

Nope. I don't need to be back there right now.

Hartman's thumb traces patterns over the back of my hand, rushing goose bumps up my arm.

"I really want to talk," he whispers. "For real."

I glance back. "Once we're there maybe."

Hartman nods. "I haven't been fair to you."

"No," I say, because he hasn't.

He squeezes my hand and my heart skips.

Bree's voice doesn't sound like Bree's voice. She's actually talking about what the *football* team is going to do next year without some of the seniors from this year. I'm just…Nobody warned me how fast people can change.

We drive in silence while everyone in the back of the car imitates hyenas—in sound at least.

When we turn off the highway and make it to the dirt road hill, Hartman releases my hand and puts both hands on the steering wheel. "Are you guys sure this car will make it up there?"

"We had a limo up here last year," Theo says. "We're good. If you need to stop, it's no big deal. We can walk up the rest of the way."

I shrug. "I'm not driving and this is our oldest hearse, so whatever."

Hartman continues slowly up the hill.

Scrubby brush has grown in further over the road since last time I was here, but the fact that the road is still here, and I can see tire tracks in the dirt, means that we're not the only ones stupid enough to navigate this road. I shift until I'm sitting on my feet and squint out the windshield.

I know the cliff for the ocean is on my right, and the mountains are on my left. This area is wide and flat enough that I shouldn't have to worry about either, but all I see in my head is the car rolling down, twisting and breaking as it goes.

Hartman squeezes my hand. "We're good. Promise."

The back tires of the hearse skid once as we reach a steeper section, and then the trail-road almost levels off. I suck in a breath.

"I got this," Hartman says quietly.

Despite the way the car is rocking up the hill, I let myself lean back in my seat.

"There it is!" Jeremy points to the tall brick building. The moonlight reflects in the bits of windows that are still intact, but everything about this place feels old and dirty and worn and used.

Hartman stops the car, and the group is out before I'm even unbuckled. Guess my body is stiff from the drive. The thought of going back *down* that hill is…I'm not even sure what.

By the time my fingers manage unbuckling my seat belt and I climb out of the car, I'm behind the group. I take a couple steps but lean on the hood. I have to walk on the balls of my feet with the small heels or I'll ruin the leather.

"Did you bring your other shoes?" Hartman asks with a smile.

"What's with all the smiling?" I ask when I stop in front of the car. "Hasn't it been rough lately?"

"It has, but…but I've also had a few great revelations." He leans slightly closer. "And I'm happy to be out with you."

I spin away as my cheeks flush again and reach underneath the passenger's seat for my dad's old shoes. I slip off the low heels and slide into comfort. Hartman grasps my hand, and I let him tug me to standing.

"Gabe!" Bree yells. "Catch up!" She waves near the gaping open doors of the old warehouse.

Meghan's light-blue dress practically glows, and Bree's pink one sparkles a little in the headlights. Tonight is supposed to be some kind of fun, magical night, but instead... Instead, I don't know what this is, but there is no way I'm going inside that decrepit building.

Suddenly Bree is at my side, looping her arm through mine. "You're not in heels." She laughs, the alcohol smell burning my nose. "You should be faster."

"I suck."

"You're clumsy, but I love you anyway." She laughs again and grasps my arm tighter. She doesn't feel like Bree holding me. She feels like someone else has taken over Bree's body. Will she go back to feeling like she used to?

"So, are we...okay?" I ask.

Bree laughs a little. She's been drinking enough that she doesn't answer, but I think we'll at least be talking again. So it was for sure worth the humiliation when I apologized to Bryce—if she's still the same Bree. *But she has to be,* I think. *Somewhere.* She's just distracted.

Darkness presses around us as we walk over the dry, uneven ground toward the old mill. Even this high up, the ocean below rushes over the rocks and sand in patterned waves of music, but I can't see the water except for the small stripe where the moon reflects.

Hartman walks on my right, and I should be glad I'm here with Bree and watching out for her, but I'm dying to know more about Hartman's revelations and his girlfriend and his trip and probably a few things I haven't thought of yet.

The hearse's headlights light up the brick building and the two large, open garage doors. Well, *open* might be a bit of a misrepresentation. I think they're busted out. The warehouse is only two stories tall, but the second-story floor is super high because the old factory equipment required a lot of height. So much of the machinery is still here, left to rust away on the main floor.

This is not a good idea.

Bree leaves my side and grasps Bryce's arm.

He reaches over and grabs her chest in a joke. My jaw clenches.

"Come *on*, Gabe!" Bree yells over her shoulder.

"I'm right here," I say next to her and she jumps, starting another round of laughter.

"You *are* right here!" she squeals.

We pause in the doorway, and Theo pulls out a flashlight. The rest use their phones.

Bree shouts, "Hello!" into the building, and her voice echoes back to us.

"It's too dark to see," I say to Bree, hoping I'm quiet enough for the others not to hear.

Our pathetic phone flashlights scan in as many directions as there are people, but the light reflects in strange patterns through and around the bits of rusted equipment. No one could possibly have a clear picture of what's inside.

"Are you sure it's safe?" Meghan asks as she clings to Theo more tightly. "I haven't been here in a while."

Jessica takes two steps forward and stops, squinting into the blackness.

"I agree," I say more loudly. "Let's come back tomorrow."

Jessica looks over her shoulder. "If we go slow, we should be able to explore at least a little."

Someone needs to be sane tonight. I grab Bree's arm, and her brows tug down. "Please just hang with me for a few?" I ask. "Let them go in and have their fun? *Please.*"

"You're paranoid." Bree shakes her head. "We're just going to poke around a little. No biggie. The worst thing that might happen is my dress will get dirty. Promise."

"I'm not paranoid."

"Gabe. Seriously." She leans toward me, her eyes swimming in whatever she just drank. "We're just walking around. This is another typical Gabe thing, and I'm not going to miss out because you worry too much."

"I just…" But she's probably right. I'm being paranoid. Her dress will get dirty. Maybe they'll all sober up in there a little. I could air out the hearse a bit before heading for home. "Please be careful, okay?"

"Let's explore!" Bryce yells into the building. The sound of his voice doesn't echo back, but disappears into the massive space.

He runs into the dark without a look back.

"Bryce!" Bree yells. Nothing but his footsteps until they go silent.

Theo and Jeremy take another step inside but pause.

"Bryce!" Hartman yells this time.

He screams from somewhere inside, and the hairs on the back of my neck stand up. My body tenses, ready to run.

"Help!" Bryce yells. "My leg!"

"Bryce!" Bree screams before running in, followed immediately by Jeremy and Theo.

Hartman shakes his head.

Bryce's raucous laughter fills the warehouse. "Suckers!"

"Asshole," I mutter under my breath.

I step back. I'm not going in there, especially if he's going to pull stupid crap like that. Meghan and Jessica smile at each other before stepping into the dark together.

Am I a hopeless wimp? I'm not sure I care right now.

"You wanna walk with me?" Hartman asks.

I peer inside the warehouse and back at the car.

"There's a group. They know how to reach us if they need anything." He wraps his hand around mine again.

He's right. They're fine. Bree's right too. I'm being paranoid. I'm also dying for more information from Hartman. I should maybe stay here, but for what? To watch my friend act crazy?

We start back to the car, and I wait for him to talk.

"I think there's a walkway down to the beach off the highway here." Instead of moving toward the front of the car, he goes to the open doors in the back. "There was a sign near the turnoff."

"After we go down the hill," I say.

Hartman looks up toward the warehouse with a smile. "The hill wasn't that big, and standing around in the dust and dirt doesn't seem all that great."

"You don't like the dirt, but you want to go find sand?"

Hartman pulls a small blanket out of the back. "Walking on the beach in formal wear is romantic gold, Gabe!" He laughs a little, and I wonder if he joked this much before he lost his dad. I like it. "Good to bring a blanket so we can sit without ruining clothes, though, right?"

"Yep. And I'll try not to trip."

He holds his arm out for me. "I'll hold you up."

I snuggle into his side, and we start down the hill. I take one last glance at the old building we've lit up with the hearse headlights and walk with Hartman into the dark.

# Chapter 23

We've hiked down the hill, and Hartman was right. It wasn't nearly as big as it felt when we were bumping our way up.

"Now across the road and down the steps over here." He points. "I saw the signs when we turned onto the dirt road."

"The beach is a big deal, huh?" I ask.

"The beach in Connecticut is like…It's not like here."

That I can understand. I can't imagine anywhere having beaches like here, but then, I do love where I live.

"So. I want to tell you everything," Hartman says as we start down the stairs that are drilled into the rock face, but then he doesn't continue.

We walk in silence for a moment.

"Okay," he says as we continue slowly stepping down. "I didn't think this would be so hard to get out."

"It's okay." What could be this huge? And should I be relieved that his distance hasn't been all about me or worried? I'd know if

Bree and I had been talking. Maybe we'll go back to how we were, and I'll have her help again. Hartman flicks on the flashlight from his phone, and instead of feeling my way down each step, I can just make out the edges of each step.

"I had a girlfriend. Back in Connecticut."

"You said."

"We'd been together for so long that we just were, and for months before my dad died, I was trying to figure out how to go back to being friends with her, but not be dating anymore.

"I'm super…I kind of suck at…" He pauses for a moment. "I was scared about what would happen if we broke up. I distanced myself from her when Dad died, and we split before I left Connecticut. We haven't talked since I moved, so I was right. I lost her as a friend when I broke up with her. And I wanted to fix that, but I felt myself starting to fall for you, and I really didn't want to miss out on a chance with you. I didn't know how to try to be friends with my ex-girlfriend while also trying to find a way to ask you out."

I clutch his hand tighter and keep following him down the stairs.

"She called me on Dad's birthday, the day after I kissed you." Hartman stops and turns to face me. With him a step lower, we're almost face to face.

"Oh."

"It was a terrible day for me, and it made both Mom and I realize how hard Christmas and holidays and everything were going to be this year because him being gone is all new." He blinks a few times.

"When Mom and I made it to Connecticut, my ex-girlfriend came to see us at my aunt's house right away."

I can't even open my mouth to pretend like I know how to respond.

"I told Ilana about you, and…"

"Ilana? Sounds exotic." I'm petty. The only comment I've made is about the girl Hartman left behind.

"Jewish," he says before tucking a few stray strands of hair over my ear. "I think she was a little upset, but I also think that I'm friends with her now. Sort of. So don't worry. You know. About how I might still feel about her, because…because I've really been in a friendship place with her for a long time. My mom's sad, but she'll be okay eventually. I'm sad, but I'll be okay and I'd really like to spend time with you. And that was a lot of words that I was panicking over trying to get out."

Hartman shifts and then releases my hand, tapping on his phone and handing it to me. "I want you to know I'm okay with you seeing everything we texted about. I want you to trust me."

Texts with Ilana fill the screen. I hand him the phone back without more than a glance. Those aren't for me, and I'm not going to be the girl who would read something so personal.

He stares at his phone. "You sure? I don't want you to think I'm hiding anything from you, but Ilana and I are close."

"Are you okay?" I ask quietly, really not needing to see his phone.

"I'm still getting used to the idea that I won't see my dad again. That a part of me is moving on, and that I don't want to feel guilty about that, but sometimes I do want to feel guilty about that. Moving on feels like moving away from him, and that's still hard.

"For weeks after he died, I'd wake up in the middle of the night terrified they made a mistake and he was buried alive. I keep thinking that being around death will help. Understanding what happened to my dad before he was put in the ground will help. I'm sorry because there's a part of me that used you, but I was more curious about you than where you lived."

I can't stop staring. Absorbing.

"When I'm around you, I feel…" He turns his phone flashlight back on. "Happy. And then I feel like my dad's dead, and I don't deserve to be happy."

I lean forward and touch my lips to his cheek.

Hartman holds my gaze as I pull away. "I should have told you. About Ilana and my mom and actually *talked* to you while I was gone. I just didn't have stuff sorted in my head yet. It's taken me this long to find a way to say everything I wanted to say. Because girls are scary." He chuckles a little.

I think about my humiliation in thinking he might have changed his mind about me, and then think about what *he's* been through.

His lips press lightly into my cheek, sending warmth racing through me. "I'm sorry. I'm sure you're thinking I'm a terrible idea right now."

"No."

His brows are wrinkled in confusion or contemplation or…He leans forward, touching his lips to mine. This wave of calm mixed with tingling energy floats through me as our lips touch again. And then again. And again.

Hartman's smile is soft as he slowly backs away.

"Beach?" I ask.

He nods before continuing down the stairs. The salty air fills my lungs, and the familiarity of that helps smooth over the newness of Hartman. Once my shoes touch sand, I stop. "Best to take your shoes off now."

"Sure?" he asks.

"When we leave, our shoes won't be filled with sand, so we'll only need to clean off our feet."

"Spoken like a pro."

We take a moment, and with the water and moonlight, I can

actually see him better now that we're down here. He turns off his flashlight and tucks his phone back into his jacket.

The road is too far above for me to even know if a car passed by, and the music from the ocean has turned into rhythmic roaring that drowns out everything but us.

He drops my hand and squints into the darkness. "Now I get why people always want a fire on the beach."

"I don't want to leave Bree for too long, and we didn't bring any wood." There's only driftwood sometimes, and with the number of people that come down to these little sections of beach, there's rarely any of that available. Also, I'm pretty sure it's illegal to burn.

Hartman spreads out the blanket and sits.

My dress rustles as I find a place to sit, and I wiggle a little to create a nice dent for my bum in the sand. Hartman crosses his legs and leans forward, taking my hand in his.

His dark eyes soften. He's closer. Closer. Grapes.

Our lips touch and sends rippling waves through my body. His lips part a little, so I follow his lead. Our lips come together again, only now they're stacked. A Hartman lip. A Gabe lip. A Hartman lip...

This time when he pulls away, the sliding of his lips sends tingles up my spine. Our tongues slide together, but then we once again get that lip slide, and I scoot closer. Our knees touch, and he feels like fire—the good kind.

I reach up and tuck my hands behind his neck. This time there's no starting or stopping kisses, because this is just all one big heavenly kiss on this heavenly blanket on this perfect beach.

He smiles as he backs away, but our faces are still so close we almost touch.

I suck in a huge breath because I think I forgot to breathe, and my smile cracks apart all the tension I've been keeping in my body for the last few days. Hartman tugs me closer, shrugging out of his jacket and resting it over my shoulders.

Pulling me carefully so I can rest my back on his chest, Hartman wraps his long limbs around me and plants another kiss on my temple. "This is pretty perfect."

"Agreed," I whisper.

His chin sits on my shoulder, and his cheek rests against mine for a minute as my spinning head wraps itself around the idea that *he kissed me. I kissed him. We kissed. And it was really, really good.*

# Chapter 24

I don't know how long Hartman and I sit together listening to the waves, making random comments, and occasionally kissing, but my body aches when we stand, so I'm thinking a long time.

Hartman stretches and yawns. "They *might* be done exploring that old place by now."

"At least they have the car if they need it," I say.

We brush the sand off our feet, and the faintest hint of light touches the edges of the mountains behind us. How long have we been gone?

After slipping on our shoes, we walk up the stairs.

"Thanks for giving me a second chance, Gabe."

"Thanks for wanting one."

He squeezes my hand, and I stop, turning to face him. Hartman's mouth quirks into a smile as I step closer and slip my arms around his neck. He's one step down and still taller than me. I kiss him, slow and soft and deep. His hands tighten on my waist, our bodies touch, and the world spins beneath my feet. I understand a little more why Bree wanted this kind of distraction—even if it was from Bryce.

Hartman pulls away enough for the world to right itself, and we continue up the stairs, which end far too soon. The beach, which felt magical a few moments ago, is now just another place.

He glances both ways before we jog across the quiet highway and hit the trail up to the warehouse.

A car slowly bumps its way down the hill, and I can't tell what it is, but it's for sure not the hearse—too small.

"Did the group invite anyone else?" Hartman asks.

I shake my head before answering, "No, well…not that I know of."

We step off the side of the small trail-like road and into the brush. Hartman squints. "Is that…"

My chest drops. "A cop car."

"Do you think they got in trouble?" he asks. "I don't know who would care if we're out here."

I hold my breath as the car stops next to us because they might care, and for sure the cops will care since the rest of the group has been drinking. And part of the reason I even drove Bree and the group was to help her stay *out* of trouble.

The cop's window rolls down. "Is one of you Gabriella Osborn?" he asks.

My knees nearly buckle. "That's me. Yeah."

The cop's dark eyes bore into me, making me shrink behind Hartman. "The hearse is registered to your parents?" he asks.

"The hearse?" I ask. "Yeah…" Whatever Bryce did to get the cops called out here, I'm gonna kill him.

"What's happening?" Hartman steps forward.

The guy looks back and forth between us—me still warm inside

Hartman's jacket, Hartman's arms tucked around me, the blanket in Hartman's arms…It all looks a lot more scandalous than it is.

"Who are you?" the cop asks.

"Hartman Smith."

The cop rubs his forehead. "One of the girls mentioned your name before the ambulance left."

I fall against Hartman. "Ambulance?"

"Floor collapsed. Everyone's on their way to the hospital. I'll call in that we found you. There wasn't much rubble, but we thought maybe we'd missed you in there."

Prickling cold passes from my forehead into that place that makes people faint from shock. I grasp Hartman's arm as my legs go weak.

"What?" My quivering voice doesn't sound like me. "Who was hurt?"

"All I know is that everyone's been taken in." He talks into his radio to say that he's found Hartman and me walking near the site and that I appear to be fine.

*Everyone's at the hospital?*

"But who was hurt?" I ask again.

The officer looks back and forth between us. "Have you two been drinking?"

"No!" I yell. "*Where's my friend?*"

"Like I said, they took everyone to the hospital." The cop clears his throat. "You might want to call your parents to tell them you're okay."

I drop Hartman's hand and sprint for the car. My phone's in the car. I should never have left. Why did I let Hartman talk me into following him? Why couldn't we have just talked in the back of the alcohol-scented car? Or on a rock? Or the dirt? I was worried about Bree. I was supposed to stay close to *Bree*.

Instead of grabbing my phone to call my parents, I call Bree. It rings and rings until it goes to voice mail.

I'm about to slide over to the driver's side of the car when Hartman folds into the driver's seat, immediately starting the engine.

Two cop cars marked with K-9 still sit between the hearse and the warehouse. Right. They thought there might be another body, maybe two. How much trouble did I cause by taking off for… "How long were we gone?"

"I don't know," Hartman says quickly. The moment he puts the car in gear, I hear a loud honk, and he slams on the brakes.

Hartman opens the door while I frantically send the whole prom group a response to the group texts that bounced around earlier.

Will someone please tell me who is hurt? How you are? Where you are?

My door pulls open, and Mom wraps her arms around me so tightly that I can't breathe. "Oh my God, I've never been so scared in my life."

"What?"

She squeezes my shoulders and sits back. "You weren't answering your phone, Gabe. We got a call to say they were looking for you… for your…"

I glance at the warehouse and the remaining two cars. "You thought I was in there?"

"Gabe!" Dad's whole body goes slack as he rests against the side of the hearse, and his hands slide down his face in relief.

"We just walked down to the beach," I say. "Do you know who's hurt?"

"No." Mom shakes her head.

Every part of me feels twisted and consumed by energy I don't know what to do with. "I should have been here."

"No!" Mom snaps.

"But you should have had your phone on you," Dad says. "You have no…" He starts blinking and purses his lips like he does when he tries not to cry.

"I'm sorry," I say, wondering how many times I'm going to be repeating that. "I have to get to the hospital. I have to know how Bree is."

Hartman's on the phone, and by the few words I hear, I figure he's talking to his mom.

"Why don't you two get in the Subaru," Dad says. "We're leaving."

"What about the hearse?"

"I'll get it tomorrow!" Dad shouts. "Get in the car."

I jump into the Subaru, mind spinning and rib cage tightening. I see Bree's sparkly gloss from middle school. The millions of times we sat next to each other making a corpse looking like they're sleeping instead of dead, all the trips to Audrey's, the late-night texts, the music…

Dad gets the keys from Hartman and locks up the hearse before following us back to our family car.

Hartman slides in the other side of the backseat. His knees pull up so he can fit behind Dad.

Mom's breaths shake. She blots a few tears. Dad's jaw flexes. All the worry I have over Bree turns heavy and spreads in my gut.

"It was my idea to go for a walk," Hartman says quietly. "I didn't think about the phones. I'm sorry."

"You'll have to give me directions to your house," Dad says.

"My mom's on her way to the hospital."

"We need to get Bree," I say. "I need to check on Bree."

The words from the cop about hospital and ambulances are like hitting my head against the wall, rattling my brain. My thoughts. He used the word *collapsed*.

Bree has to be okay. I can't watch Matthew embalm my best friend. Cannot.

My knuckles are white from clutching my phone, but not one person from the group has gotten back to me. Hartman rests his hand on the seat between us. I take that as an invitation and slip my fingers through his.

But he can't help me rewind our night. I should have been there. I was worried about Bree and Bryce, but still I left. For Hartman.

I should have been there.

# Chapter 25

The hospital grows larger with every step.

I'm not sure when I went from sitting to walking or how we moved from one side of the parking lot to the other, but now we're here. Going through hospital doors. This isn't a big hospital. I can already see flits of color and sparkle that belong to prom dresses in the waiting room of the ER.

I need Bree's pink dress, but it's not here.

A waft of cold, manufactured air hits me in a rush. The sterile room is quiet and loud at the same time. Grief weighs the air.

Bryce's mom and stepdad stand against a wall. She's shaking in his arms. Two prom dresses have turned into one single, warped form with too many arms, heads, and feelings. No Bree. I need to see Bree. If she's not here, she could be in a room. She could be…My brain shuts off the thought before it forms.

Hartman's hand envelops mine, and I feel a tug on my arm as he moves forward.

"Hartman!" Bryce's mom wails as she throws her arms around him, and Hartman is forced to drop my hand.

Right. His mom was maybe also told he was there with us.

I'm just standing here like a moron whose throat is too swollen to talk. Whose brain is too scattered to think. Whose legs won't move forward.

This night still doesn't feel real. I'm both stuck in the nightmare and watching from outside. Everything happened so fast. But not fast. I don't even know. I left. Kissed a boy on the beach. And now my world is different.

Suddenly I'm moving. Walking around a row of depressing office-like chairs to Meghan and Jessica.

"Hey," I whisper. "Where's Bree?"

"Outside. She wants to be alone."

My lips tremble. "She's okay?"

She shakes her head. "He died, Gabe. Bryce died. Bree's not okay."

*Died.*

*Bryce.*

As much as logic and experience tell me that this happens all the time, it doesn't happen to me. To my people. I can't...

Nothing.

Nothing comes.

Meghan's mom shows up behind Meghan, and Meghan lets out a keening sob as she leans against her.

"I'm going to go change into the clothes my parents brought," Jessica says quietly. "Jeremy's in X-ray and Theo's in surgery... We were standing on the stairs when the boys fell through."

I wasn't there.

I've been around death my whole life. I stood next to my grandparents' open caskets and smiled at their bodies, knowing they were long gone, but being okay with saying good-bye.

This.

Bryce.

I don't even know how I feel.

"Where's Bree?" I ask again. She'll need me. She'll need me like she did when her parents divorced—only so much more.

Jessica points to a pair of doors, and I start in that direction, trying to figure out how to make this better.

Bree jumps when the door clicks shut behind me.

"Bree?"

I have to know what to say. Have to. Bree's my best friend.

She slowly turns to face me. "I don't even have more than a small scratch," she says. "And he's gone. So fast."

Even though it's our fallback when things go bad, asking her if she wants to share a doughnut right now feels absurd. Childish. This is so much bigger than sand and sugar.

"I'm so glad you're safe." My thoughts can't get past this piece of information, but I have to. I finally get why she was with Bryce. How she got so distracted. How it feels to stand next to a guy who looks at you the way Hartman looks at me.

How would I feel if I'd just lost Hartman?

My chest crumples. I can't feel this. I need air. Dragging in a breath doesn't calm me. I have to be calm enough for my three even breathe-ins. Instead of focusing on what I feel, I focus on Bree.

Her defeated stance and the grief on her face kick me back to my familiar place. The place where I know how to deal with grief. Know what to say. How to act. But I know it's not right.

Bree's eyes are broken. Broken deeper than I've seen of her before. The toppling wreck inside me burns and aches.

Self-preservation or stupidity begins to take over. My body shifts into the Gabe that I am when I'm at work, starting with my three breaths. There's too much feeling to deal with otherwise.

*Loss. Dark. Black. Hollow.*

Three breaths. Again. Work calm. Slow. Succinct. Smooth. I can't keep feeling so much if I'm going to help.

I reach out and grasp her bicep because I can't just stand here. I have to do something. *Help. Fix.* Sentences start to form. These words aren't the right words. Not for my best friend. Not even close. They're coming out, and I don't know if I should stop them or let them out or hug her or just drag her out of this horrid hospital.

"I'm so sorry for your…loss," I finish lamely.

The words hang between us. My work voice hangs between us. The fact that we both know Bryce wasn't my favorite person hangs between us.

Her head tilts slightly to the side, and her brows begin to pinch together—like she's studying me for the first time and doesn't like what she sees.

Bree knows these words aren't for her. They're for me. They're what I use to keep myself safe. Bree doesn't want me to be safe. She needs my help.

My mouth opens and closes.

She shakes off my arm and jerks open the hospital door.

I cover my face with my hands as my body weakens enough that I lean against the railing.

"How do I even fix this?" I whisper. My gut tells me to run after my friend, but I still don't know what to do. What to say. How to help.

I'm supposed to know how to help my friend. Friends know these things. I knew what to do when she got her first kiss and when her parents were divorced. When she and Peter broke up.

Why don't I know what to do now?

Before letting myself think too hard, I push back through the doors.

Dad is talking in his low voice to Bryce's stepdad. "...*anything you need...please... All on us...We are so incredibly sorry... Anything...*"

I scan the room. No Bree.

"Gabe?" Jessica asks.

I pause.

"Bree said she was meeting you out front to go to your house?"

Okay. I may not know what to do for my friend right now, but I do know there's no way she'd voluntarily go to my house after what just passed between us.

"Um..." I say. "I don't know."

*I don't know.*

Sprinting out the main doors, I run into the brightly lit parking lot but see only rows of parked cars.

No footsteps. No movement. Just my breathing in the open space. "Bree?" I yell. "Bree!" I yell again.

Nothing.

How could she disappear so fast?

Hartman stops behind me, and touches my shoulder. "What's going on?"

I turn to face him, and I want to hug him for comfort, but start running to find my friend at the same time. "I think Bree just took off." *Because I screwed up again.*

If Jessica's right and Bree did go to my house, then I need to see her. Help. Somehow. I can't imagine she'd go there, but it's all I have.

Mom and Dad stop next to us. "Gabe. It's time to go."

I reach over and take Hartman's hand.

"Are you okay?" he asks.

"Are you?" I whisper back.

"My perception is warped. I'm in shock, but so glad I didn't lose you or my mom."

My parents are silent—probably somewhere between worried and angry.

"I'm sorry," Hartman tells my parents. "And thank you again."

Dad gives him a curt nod, and Mom waves as Hartman heads back toward the hospital.

I'm not ready for our night to be over. I don't want it to end this way. I want him to help me find Bree, and I want a kiss good night or a hug or something. I run up behind him and grasp his hand with my two.

Hartman pauses and turns to face me. A million apologies for the crappiness of our night and the thank-you's for the awesomeness of our night and promises that we'll see each other again soon pass without a word.

So many things about guys and love and togetherness make sense now. One look can convey a whole night's worth of experiences, future wants, and feelings I don't totally understand.

His lips press together, and he gives me a slow nod like he understands what I'm thinking.

"Text me whenever," he says quietly. "I don't care if you wake me up."

"Okay."

And then he's back inside, and we're in the car and driving for home.

"I'm sorry about—"

"Not right now," Dad growls.

"We need to find Bree," I say. "I'm...worried."

I'm more than worried. I'm stupid. I screwed up. First by leaving

Bree with Bryce in that awful warehouse. And second by saying the absolute worst thing in the absolute worst way.

Mom and Dad are silent.

"She probably went home," I say.

"We'll check *after* we drop you off," Dad says.

Dad breaks pretty much every traffic law on our way home. No one speaks. At this point, I'd probably rather they yell.

I text Bree ten times with no response.

I'm sorry

Let's talk.

Come over.

Text back...

The second we're in the driveway, I jump from the car. There's a small chance Bree is here. Not a great one, but enough to make me move. I sprint to the front doors of the lobby. No Bree. I run around to our family door. No Bree. I jog down the gentle hill to the back doors. No Bree. Did she get inside?

Mom has the door open.

"I don't see her." Not that I expected I'd find her here.

Mom nods. "We'll go check her house."

I kick off my shoes and go for my room. Empty. Mickey's room just has Mickey's sleeping form. I move up the hallway opening each door, even though I know Bree's not here. Did I really think she walked out of the hospital and all the way here on her own? Where else would she be?

"I bet she's at her grammy's," I say as I jog back to the living room, out of breath. "Or at the beach. Or maybe just sitting in front of Audrey's, or getting a doughnut. We need to check the beach, or—"

Dad points to the kitchen table. "Sit."

I lean for the front door. "But Bree."

"Sit. Down. Now."

I freeze, my body's like drying play-doh, thick and heavy. I sit.

Dad folds his arms on the table. "First off, you didn't have your phone on you."

"Sorry," I mumble, but I'm clutching it now, praying Bree will send me a note.

"And you said you were driving, you and Hartman," Mom says, her jaw clenched in anger. "You had a group."

"And you were *drinking*," Dad adds through clenched teeth.

"I wasn't. I swear." I shake my head.

Mom holds her hand up to silence me. "We were terrified, Gabriella. Terrified. We get a call that some kids were in the warehouse. The car was there, and you weren't answering your phone. Everyone assumed the worst."

"I'm sorry." I stare at the smooth table, wishing I could redo my night.

"And how could you let open alcohol be in the car? How were you with kids who were drinking at all?" Mom asks.

I stare at my fingertips as I slide them across the table.

"I was worried about Bree," I finally say. "She hasn't been acting like herself. I'm scared now. She said she was coming here. She's not here. Her boyfriend just…He just…" Bryce died. I didn't like him, but this…Nobody deserves to die at seventeen.

I'm in shock. People like Bryce don't die. They grow up, live charmed lives, and end up on the covers of magazines.

"How did you not hear the sirens?" Mom asks.

I glance back and forth between them, wishing that I could somehow force them to feel how torn up I am. "I don't know. We walked down to the beach. Between the noise of the ocean and

216

being so much lower than the road…I don't know."

"We do *not*"—Dad shifts in his chair, bringing him even closer to me—"appreciate being lied to."

"You were having a party in the back of that car," Mom says. "This isn't like you."

I blink and tears roll down my cheeks. "I just wanted to try to be friends with Bree."

Mom and Dad exchange one of those parent looks that says neither understands.

"But you're already friends with Bree," Mom says.

I shake my head. "Bryce…I just…And we just…We drifted so far apart so fast, and it doesn't make sense. I was trying…to fix that."

Mom and Dad glance at each other. Dad sits back. "We're not sure what we're going to do with you yet, Gabe."

"I just want to find my friend."

Dad points, his whole body quivering with tension. "I thought I *lost* you tonight! I thought you'd been buried in pieces of that old building because you didn't do the *very few* simple things we asked you to do! You are *not* to leave this house!"

I cringe back in my seat, unable to control my tears. *I'm sorry* comes out in a whine.

Everything trembles, and the world is spinning too fast around me and *where is Bree?*

"We'll go look for your friend," Mom says. "You go to your room."

My parents go look for Bree? "But I—"

"Not another word." Everything about Dad is tight—his face, his shoulders. Everything.

Mom stands. "Ready?"

"We need to take one of the hearses or the van. We'll be picking up Bryce when his parents and the hospital give the okay," Dad says.

Bryce is now a body. A corpse. A cadaver. The deceased. I can't sort out my thoughts. Hartman was right—of course people are shocked when someone dies.

I want this horrible night to be over already. No. I want to erase this night. And maybe a lot of other things as well. I really should have stayed with my friend. Why did I let Hartman pull me away?

My phone sings in a text, and I immediately read the short note.

Bree crashing at my place tonight.

At Jessica's? I blink, and tears roll down my face. "I guess we found Bree."

And she's found somewhere to be that's not with me.

# Chapter 26

The house is quiet once Mom and Dad leave. They're picking up Bryce's body.

I lie in bed and stare at the ceiling, the sun on the horizon slowly lightening my room.

My phone is still clutched in my hand, and my prom dress is slumped over a chair.

"Uptown Funk" sounds on my phone, and I glance to see a text from Hartman.

Can't sleep. You?

**Nope. Bree's at Jessica's.**

I'm sorry. You two will work it out.

Maybe. I can't even believe that I'm in a position to need to work things out with Bree.

I'm sorry I asked you to leave with me.

But the alternative would have been to hear the tragedy from the car and then run inside too late to change anything aside from me being able to be there for Bree. My heart twists so fast and hard that I gasp. But my choice in the moment he asked me to go to the beach was simple—of course I wanted to be away from everyone and to be alone with him.

**Don't be sorry. I wanted to go.**

I wanted to go with Hartman because I wanted to get to know him better. Because I like how he makes me feel. And we were gone for so long because we got distracted and lost track of time. These are all things Bree has done since Bryce. So, I'm guilty too.

Is it weird that I miss you?

**Miss you too.**

Text if you connect with her. Are your parents as angry as they seemed?

**Pretty much, yep.**

If you're on lockdown, you might as well try to sleep.

I might as well.

G'night/morning

**G'night/morning**

My body starts to warm up again just thinking about him—how magical is that? I have to focus on this feeling. I'll be no good to my friend or anyone else if I don't get any sleep.

\* \* \*

Vibrating on my head makes me blink. Slivers of light flash as I keep blinking. The sun is fully up, and I have no idea what time it is.

I sit up, and now the vibrating is against my hand.

My phone.

*Idiot.*

I pick it off my mattress and stare at a text that makes zero sense.

How's Bree today? Jessica asks.

How's Bree? Bree's with her. Maybe I somehow input her phone number wrong.

Is this Jessica? I text.

Yep

You said Bree was staying with you

She told me she couldn't get into your house, so she was coming to mine, and then she said you came home so she was staying with you

I'm wide awake. Brain running, spinning, trying to put this together. Why would Bree need us both to think she was with the other?

Where are you?

Back at the hospital having breakfast with Jeremy. Theo's still sleeping after his surgery, but they say he should wake up later today.

I can't imagine anything hurting that massive guy, but I guess I've seen bodies that were larger. So different when it's someone I know.

I shove off my blankets.

I'm going to head out to find Bree. If you hear anything, please text me.

She's not there?

I haven't spoken with her since last night at the hospital. When she ran away from me.

Of course. I'll help once I'm done here.

I don't bother changing out of my pajama shorts, just slip on a bra under my old T-shirt. It's going to be hot out today anyway. I run downstairs and see Mom sitting at the kitchen table and staring out the window, her mug of coffee to her lips.

"Mom?"

She jumps.

"Bree's not at Jessica's. Jessica texted me to see how she is."

Mom sets down her coffee and stands, her eyes glassy with tears. "I'm sorry we were so angry last night."

"What?"

"Your dad and I." Her fingertips turn white as she presses them against the top of the table. "We were so scared, Gabe."

I nod. "Well, I'm scared about my friend. I know I'm in trouble, but please—"

Mom picks the Subaru keys off the hook. "If you miss one call from me, your freedom is done. Understand?"

"I understand." I snatch the keys and head for the door.

"I'll make some calls to see if I can find her from here. Let me know the second you find her, okay?" Mom asks.

"Yep!" I yell as I run down the steps for the car. I'm not even sure where to start except at her house. I can't imagine why she'd tell Jessica she was with me, and me she was with Jessica, if she was just going home, but I have to start somewhere.

\* \* \*

The windows in Bree's grammy's house are dark instead of having lace-printed curtains, making the place look emptier than usual.

I knock on the door and wait. And wait. And wait.

The door opens with a jerk to reveal a man I don't know. About my dad's age, only with Bree's big, brown eyes. "I'm looking for Bree?" I ask.

"I'm her uncle Greg." He swipes his brow, and as I glance around him, I see the living room is full of boxes. "We're in the process of moving my mother to Seattle so she can be closer to me."

I knew *none* of this. "Oh." But. "Where's Bree?"

"She's staying with a friend until her parents sort out what will happen next."

"Which friend?"

"A"—he scratches his head—"Gabriella?"

"Are you sure?"

"I'm sure." He nods. "My mom said she spends a lot of time over there anyway, so…"

I think about how I didn't tell the principal that Bree was drinking that day at school. I knew she would have gotten in trouble, and that would have been awful, but it also might have kept her from prom. I'm not sure what the right thing is here, but with her grammy moving, it's not like I have anything to lose.

"I'm Gabriella," I say. "She's not with me."

The man frowns and sags. "You have any ideas?"

"When was the last time you talked to her?" I'm breaking every friend code right now by telling someone from her family that she's disappeared, but what else am I supposed to do? I'm more worried about her safety than I am about how much she likes me after this mess is over.

He shrugs. "A couple days ago?"

He doesn't know.

Do I tell him? Do I not?

"Prom was last night. There was an accident. Bree's okay. She's just disappeared since then, so…"

His lips pull into a thin, worried line. "I'll call her parents, and then probably the police."

Police make this real again. Bree's missing because she *wants* to be missing.

He hands me a black marker and rips the corner off a box behind him. "Just write your number so I can call if I find her."

I scribble my number. "I'll call here too."

"Thank you, Gabriella," he says as I turn and start running for my car.

Bryce texted me all the addresses I might need for my chauffeuring gig, and it's so weird to pull up something I got from him now that he's gone, but I'm after Bree. I copy Meghan's address into my maps from Bryce's text and let my phone guide me there.

Another typical California home—stucco sides and tiled roof.

I park out front, run to the door, and then cringe a little as I look down at my worn-out pajamas. Oh well. Bree's important, not my clothes.

Tapping my feet, I wait for someone to come to the door. And wait. And wait. Finally it opens to reveal who I guess is Meghan's father—dark circles under his eyes.

"Sorry." I fold my arms. "I'm looking for Jessica or Meghan or Bree."

"They're all at the hospital," he says.

"Bree too?"

The man shrugs. "I'd assume so, but I don't know."

"Thanks." I back up and then turn and jog for the car.

Once I'm in the driver's seat, I slide my phone out and type a text to both Jessica and Meghan. Bree isn't at my house, and she isn't at home. A guy who I think is her uncle is going to call the cops, so if you know where she is, please tell me.

OMG!! Meghan texts. I haven't seen her since she left last night!

Jessica replies, We'll watch out for her here.

This is bigger than Bree getting in trouble. Everyone thinks that Bree is somewhere else. Because she led them each to believe she was somewhere else. Nothing good can come from a person wanting to disappear this way.

I call Bree's phone again, but it goes straight to voice mail.

She won't answer me. What if it's for a much bigger reason than her just not wanting to talk?

Why would she need to disappear?

I clutch my phone and call Hartman. "I'm freaking out," I say as he answers.

I give him the rundown of where I've been and what people have said. By the time I'm done, my hands tremble. "I can't lose my friend. Why would she lie to everyone?"

*She wants to run away.*

*She hates us all.*

*She doesn't want to live anymore.*

I sniff as my nose starts to drip. "I don't know what to do."

"Do you want to come here for a minute and regroup?" he asks. "Or do you want me to come with you?"

Am I just going to screw up by going to Hartman's? I don't know. "Yeah."

"I'll text the address to your phone, okay?"

And in about two minutes, I'm following my phone's directions to Hartman's house. I'm trying to make a mental list of all the places I should stop to try to find Bree. The diner near my house. Audrey's. The beach. The school. Am I screwing up by taking the time to pick Hartman up?

I'm at his house in only a couple minutes, and he jumps in as I pull to a stop.

"Where to first?" he asks.

"Audrey's?" It seems like a good place to start.

# Chapter 27

I'm one of the unsafe drivers.

My eyes can't focus. I want to drive a hundred miles an hour to every stop on my list. A million horrible scenarios race through my mind.

Every light stops me. Every stop sign has a person waiting to cross. I itch and tick and bounce in my seat as I drive.

"It's okay," Hartman says.

I shake my head. "It's not okay. I didn't take the time to understand what Bryce did for her, and now I do, but she's taken off, and I can't even think about why she'd need to disappear."

My phone vibrates, and I hand it to Hartman so he can read the text.

"Your mom," he says. "She talked to Bree's mom, and her mom has no ideas."

"Is her mom coming up?"

Hartman reads the text. Of course her mom doesn't say.

We go to Audrey's with no luck.

Bree's not at school.

Not at her favorite places to eat.

Not at the beach.

Not at the doughnut shop.

Bree is nowhere.

We stop in the parking lot in front of my house, and I'm so weak that I'm not sure how to keep moving forward.

"Hey…" Hartman whispers as he slides his fingers over my cheek, wiping my tears away. "We'll find her."

But she doesn't want to be found. People who don't want to be found are incredibly hard to locate. I sniff. "Maybe."

Mom jogs down the steps of the house entrance and to the driver's side of the car. I roll down the window, not quite ready to move.

"No luck?" she asks.

I shake my head.

How is this happening?

Mom glances at Hartman. I'm waiting for her to say something about how I should be on lockdown and for sure shouldn't be running around with a guy, but she says nothing.

"I can't lose my friend, Mom. I can't…" I suck in a ragged breath.

"Breathe," Mom whispers.

"I should have stuck closer." I sniff again. "Should have known she was…I don't know! I should have not cared that she was mad and made her be close to me, or something. *Anything.*"

"Why don't you two get out. We can sit on the back porch for a few minutes and regroup."

Hartman jumps out of the car and starts for my side, but Mom already has the door open. We walk to the back patio and sit on the faded furniture with the cemetery spread out in front of us.

"How are you?" Mom asks Hartman.

"I've been better," he says. "I wasn't close with Bryce, but I've known him since I was a kid, on and off."

"I'm sorry."

I'm so horrible. I haven't even thought about Hartman. I reach out and take his hand. His fingers slip through mine.

Matthew pushes out the back door, sunglasses on his tanned face and wearing surfing shorts. "Hey." He pauses. "How you holding up?"

"We spoke," Mom says with a tone that I recognize well. She and Matthew have discussed something that probably has to do with Bryce.

He comes up the few steps from the lower door and flops in a chair, studying me too closely. "You look like hell."

"Rough night."

"Wasn't aware you were so close with Bryce," Matthew says.

"It's not that." I stare out at the cemetery. "Bree's missing."

Matthew shifts. "What?"

"Bree's gone."

He looks over his sunglasses now that he's under one of the umbrellas. "She, um…couldn't get in to your house…so she came to my house…She's crashed in the guest room…"

"Wait." I sit up. "Bree's at *your* house?"

"Yeah." He looks at each of us. "She, um, didn't say?"

With all the pauses and "ums," I'm wondering if there's more to his story than he's letting on, but I don't care.

I have no idea how many wires had to cross for me to not know this. It doesn't even feel possible. "What? Bree's at your house. Right now?"

"I don't think she slept all that well, but she was still in the room when I left about an hour ago."

My chair topples to the ground as I stand. I run across the grass, pushing as hard as my tired legs will carry me between the grave markers. When I get to Matthew's house, I don't pause, just run inside and head up the stairs to the bedrooms.

"Bree?" I ask.

"Hmm?" Her voice is sleepy, scratchy, and mumbly.

I pause in the doorway to see her blinking my direction. I fall against the doorjamb and just stare. More tears. More water. More sorrow and worry and shame and wishes fall down my face.

She's here.

She's safe.

"You scared the crap out of me," I whisper.

"What?" She sits up, blinking.

"I thought you were at Jessica's. Jessica thought you were at my house..." *I thought you'd tried to disappear.*

"I couldn't stay at the hospital, Gabe. I couldn't..." Her voice turns high pitched, and she sniffs before tears start spilling over her dirty cheeks. "I was mad at you, but I know you. I just...This is... where I ended up."

I move across the room and sit next to her. "I'm so sorry. I'm sorry I left the warehouse. I'm sorry I didn't get home sooner. That I didn't know where you were."

Bree's fingers fumble over one another as she stares down at her lap. "I don't know what to do. It's like I forgot how to function. Like everything hurts, and I can't deal with the hurt. I can't."

Grabbing Bree from the side, I hold her against me until her body relaxes. Voices carry from downstairs so I'm guessing Mom and Hartman are here.

"I get why you wanted to be with him," I say. "With Bryce." My ribs smash together as grief begins to suffocate me. "I get it." My voice is tight, spoken through a swollen throat. "I'm so sorry."

She tugs me closer, and we sit together, each clutching the other. Her body shakes against mine as she cries, and the same ripping pain spreads through my chest again. How much crying alone did she do last night? If I'd said the right thing at the hospital, she wouldn't have had to be alone.

"I'm so, so sorry," I whimper.

"This is what I need from you, Gabe." Bree's voice sounds stretched and soft.

Her arms slowly loosen, so I loosen mine too. Slowly. Bree slips her arm under my elbow and rests her head on my shoulder. Instead of saying something stupid, I sit silent. I'm here. I hurt. I hope that's enough.

"You don't get what he did for me, Gabe. And you were my voice of reason when I didn't want one. I didn't want to be smart or sensible or any of the things you are. I'm sorry too."

Hartman's low voice carries up the stairs. "Can I…"

"Go ahead," Mom says.

And then he appears in the doorway, a slight frown on his face.

Bree's breath hitches a few times, and her head comes up a little. "Hey," she says quietly, tugging the down blanket more tightly around her. "Did you two have fun?"

There's no malice or frustration or anything.

A corner of Hartman's mouth kicks up.

"Never mind," Bree says as she swipes at her eyes. "I'm glad."

"I should go." Hartman gestures with his head back down the hall.

I'm not letting go of Bree again. "Yeah. Okay."

"Your mom said she'd give me a ride. Or your dad. My mom said she could come. So I'm totally covered there."

Bree sniffs a few times. "You go say good-bye for real, okay?" And then gives me a shove off the bed.

I nearly slip to the floor but push myself up and step into the hallway with Hartman. My bones feel as if someone's put them together all wrong.

"I'm so glad you found her," he whispers.

"Me too," I whisper back.

The now familiar energy of firsts and newness and *like* bounces back and forth between us.

"You spend time with your friend. Call me later, okay?"

"Okay."

He dips his head down and pauses just before we touch. I close the distance and Hartman kisses me twice softly. "See you soon."

"Soon."

He kisses my cheek before releasing me. Hartman knows. Bree comes first. Especially now. And he's okay with it. Aunt Liza was right—he's a total keeper.

I walk back in the room to see Bree sitting on the edge of the bed in one of Matthew's T-shirts.

"Oh." Bree looks down. "I stole it when I couldn't sleep."

"Everybody's crazy worried."

"How are Jeremy and Theo?" she asks.

"Sounds like Jeremy is good, all things considered. Theo's still sleeping."

"I need a shower, and then I want something to help me sleep and not feel so much—at least for a while."

Mom stops in the doorway. "Come on over to our house. I can help with both of those things."

Bree nods and lets herself be led from the room in the oversize T-shirt.

"I'm sorry, Bree."

Her familiar chocolaty eyes rest on mine.

"I'm sorry for not taking time to get to know Bryce or understand and just generally being a brat."

"Me too. I just wanted to have fun. That's all…" Her chin starts to quiver again, and she wraps her arms around her waist. "I wonder if this aching will ever end."

"It will," Mom promises. "It'll just take a while."

I've heard a version of this interchange thousands of times in my life, but only now do I actually internalize it. Losing my grandparents still hurts. Sometimes enough to make me stop for a moment. Some days I smile when I think about them, but they're always there. The idea that I had them in my life, and now I don't…that's always there. The second I let myself feel was the second I began to understand Bree. I can't keep closed off and expect that I'll help anyone in any kind of real way.

Bryce was a guy who understood things about her that I couldn't. I hated him for it. I hated him for taking Bree from me. Lots of things. But I'd bring him back in a second, even if it meant that Bree and I weren't talking.

We are both changed forever.

# Chapter 28

After a hot shower and a few of Mom's sleeping pills, Bree crashes.
I'm relieved, exhausted, and unable to sleep. Bored, I head downstairs
and jerk open the elevator. Matthew frowns when I enter the
embalming room. "You're not supposed to be here."

I glance at the overly tanned hand that sticks out from under the
sheet. I'm no longer part of my body.

"I can guess this one."

Matthew's head cocks to the side. He already knows, of course.

"He died by falling through the floor of the old Tanner
Warehouse. Got it right on guess *one*."

Matthew's face falls further. "I'm sorry, Cuz."

I stare at the hand. "He wasn't my friend."

But Bree liked him. That should have meant more to me. Maybe
she has every right to be furious. Those thoughts don't stop my
mouth. "If someone gave me a lineup of all the people who went
into that warehouse that night and then said one had to die and

which one should it be, I'd have chosen him. What does that say about me? About what kind of friend I am?"

Matthew shifts. Folds his arms. Unfolds them. "Um…You're not a terrible person. Bryce wasn't good for Bree, yeah? We both know Bree deserves better. And she was your friend, so…" He shrugs. "Maybe that makes you a good friend."

No. A good friend would have tried harder to see how Bryce made Bree feel. Bryce might still be alive if Bree and I hadn't been fighting. I might have been able to talk them into doing something different. I wouldn't have the guilt of leaving for the beach with Hartman.

I think to what Hartman said about how no amount of preplanning or knowledge would have saved his dad. He went to work. He collapsed and died. But Bryce's death is so different. How many little decisions killed Bryce? How many little decisions *of mine* led to Bryce dying?

Matthew drags in a long breath. "Why don't you head back upstairs so I can finish up?"

I step closer.

"Now, get out of here." He seriously shoos me, rubber gloves and all.

I don't move.

"I want to see him," I say.

Matthew steps back but makes no move to uncover him. Maybe I don't want to see Bryce.

I reach forward and tug the sheet off his face anyway. Matthew's already set his face, and the embalming fluid has almost made him look alive. I stare and stare and try to find the guy I didn't like, but he's just another face of a shell that died too young. Nothing of Bryce is there. This seventeen-year-old boy won't get to live a life. Seventeen years is not long enough.

"Services for him are in two days," Matthew says. "Private. Family only."

"What? That's not okay. What about the people who were with him that night? What about Bree?"

Matthew shrugs. "I follow orders. Wanted you to know. And… Bree to know."

I tug the sheet up and drop it back over his face.

"Okay, Gabe. Out."

I head back up the stairs, but my mind is stuck on Bryce. On how he's really gone. On how Bree has lost yet another person she cares about.

* * *

Finding sleep while my best friend snores on the other side of the room is proving to be more difficult than I originally thought it would be—even after my trip to see Matthew.

Giving up on sleep, again, I roll over, pick up my phone, and send a message to Hartman.

Are you awake?

Yes

Can I call?

Yes!

I hit Call almost immediately.

"Hey," he whispers.

"Hey," I whisper back, blinking in the dark and holding my breath to see if Bree will wake up.

"I have a confession."

There's enough tease in his voice to make me smile like an idiot. "What?"

"I wasn't really awake."

My hand flies to my mouth. "I'm so sorry!"

He chuckles. "I wanted to talk to you. Don't be sorry."

Resting on my side, I slowly lie back down.

"So you called," he says.

"I..." I just realized that everything I'm thinking about right now is sorta dark to be waking someone up in the middle of the night over.

"I'm starting to think you wanted to wake me up for fun."

"No!" I pause again. "I want to ask you what I should do for Bree."

"Oh." There's a pause where I really hope he's thinking about it. "Just talk to her, Gabe."

"What if I don't know how? What if the wrong thing comes out again? I know the generic lines. That's it." But I have gotten to the point where I know how to *feel* with her, which is maybe already the biggest obstacle.

"Ask her questions about Bryce. About her favorite things about him. Make her feel like even though he's gone, he's not gone. I'd have done anything for that after I lost Dad."

"But he *is* gone. He was temporary, just like everything."

Hartman sighs. "My dad will live forever. I'm not saying that in a religious sense. I'm saying that because I will always remember my dad. I'll remember him until I die. And for me, that's what's important. My forever is his forever too. And I might have kids one day, and they'll carry part of me with them. We're all forever."

I shake my head, which is stupid because we're on the phone.

"You there?" he asks.

"Everything is temporary." I've seen it, learned it, and lived it.

"And what does that mean to you?" he asks.

"That maybe we put effort into things we shouldn't. Everything ends." I shift under my blankets, pulling them just under my chin.

"Do you know what it's starting to mean to me? And the more I think about it—life and death and everything else?"

"Hmm?" I let my eyes fall closed.

"Because after my dad, I never wanted to feel sad about anything else, but then watching my mom and watching you and Bree, I realized that's inevitable. Knowing there's sadness out there, and trying to stay away from it, doesn't mean it won't find us."

"Is this supposed to make me feel better?" I ask.

"Yes. Because there's something to be learned from every moment. Even the sucky ones. And even the great ones, like the one we're having right now on the phone."

My cheeks warm. "What do you miss most about your dad?" I ask. I can do this. This is what he said he wanted. What Bree would want. I'm practicing, but I also really do want to know.

"You sure you want to hear this?" he asks.

"You don't have to share, but yeah."

"I miss that he was always ready to give advice, but wouldn't be offended if you didn't take it. I miss that he did everything in his power to be at any major school event. And I love that he'd come home sometimes and just say, 'Happy Wednesday everybody! Let's go out to dinner!'"

I'm smiling at the exuberance in Hartman's words, but the horrible part of me wonders—how can you think your dad will live forever if when you die, you take those memories with you? "I sometimes wish it was forever. Life was."

"Forevers are personal, Gabe. My father's existence may not matter to a star a million miles away, or even to someone else who lived on my street. But my father's life was so much to me. The way I live my life will always be influenced by knowing him. So, in my world, my father is forever. In my world, that time we spent on the beach is forever. I will never forget that. Forevers are everywhere."

"You're full of interesting insights and adult speak," I say.

"Good," he says quietly.

"Good."

"And now that we've met, and that I like you…you're a part of me. Whether we stay together or not, you'll always be the girl who helped me feel better about my dad without realizing it, and the girl who kissed my cheek even after I disappeared for a few days."

I grin. "And Bree will be my forever because we'll always be friends."

"But she's part of your experience, even if your friendship ended tomorrow. You'd always remember Bree as the girl who you shopped with and who you shared a love of vintage with and who you Internetted with."

"I don't think Internetted is a word."

"But it *should* be." He chuckles.

"It totally should."

"So everything lasts forever. Even made-up things," he says.

"I like this." Every person and experience can be a forever thing, just maybe not the way we expect it to.

We sit on the phone in silence. I'm not sure what else I want to tell him, but I do know I'm not ready to be alone.

"Will you be at school tomorrow?" he asks.

"I'm not sure."

"When you're ready to go back, can I give you a ride?" he asks.

"So, is this where my life settles back into routine?"

"Not yet."

"Why not?"

"Because Bryce isn't buried. Because Bree still has a lot going on.

Because you have more to sort out in your head than you think you do. Because routines are overrated, and once we find them, we're thrown back out. Best to embrace the chaos."

I open my mouth to argue, but he's right. "Normal is boring anyway."

He laughs a little. "Night, Gabe."

"Night, Hartman." I close my eyes as I end the call and let out a long sigh.

# Chapter 29

My argument of not going back to school is met with blank stares from my parents, and then my dad cracking a smile and saying, "Nice try."

School is bearable only because Hartman's here. Both Jessica and Meghan seek me out first thing. Jeremy and Theo won't come back this year, but they're alive and doing better every day.

"I just want home," Meghan says as she flops against the locker near mine. "People ask the most horrible things."

"Just don't answer," I say, a bit amazed that she's still talking to me. I was just her driver for a night, but today she sought me out like we're friends.

Both girls look at me, and I take a half step back.

"No, that's good." Jessica holds her books more tightly against her chest. "I mean, I can't even think about that night without my body going cold, and…"

"I keep seeing them fall through the floor, and my stomach drops again." Meghan closes her eyes.

"So. Stony looks of coldness then?" I ask. "Or maybe we can just say we're not ready to talk about it." They're including me even though I wasn't there when the group needed me.

This is the same feeling I had when Bree first came to my house in seventh grade—possibility. Excitement.

"I like that." Jessica nods.

"Me too." Meghan nods as well.

"How's Bree?" Jessica asks.

One person should never have to deal with so much. "She's been better. She's going to stay with me for…for a while, I guess."

Meghan rolls her eyes. "Her parents are such assholes. My dad moved out two years ago and married a woman who was five when I was born, so I've been through the parental midlife crisis," she says. "It's ridiculous. Harder when—" Her eyes drop to the floor.

"What?"

"I think Bree was jealous of how great your family is. She talked you up a lot, you know."

"Oh." I've always looked at Bree as the brighter, smarter, better, and cooler of the two of us.

These girls were friends to Bree when Bree and I weren't so close. I want to hug them for it instead of being jealous.

"See you at lunch?" Meghan asks me.

"I'll be with Hartman."

"Great. So we'll see both of you then," Jessica says before she and Meghan walk away.

Hartman stops next to me and squeezes my shoulder. I lean back, letting my body fall against his. It's almost scary how easy it is to be around him. Maybe just because it became easy so fast.

"I'm glad you're here," he says into my hair.

I turn and lean into him again. "I'm glad I'm here too."

Only, as the day progresses, I wished more than once that I wasn't at school. The rumors are insane.

*They were playing Truth or Dare, and Bryce lured the others guys to where they knew it wasn't safe…Jessica doesn't want to be with Jeremy anymore so she led the guys onto the floor…Bryce was the nicest ever… What a tragedy…*

Freshmen cry in class over a guy they'd never met, and if they had exchanged words with him, it probably was him throwing an insult their way. There are hand-drawn posters on the wall, pictures of Bryce.

The counselor comes over the intercom to say she'll meet with any students having a hard time dealing with Bryce's death.

If a new student were to walk through my school today, they would think that Bryce was some kind of hero philanthropist instead of the guy most likely to shove someone in a trash can. Just because I'm starting to understand what he did for my friend doesn't mean I'll remember him differently. It also doesn't mean he deserved to die.

By sixth period, I feel like a grenade with the pin half pulled— one wrong word or phrase…*Boom.*

Jessica stops next to my locker, her backpack over her back. "I signed us out of school. Had my mom call to say that we were all going to her therapist for a grief-counseling session."

"Oh," I say.

Hartman chuckles. "Good."

"We need out," Meghan adds. "After you check on Bree, call us, okay?"

I nod.

"And maybe we can get together today or tomorrow?" Jessica asks.

I'm nodding again because my body apparently now only does one thing. "I'll go chat with Bree and let you know."

"Do you need a ride?" Meghan asks.

"If she's okay with it, I got her." Hartman gives me a squeeze.

I glance up at him before looking back toward the two girls. "I'll go with Hartman, but thanks."

"Let us know when we all want to get together."

"Yeah...okay..." We're going to end up as friends.

Jessica and Meghan walk up the hall, and instead of pulling out my English text for sixth period, I start packing my bag.

"Look at you with friends, Gabe." Hartman kisses my cheek with a smile.

I shut my locker and hoist my pack on my back. "Who knew that anyone could like the girl armed with sarcasm to protect her cold, cold heart?"

"*What?*" he asks.

"Nothing. My cousin." Who was only half right. But I'm changing all the time. I hope for the better.

\* \* \*

Hartman's car stops in the parking lot in front of my house, but neither of us moves. Energy zaps between us, and I shift in my seat twice to keep myself from leaping over the car and attacking him with kisses.

I've turned into someone new.

His fingers slide through mine. "You with me, Gabe?" he teases.

"I'd really like to kiss you."

He leans forward.

I lean forward.

His thin fingers stroke my cheek before his lips touch mine. I know more what I'm doing now, so after two small kisses, we're locked for a moment. Or two. Or several.

When people start kissing, how do they stop? I reach out for him, but with the center console, it's an awkward stretch.

Hartman breaks away first, and scoots back slightly. He nods a few times with a partial smile and flushed cheeks.

My cheeks are on fire, so I turn and push out of the car before he can comment. Hartman jerks to attention and sprints around, but I'm already out.

His hand touches my shoulder.

He leans down.

I hold my breath.

Waiting.

Instead of a kiss, his forehead touches mine. We just stand there for a moment, the world spinning around us.

"So, are you going to come swimming with me this summer?" he asks.

More grape smell. "In the pool."

"No beach?"

"I'll come to the beach. My fingers will hover over 911 and I'll stand by the lifeguard, but I'm *not* swimming in the ocean."

"I'm going to make it my goal to get you to swim in the ocean."

"I'm very sorry that you won't make your goal."

He kisses me again. "I think I could fall in love with you, Gabriella."

"I think I could fall in love with you too…" I narrow my eyes as if deciding, but I know my grin has completely given me away. "But it might take some time."

He kisses my nose. "I've got time."

I reach out and take his waist, pulling him against me. This is infinitely better. His stomach against my stomach and his mouth against my mouth. Our hands on each other's backs…

"Okay." He gives me a little peck. And then another one. "Okay, I have to…" He leans back. "I'm waiting for one of your parents to burst out of your house and attack me with a shovel or something."

"They don't use shovels. That's *so* last century," I tease.

"Nice." He laughs a little. "Call me later?"

I take a step back and then another and then another. Hartman's still grinning. He tugs a piece of gum from his pocket.

Grape gum. Aha.

I'm so buying like ten packs of that stuff to put next to my bed. Maybe I'll start dreaming about him if I smell him all night.

He climbs in his car and drives away while I watch. I step inside the lobby. I could for sure get used to this flying feeling.

Bree grabs my shoulders the moment I'm through the house door. "His parents refuse to let us see him before he's buried, Gabe."

"I know."

"I saw their car drive up today, and your parents were so obviously weird…" She shakes her head.

"They do that."

"Anyway, I knew something was up, so I snuck downstairs and listened to them talking. No open casket. No…nothing. A small, private service. Invitation only. I can't…" Bree shakes her head, and a couple tears leak down her cheek. "I can't just listen to someone talk about him and be okay with that being the end. I need to say good-bye. Do you get that? I even tried to go downstairs, but your parents have the place on lockdown. I don't know if Bryce's family will let *any* of his friends in."

"You need to say good-bye." I sat in the morgue and chatted with both of my grandparents for hours after they died. They weren't there. It didn't matter. I felt better, and that's what was important. Bree needs that too. I think about how many hours Mr. Nichols just sat with his wife, even knowing she was gone.

"Is it okay if we invite a few other people?" I ask. "Theo's still stuck in bed, but Jeremy and Jessica and Meghan?"

Bree's hands tighten on my shoulders, and her eyes fill with hope. "You can do that?"

I nod, only about half sure I can do that.

"Thank you, Gabe." Bree tugs me into a tight hug. "I need this."

And I get that she does. I just have to make sure we don't get caught. I'm about to ask Matthew for maybe the biggest favor ever.

# Chapter 30

The whole time Mom and Dad talk, I'm mostly thinking—*I'm going to sneak friends into the basement to see Bryce tonight.*

"I sat down with Bree and found a counselor today," Mom says.

"Oh."

I glance toward the living room, but Mickey seems to be absorbed in her show.

"Bree won't go back to school this year. I've already talked to her teachers so she can finish up from here."

I'd really love that offer.

Dad rests his elbows on the table. "We've talked about possibly offering Bree a home here for senior year. I don't think her mom's in a good place to create a stable home for Bree. Her father's about to have a baby. But we also know that your friendship with Bree has suffered a bit, and I don't want to add strain to that."

Bree would live with me? How crazy awesome would that be?

"Living with a friend is hard, Gabe," Mom warns.

I shake my head. "We'll be good. It'll be so, so good."

Dad releases a breath. "We've been pretty lax with you as far as rules and curfews, but considering what Bree's been through this year—"

"And your behavior over prom," Mom cuts in.

"We're going to have to be a little more strict," Dad adds.

Well, that sucks, but I can deal. "Okay."

"Don't say anything to Bree until we talk to her parents," Mom says.

*Fat chance.*

"Is that all?"

Dad nods. "Go spend time with Bree. She really needs you right now."

I sprint from the table and find Bree curled in a ball on her bed. "I don't think I can do this."

I sit next to her, the excitement over the possibility of her living with me for senior year deflating. "You don't have to do it alone."

"I know." She turns her head to rest a cheek on her knees. "I can't explain the panic I feel."

I'm afraid to speak.

"Running down the stairs after watching them just fall through the floor. It didn't seem real until we found the guys." She hiccups. "I thought they were all dead until I heard him wheezing..." Bree shudders and I rub her back. "It was so fast, Gabe. Like everyone was laughing, and the guys were doing this dance. There was a creak, and then total chaos."

"I can't imagine." And I can't. I've heard about accidents. Seen the results of more than I could ever hope to name, but to be there... Just seeing the cop cars *after* the fact sent me into hyper-overdrive.

She closes her eyes. "I don't think I'll ever forget."

She probably won't. I won't forget the cop telling me everyone had been taken to the hospital either.

"Mom and Dad are going to talk to your parents about you staying with us through senior year, but I'm not supposed to say anything." Maybe distracting her would be good.

Bree blinks and sits up. "Are you serious? Your parents would do that?"

I shrug. "They said not to tell you, but…"

A corner of Bree's mouth twitches. "But they had to know you'd never keep that a secret."

I cross my legs on the bed.

Bree stares at the blanket. I've known her long enough to know that she's trying to process too many things at once right now. "I could live in this house," she says quietly.

"Yep." If Bree wasn't dealing with so much, we'd be squealing and jumping and dancing. Still, I think if nothing else, it'll give us something to plan and talk about and work on together. A distraction for her at the very least.

"How do you…" Her body seems to shrink as she watches me. "How do you work in the middle of death and not want to just give up?"

"I…" But my mouth just hangs open. "I…"

Why do I?

"Oh great." Her brows go up. "Even you can't answer."

And then I think about what Hartman said—about spending as many moments together as we can. And about how Mom is always talking about actually *living* life instead of just walking through it. "Because life is worth it."

"Are you sure?" Her voice is so hollow that I ache for her. I also wonder what really happened the night she disappeared, but I don't think I'll get the full story on that one for a while.

Goose bumps wash over my skin. "Remember that poster in our freshman English class that we used to make fun of? 'The best things that are going to happen to you in this life are probably things you haven't even thought of yet'?"

She clutches her sides. "I sort of remember that."

"We used to think it was stupid," I say.

"And then…And then…Or I guess now, it's not so stupid."

I nod once, studying her. She's thinner.

"Do you know what it feels like to be left by so many people?" she asks absently.

I'm not sure she would even care who was here right now, but maybe I'm wrong. I sit silently, like I seem to do a lot around her.

"My dad left me for a promotion. I mean, he offered to take me with him, but that's hardly…I don't know. He's starting a whole new family now, so he won't even pay for the few things he promised. Mom left me for what I'm guessing is a total craphole apartment in LA, based on the few conversations we've had. My grammy, who stepped up to help, is now being carted away. Bryce wanted me, but my best friend didn't approve, and it just made me feel guilty and angry for feeling guilty because I was finally wanted. The whole time I was with Bryce, I half knew it wasn't a good idea, but doing the safe thing had gotten me missing parents and a crazy grammy. And then Bryce died…" Her voice is monotone and unflinching.

Just looking at how sad and broken Bree is kills me a little.

"I'm sorry," I say again because that's all I know to say right now.

And we sit. In silence. Our shoulders touching and the breeze washing over us through the window. We'll never be the same Bree and Gabe again, and maybe that's okay.

# Chapter 31

Bree clutches my arm so tightly that my fingers are going numb. "How many bodies are down there? It's weird when there are a lot."

"One under a sheet. Matthew placed Bryce in his casket yesterday."

"And he's not…" She sniffs. "I mean, I'm not going to see…"

"Bryce's suit is on. He's dressed. Promise. You know Matthew does good work."

"Not as good as us," she jokes, but her voice quakes on every word. She's *trying* to joke though—another sign she'll be okay.

The basement door kicks open, and Matthew's hair is a blond halo with the way the light's shining behind him. "You two coming?"

"Yep," I call quietly as we take another step down together.

"I can do this," Bree says quietly.

"You'll be sorry if you don't," I whisper.

Her steps even out as we keep walking down, and once we're at the bottom, Matthew gives me an *Are you sure?* look.

"Even if I get in trouble, how bad could it be?" I ask.

"After prom night?" Matthew asks. "It could be bad."

He has an excellent point.

Bree has stopped two steps into the room.

Bryce is in his suit, the top of the coffin resting open. The other body is gone, but the doors to the embalming room are closed, so my guess is that Matthew tucked the corpse in there. My cousin can be a good guy when he wants to be.

I stand next to Bree, but when I look over at her, her eyes are closed.

"I'll step out the back door," Matthew says. "Watch for your people."

I don't even acknowledge him. My attention is on Bree.

Her hands loosen and tighten a few times before her eyes open.

Bryce is solid. Still. Cold. Stuffed into a suit.

This thing lying in front of us makes no sense when I think about Bryce in the hallways of school. He was so full of life.

Every part of my body stills. *He was so full of life.* I've always thought of that as the stupidest cliché, and now, even faced with someone I didn't like, I feel the impossibility of him being gone. But he's gone just the same.

The shock suddenly makes sense. This is a revelation I should have had with my grandparents, but maybe because they were both so prepared for this phase of their existence, I was too.

I stay back by the door to upstairs. Matthew steps outside one of the double doors behind the house. No way for me to know how creative he'll be with payback, but I suspect I'll be his go-getter and errand runner until I'm the one lying still. Stuffed in a dress I hate.

"Hey," Hartman whispers behind me.

I spin to face him and lean into his chest.

"Gabe?" Bree's voice shakes a little.

Turning from Hartman, I take three small steps toward Bree and Bryce. I stare down at Bryce's body. I recognize which foundation Matthew used on his skin, and the signs of his jaw and mouth being shut and the subtle edge of the eye cap under his eyelid.

"This is so…weird," Bree says. "I've sat down here to do other people, but to see him this way…"

"Hey," Jeremy's voice echoes a little in the sterile room. "Whoa…"

Pretty soon we're all standing around Bryce in a strange half circle. Meghan and Jessica have locked arms. Jeremy rests on a sturdy set of crutches, but he looks thinner and paler than I've ever seen him. I'm guessing he's still in a lot of pain. Bree leans into me, and Hartman stands behind me, a hand on my shoulder.

"You're right," Jessica whispers. "So weird."

Meghan says a few things into her phone and then scans the room with it. "Theo is here on FaceTime."

I glance back at Hartman, and he has a *What the…?* look on his face. At least I'm not alone in thinking that FaceTime seems super strange in this moment. But maybe we should be glad for Theo that it's even an option.

"What do you even say?" Meghan asks. "I can't believe he's dead, but at the same time, he was insane, so part of me wonders how he lived this long."

Jeremy smiles a little as his head drops. "Yeah…I…Yeah."

Meghan's phone talks, and it takes me a moment to register that it's Theo's voice. "I think we should all share a story. Isn't that something people do? Ask Gabe. Hey, Gabe, isn't that something people do?"

"Uh…yep." I really hope I don't have to share a story because I have no idea what I'd say. *Thanks for not stuffing me in a trash can when I apologized to you at school?*

Bree and I grasp hands. I lean back against Hartman. People who might start to become my friends are talking about Bryce, but not in a way that makes him sound perfect. In a way that makes him sound real. He was a real person. Now he's not.

I blink and see him jumping around at school, and the look of shock on his face after I hit him, which was so satisfying.

Jessica says something about how much Bryce would love the attention he's getting at school right now, and a new thought walks through my brain. Pieces of Bryce's death will always be around. Some pieces of his life. I see the people in this room, and he gave us all something to bond over. Shaped parts of who we are—some for good, some for not so good. So really, he's influencing us, even in death. Maybe it's that our function after we die just changes, whether we live in any kind of afterlife or not. Just like people can be forevers to us, even when they aren't around anymore, because we remember them.

The elevator sounds, and my stomach rolls over. Everyone in the room stares at the wall as the cranky lift lurches and groans.

No one moves as the elevator door slides open to reveal both my parents. Both wearing robes, pajamas, and scowls.

Dad's jaw tightens as he takes in the scene. Me, four of my friends, Matthew, and Bryce.

"Gabby!" Dad barks as he steps forward, and Mom reaches an arm out to stop him.

"What is going *on* here?" Mom asks, her hand still on Dad's arm.

Hartman moves from the group and pauses in front of Mom and Dad. "Bree needed this. I needed this with my dad and never got it. And your daughter…" He glances over his shoulder, giving me a small smile. "Your daughter risked getting in trouble so we could all get…closure, I guess."

"But this is…" Dad sputters.

Bree's lip trembles. "Please?" She sniffs once. "We're not doing anything bad. We're not rearranging anything. Just…" She glances down at Bryce. "We all needed a few minutes."

Jeremy readjusts his crutches. "Five more. Maybe less?"

Even he sounds pleading. I can see Mom and Dad deflating as their faces and shoulders relax.

Dad's glare is on me. "Gabby?"

He points to the floor in front of him.

*Nice, Dad.*

I walk around Bree and toward my parents. Hartman gives me a small smile before we pass on his way back across the room to the group.

Mom steps backward until the three of us are in the back corner of the large elevator.

"You could have just asked," Dad says.

"And if you'd said no, this would have been so much worse."

"Because you'd have done it anyway?" His voice is high-pitched and incredulous.

"Dad…" I plead in a whisper. "I've never had…I've never had people. Friends. This was something I could do for them. For my best friend. For the girl who has saved me from my awkward self through most of high school. His parents are doing private services. And the viewing is family only. I'd have done it anyway."

He presses on the bridge of his nose. "Gabriella…"

"I know." I fold my arms and glance at the floor, trying to look somewhat contrite. "I've spent enough time with Hartman to know how much *not* getting this kind of closure with his dad has hurt him. I didn't want to see my friends hurt that way."

Dad lets out a sigh and glances back at the group standing over Bryce.

"Please?" I ask. "Let me back in there, and I promise this was a good thing. And I promise Bryce will be in the exact condition that Matthew wants him in. Just...*please*."

Mom sighs. Dad frowns. They whisper for a moment before Dad turns back around. "Five more minutes."

I give them a nod, and just as promised, I step back out of the elevator door, which is open just long enough for Dad to give everyone a very stern look. The elevator door closes with a *thunk* and once again groans as it creeps slowly back upstairs. I walk back to my friends.

"All okay?" Hartman asks.

"Not so much," I say. "But okay for now."

"We should finish up," Jessica adds.

I nod once. "We should."

Jeremy leans further forward on his crutches. "You would have been an asshole if you'd had a chance to grow up, Bryce. But a good asshole."

Even Bree smiles a little. "And a great kisser."

I wrinkle my nose, and Hartman smirks but shakes his head for me to stop. Now I have two people helping me. There might be hope for me yet. But I might care a little less how people see me, so I might not need the help in quite the same way.

"Okay?" I ask quietly as I step forward.

Bree clutches her arms as I release the top of the casket and slowly lower it. There's a messy mix of relief and sadness. And then guilt over the relief part.

"Thank you so much, Gabe," Bree says.

I nod once.

"I can't imagine how much easier the last months would have been if I'd had that with my dad," Hartman says quietly. "This was a good thing."

"Thanks, Gabe." Jeremy gives my shoulder a gentle slap.

Jessica gives me a half hug, followed immediately by Meghan.

Matthew tugs open the back door from the outside, and we all walk out together.

"And we'll be back here tomorrow." Jeremy sighs. "The few of us with invites." He rolls his eyes. "But that will be for show. Tonight was for real."

"For real," Theo agrees from within Meghan's phone.

We exchange waves as Jessica and Meghan help Jeremy into her car, and they pull away.

Bree's smile is faint. I can only imagine what she's dealing with. I can't really know.

I tug her into a hug, and her arms tighten around me. "Thank you, Gabe. Thank you so much. For everything."

I'm blinking back stinging heat on my eyes as I hold her back. "Anytime."

"But hopefully never again." She sniffs. Bree's trying to tease. She'll for sure be okay.

"Never again," I agree.

"I'm starving. Is that weird?"

Hartman tugs me in to his side and kisses my forehead. "Why don't you two go to breakfast. You can call me later."

I'm already in trouble with Mom and Dad, and food sounds pretty amazing. I glance at Bree who nods.

Hartman takes my hand and I walk him to his car. There's no asking or questioning anymore. We're dating. And it's so good.

He takes my face in his hands and kisses me lightly. "Be careful with yourself. I'm paranoid. I've lost two people in a very short time, and I don't want to lose another."

"Then you're dating the right girl." I smile.

He pulls me against him, his lips on mine, his kiss long and slow and perfect. I feel like every time we're together I'm just soaking up as much of him as I can get.

And then the warmth of him is gone. In his car with a wave and a sad smile.

I watch him go, knowing he'll be back.

Bree is suddenly at my side. "I'm happy you're doing this. Hartman, I mean."

"Me too."

"He seems pretty great." She nudges me. "So me pushing you that way maybe wasn't the worst thing."

"He's so, so great."

We start slowly walking up the dark street.

"I'm barely hanging on, Gabe," she says quietly.

I slip my arm through hers. "I know. But you're doing a fab job on the ledge."

"You know what I think speaks volumes?" Bree says more quietly, her face falling into something more serious.

"Hmm?"

"The fact that the stereotypical pretty boy, gorgeous boy, popular boy took the time to get to know someone who only fits into the stereotype of quirky. And did he push me? Yep. But I was ready to be pushed. Wanted to be. I was furious with my parents, more than I admitted to myself, and he gave me distraction." She sniffs and swipes under her eyes quickly.

Her simple phrase really does sum up a lot.

"I still did some stupid things," she says. "But he was exactly what I needed."

Our footsteps echo in the quiet night.

"I can be sort of an asshole," I say.

We stop at the light, even though I can't see any cars in any direction.

"We're all assholes sometimes."

The crosswalk lights up, and we start across to the small restaurant on the corner.

"I'm not ready for doughnuts and sand," Bree says. "I'm saving that for when I think I'm getting close to ready to move on."

"Sounds good."

We're people. We're imperfect. At some point I'm going to hurt Hartman's feelings, and at some point he's going to hurt mine. We might last a few months. We might last a few years. We might last a lifetime. But I'll always remember him. He'll be forever. So will Bryce and my grandparents, and my Aunt Liza's closet.

But me and Bree? We're solid. We're messy and we get angry and we will fight again over something big or something small, but her and me? We're the forever kind of friends. Not the kind I'll remember when I'm eighty, but the kind I'll live next to when I'm eighty.

"I promise to tell you when you're too old to go commando."

She snorts, and I trip over the curb. I love how random everyday things are part of big revelations.

"After breakfast, and before my parents probably ground me, let's put nose and handprints on the outside windows of Audrey's," I say.

"Done."

# Epilogue

Bree is in her blacks but has asked to do nothing but welcome people, hand out programs, and keep the snack table filled. She'll answer the phone if needed. This keeps her near the front and away from the viewing room, which has been harder for her since losing Bryce.

Her bedroom is up the hall from mine, decorated in sixties pastels, and is all Bree. She's back to her regular "Bree" wardrobe, which makes me endlessly happy. Also, having a sister in the house my age means that we're always two against one for the remote—except for *Jessie*. Bree totally takes Mickey's side on that one. With Bree wanting to spend her senior year at Paradise Hill High, and my parents being awesome, she'll be with us for the year.

Bryce has been gone two months.

Today a family is burying a man who is a father and a grandfather, an uncle, a nephew, a friend, and a great-grandfather. I don't know the family, but still, my eyes fill with tears as I think about how much life he lived.

Aunt Liza sighs, tapping the cigarette in her fingers with a frown. She knows she can't light up in here, but that doesn't prevent her from carrying her smoke around, just in case she gets a moment.

"I used to be built just like your friend," Aunt Liza says, pointing at Bree.

"Oh yeah?" I ask. "How's that?"

"Curvy and gorgeous. Like a brick shithouse."

"Um…" My cheeks warm up. "I don't even know what that means."

Liza grunts and taps her cigarette a few more times. "I'm going to step outside. That Angel guy better get back from vacation soon. The phones here are a bitch."

So very Aunt Liza.

I scan the crowd again, hoping to catch Mom or Dad's eye to see if anything needs to be done. A boy about my sister's age sits alone on a bench near the entrance to the chapel, his chin quivering.

As I walk toward him, I do a quick scan to see if I can make out who his parents are, but no one's giving him extra glances. He's still enough to have blended into the furniture.

I sit next to him and he scoots slightly away, like he's being polite and giving me more space.

"It's hard to say good-bye," I say quietly. "I had to do it with my grandparents. We all worked here together. What did you and your granddad do together?"

"He liked to fish."

"Gross." I chuckle, and the kid's mouth almost tugs into a smile.

He lets out a sigh and stares at the ceiling, blinking.

"You hold on to those memories, okay?" I tell him. "That's how we make someone last forever. You tell your friends about what you did together. And someday when you meet some amazing girl and get married, you can tell her, and then you can tell your kids about this very cool man that you knew."

He blinks, and a few tears stream down his small cheeks.

My heart aches for him, but it's some of the sad kind and some of the empathetic kind and some of the warm kind too.

"And then, your kids will tell their kids about this guy who used to take their dad fishing. And that's how you keep someone around. You talk about them, even though it hurts."

He swipes at his tears a few times.

I lean closer. "It's okay to cry, you know. Good even. It helps that really harsh sadness slip away, and then all you have left is missing him and lots and lots and lots of good memories."

He nods quickly, and suddenly a woman is kneeling in front of him. "Oh, honey," she says softly.

"We'll see you around, okay?" I tell the kid as I stand.

I close my eyes and take my three deep breaths. But I'm learning that letting myself feel a little with the people around me helps us both.

The woman takes my place on the bench, and I start back toward the offices. I get why Mom lets herself cry. Feel. I also understand what we do now. How we help people through this process. Why Dad never comes up for dinner. Finally.

Bree bumps my hip as I near the offices. "Look at you being all sensitive."

My job is harder than it's ever been, but I love it more too.

"There's a tall guy in the offices asking for a kiss," she teases. Funny how she used to prefer the bodies to the mourners and has now switched. Either way, I'm glad she's here and happy for the help.

I grin and swipe at the outside corners of my eyes.

The second I push through the swinging door into the offices,

Hartman tugs me into his arms and plants a kiss on my lips.

I playfully push him away. "I could have terrible breath!"

"I couldn't care less." He holds me tighter, and in seconds we're wrapped up together in one of those fantastic kisses that doesn't have a solid start or stop.

When we break away, we both gasp for air.

His fingers slide over the fabric of my dress, making me shiver.

"Dinner tonight?" he asks.

"Audrey's tonight. No boys allowed."

"That's right," Bree says as she steps into the room. "But why don't you two go out after? Mickey and I want to watch *Jessie*, and we could do without Gabe commentary."

"Is she that bad with the interruptions?" Hartman laughs a little, his body shaking against mine.

"Worse." Bree's smile is teasing. She picks up another prepared plate for the table. "Sad people eat a lot."

"You go work." Hartman taps my rear. "I'll see you tonight after Audrey's. I just had a few minutes, and I wanted to see you."

I slowly pull myself away. "See you tonight."

And then I hold open the door for Bree, who makes a kissy face and laughs.

I lean in the doorway of the offices and look out at my life in the lobby of the funeral home. People talk in quiet voices in small groups. Matthew winks at Bree, who rolls her eyes. Mom touches Dad on the shoulder as she passes him by. Liza stands just outside the glass door with her cigarette, even though she *knows* she needs to be farther away than that to smoke.

Bree still misses Bryce. Her parents are still going through their own crisis instead of helping Bree with hers. My little sister makes me almost as insane as my Aunt Liza. But all this madness is what makes my story interesting, worth telling, worth lasting. All the good and bad and terrible and wonderful things have become a part of me.

I get it now. Forevers are everywhere.

# Acknowledgments

I will say this every time a book releases—writing a book to put out in the world is a group effort. From readers to friends to publishers to agents to families, a lot more people are involved than just the author.

To my always amazing agent, Jane Dystel, thank you for taking care of all the boring stuff so I can save my brain for the fun stuff. In other words, thank you for helping me continue to grasp on to the small bits of sanity I hold dear.

A huge thank-you to the author-readers for this book: Christa Desir, Melanie Jacobson, Tiffany Odekirk, and Allison Martin—boy, did you read rough drafts.

And another huge thank-you to my Sisters in Writing, my Suite Sisters, my Storymakers Tribe, and my Binders. You are proof that there is power in numbers.

There have been so many author friends who are just stellar human beings, and I call myself lucky to know them and have their support—Jenny Proctor, Wendy Jessen, Courtney Stevens, Steph

Campbell, Nyrae Dawn, Amber Argyle, Rachel Larsen, J. Scott Savage, Steve Bohls, Kaylee Baldwin, Chantele Sedgwick...and so many more.

As always, massive thanks to the Albert Whitman team. Wendy, you seem to always know what I'm trying to do and help me bring that out in my story.

Every year, I'm grateful again that people are still reading books. Thank you, thank you, readers.

And finally, no book would make it out into the world without my family being amazingly patient with my scattered writer brain. Love you.

# More Great Reads from Jolene Perry

THE SUMMER
I FOUND YOU

"Sweet, hopeful, uplifting"
—Christa Desir, author of Fault Line

JOLENE PERRY

HC 978-0-8075-8369-2
PB 978-0-8075-8367-8

Stronger
than you
Know

"A moving
survival story."
—Booklist

JOLENE PERRY

HC 978-0-8075-3155-6
PB 978-0-8075-3158-7

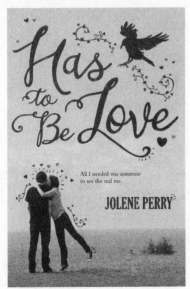

Has
to
Be Love

All I needed was someone
to see the real me.

JOLENE PERRY

HC 978-0-8075-6557-5
PB 978-0-8075-3167-9

**Praise for Jolene Perry:**

"The romance is sweet and believable."—*Kirkus Reviews* on *The Summer I Found You*

"[Perry] offers a portrait, rare in YA, of the way compassionate, functional families work and the good effects they can produce."—*Bulletin of the Center for Children's Books* on *Stronger Than You Know*

"Breathlessly captures that adolescent moment of being torn between an old life and the possibility of the new as well as romance and the dangers and exhilarations of physical contact." —*School Library Journal* on *Has to Be Love*

**Jolene Perry** is a middle and high school teacher turned author. She married the guy she kissed on her high school graduation night, has spent months sailing in the Caribbean, and lives in the mountains of Alaska. She is the author of several novels for young adults, including *Has to Be Love*, Stronger Than You Know, and *The Summer I Found You*.